SWEET POTATO JONES

JEN LOWRY

This book is a work of fiction. Names, characters, places, and incidents are either products of the author's imagination or are used fictitiously. Any resemblance to actual persons, living or dead, business establishments, events, or locales is entirely coincidental. The author makes no claims to, but instead acknowledges the trademarked status and trademark owners of the word marks mentioned in this work of fiction.

Copyright © 2020 by Jen Lowry

SWEET POTATO JONES by Jen Lowry
All rights reserved. Published in the United States of America by Swoon Romance. Swoon Romance and its related logo are registered trademarks of Georgia McBride Media Group, LLC.
No part of this book may be used or reproduced in any manner whatsoever without written permission of the publisher, except in the case of brief quotations embodied in critical articles and reviews.

Trade Paperback ISBN: 978-1-948671-70-5
ePub ISBN: 978-1-948671-78-1
Mobi ISBN: 978-1-948671-79-8

Published by Swoon Romance, Raleigh, NC 27609
Cover design: Beetiful Book Covers

To Eli, for dreaming with me
To Solomon and Samuel, my loves forever
To Aunt Dot, for always believing in me

SWEET POTATO JONES

ONE

Everything used to always look different on Sundays. Why that was, is hard to say. I just knew it did. On Sundays, the air seemed to be a little cleaner, my vision better. Within me, a hope burned that no matter what had happened in my life before then, Sunday would make it all better.

The grass prickled my bare feet as I spun the kids in helicopter circles, individual sprigs like a spiky hairdo, would tickle us as we fell softly together in our small backyard. We would lay back imaging cloud dragons and stare up at the Carolina-blue sky.

My heart swelled as I remembered sitting with Daddy on the front porch glider on Sundays at the old place. I'd stare across the railroad tracks and see the same exact water tower and the same exact burned-down mill. They're both probably still standing today, since around there, broken things aren't demolished to make way for something new. They're left in pieces to remind us how shattered we are. Even though we had nothing pretty to look at, only shambles and stacks of rotted wood, those were the most wonderful moments of my existence. That was how it once was for me, before she stole Sunday. All the miles had left me a hollow girl robotically moving from one day to the next. On most days, I found myself feeling more like a dead stump where nothing would ever grow again.

The Sunday Momma died was the day all the goodness in my life flew away on angel's wings—if angels even came for the broken ones.

"Do me a favor." She spoke to me in a fragmented whisper.

We needed her to give us last words of wisdom, to tell us about her legacy, our grand purpose in life. We deserved words to hold on to, the ones to help push us through the hard days. But these words never came. Her speech would dwindle to a dreamy whisper, and then she would say, "Do me a favor ..."

By the time she expended all her energy on those four words, she didn't have the strength to say anything more.

When she seemed on the verge of speaking again, we would say, "Don't ask us to do the favor. Just tell us what the favor is." But she could not continue.

Daddy shook her, and she lolled her head to the side and held out her arm, asking for a release, dancing those frail arms in her pantomime even as she fell into a comatose state. "One more hit, baby."

Daddy, give her one more try at it, why don't you? I wanted to scream.

But all the words I had wanted to say were closed up inside of me.

Whether she couldn't or wouldn't tell me her last wishes is something left to the mysteries of this life. What was that favor? Why couldn't she have said all the things that she needed to say when we were by ourselves, singing gospel songs and hanging clothes out on the line? She could stare down that preacher like the best of them—go hide out in the basement by the hot water heater and shoot up, as if we didn't know what she was doing down there. Why couldn't she talk to me instead?

Why didn't she tell me what I was meant to be? Why her love for me wasn't enough to keep her on the straight and narrow? She could've even told us about our family tree—given names and faces to our ancestors. A generational connection would've been something I could hold on to in times like these. But instead, that overdose messed with her mind to the point where unanswered wishes or last requests were never granted, because she had already lost all her ability to speak and eat and urinate and move and breathe independently. Momma had lost her ability to *be*.

"Do me a favor. Give me a proper life," I whispered in the dark, as the sweat clung to my skin like sticky rain.

I felt cheated. And scared. And alone. And mad. I felt everything and nothing at once.

In the days before her overdose, a sense of paranoia hit her strong like she knew the reaper would soon be coming to claim her soul. She had been scared, too, and I'd lied to her. When she whispered to me that she was afraid of death, I told her there was nothing to be frightened about. I tried to reassure her she was going to Heaven— why should anyone fear that? But I lost my real, deep-running faith the day her eyes turned this strange, oil-pumping color, like her pupils had filled up with mud. Almost like Satan had already staked his claim on her, and it showed not just in the spider-web veins all along her arms and neck, but in those orbed, blank eyes that looked but did not see.

I kept wanting to grab that faith I once believed existed on those Sundays of my childhood. My insides yearned for it again. I even found myself praying it would show up in my times of despair. I needed it now so desperately, and I begged God would give us a chance, but it had been proven, time and again, God wasn't taking calls from me.

But maybe he was still listening to my brothers and sister. In her ten-year-old eyes, Bell's world was adventure and freedom, without the restraint of the system. She never saw the danger or felt the cold or had those longings for a porch swing, like I did. She was an infant when we started hopping trains. She's never known anything different. Bean was barely out of diapers then, and who's to say what an almost-three-year-old could remember. It was something we never openly discussed with the youngins. I did know for a fact Maize had flashes of it. He was only three years younger than me, and despite all our apparent differences, he was more than a brother to me. He was my soul friend.

I had pains for Maize like I had for no other—deep ones that would take my breath away if I allowed myself to dwell on them long enough. It might not be all in what he said, and he sure had lots to say on the subject of our life. It was in his blank eyes, his rough edge. He remembered our past life, knew all about this transient one, and had the comparison of what normal folks had. He'd once said we'd be cursed forever. I knew how long eternity was and wasn't so sure about all of that. Not that I didn't believe we were the unluckiest family in the world. I had learned the art of suffering in silence, because I knew no words in the world would ever change the circumstances of our life.

"Sweet Potato," Maize whispered harshly from the corner of the shed. "This is it. The last stop."

"What are you rambling on about now?" I grumbled in the dark, trying to hide my growing fear. I knew exactly what he meant.

"I'm running away after this one. I'm calculating me a plan."

His voice was shaking leaves, but there was something there that made me believe him deep down to my roots. I had to put this to rest now, before the idea festered within him.

"No, you hush up now. I'm too tired for this. The only plan we're making is one that involves us staying together, so stop talking about tearing us apart. We're all we've got, bottom line."

"You ain't gonna stop me. You've got Bean and Bell to mess over. With me gone, it's one less to worry about. More food for the kids. I don't like the way Bean is looking."

"You know you lie, Maize. Shut up and go to sleep. I'd worry about you to my death if you ran off. You can't up and leave like that. Losing yourself in the world will never erase who you are."

"It has to be better than who I am now. I want to be lost, and that'll be the ticket that sets me free."

Didn't he know how lost we already were? Our souls held the dreaded black spot, marked with the sin of our beloved, dearly departed mother and the rambling sins of our father.

I whispered, "If you leave, we won't survive. I can't do any of this without you. You're the rock, Maize. No matter what, we've got to stick together."

I pulled the frayed, plastic tarp over Bell's tiny-boned shoulders and watched as her soft, even breathing rose and fell. It was too hot in the shed for a blanket, but for some reason, it made me feel better that I could cover her, as if it was a natural thing I should be doing. Bean was sprawled out on the dirty floor with his shirt off, swatting at flies that weren't there. He was faking sleep, and my voice lowered once more to a plea.

"You have to stay, Maize."

"Why?" He sat up, his shoulders slumping over in the dark. "I gotta go. You can't make me stay."

Bell sighed, stirring. My heart sank straight down like an anchor, crashing through my feet to hit rock bottom. She didn't need to hear Maize's desperation, and neither did Bean. When would he learn to keep his mouth shut?

Bean sat right up with his hands crossed over his chest like he'd popped out of a casket.

Bell sang a sweet melody, her voice rising above my fear. "Stay on, brother. Roll on, sister. Just for a little while. We got miles to go."

"That's what I'm saying, Bell. We've got to find us a place." Maize tumbled off the crate he'd been sitting on. One of the soda bottle crates crashed to the floor with a thud, and his butt sank into it.

He crawled over to my side, putting his hand out to me. He

squeezed my fingers like a vise. Panic attacks often rose up in him at unforeseen times, mostly in school or when we were out in the public, but never really when it was us alone in our sanctuary. He must've been losing his grip, because he was holding on to me with all the strength he had left.

"Daddy said we're all deciding this time," Bell chirped in optimistically.

I broke the silence beginning to make my heart ache and said, "Don't get Bell all into this. We'll let you decide, Bell. Won't we, Maize? Bean, let's give Bell a spin at it." My voice rose a little, giving them a clear sign we had to play along, for Bell's sake.

Maize put his head down shamefully. He loved our little Bell Pepper Jones, our sweet-singing little angel of music. He relented. I felt a whoosh of wind release from him, and I sighed when he relaxed his hold on my hand.

Maize mustered up spirit and announced, "Alrighty then, Bell. You got it. Where to?"

I pulled the flashlight from my bag, and Maize unrolled the map Daddy had marked and circled so many times before. Bean kept swatting imaginary flies.

"Now? Without Daddy here?" The disappointment crept into Bell's voice.

She saw Daddy as a knight shining bright and polished, and for reasons unfathomable, so did I.

I reassured her. "He's working down at the cleanup site, and you know it's a long-day work. When he gets back, he'll be glad we've taken care of the logistics of the matter for him. So, where will it be? Let us see."

My flashlight strode across the interstates and highways of North Carolina, along the mountain ranges we hadn't had the chance to travel yet, touching the coastal waters that I'd seen only in books. We'd somehow stuck to the main cities and the little sideways towns labeled in such small print that it was hard to make them out even with the flashlight.

"We gonna do this right this time," Bell said, her smile breaking all speed limits across her tiny face.

"You act like we've been doing it all wrong." Maize chuckled.

"You know Daddy don't do no wrong." His sarcasm fell on deaf ears.

This was a big night for us, laying out future plans. The unknown was always our shadow, but hopelessness wouldn't be, not anymore. I only had to look at Bell to see there was hope left in the world. Maybe not for me, but for her sake, I'd try to summon all my courage and smile. Smile even in the darkness, no matter how forced it was. In all honesty, the anticipation was there for me, too. The ceremony was about to begin, and I felt all sorts of feelings trying to attack me at once.

"We never prayed about the thing before," Bell said, pulling her weather-worn New Testament out from the back pocket of her jeans and fitting it into the palm of her hand.

My heart ached when she mentioned prayer, because she said it with the innocence of a child, the way Jesus would've wanted it. That little, dark hole had once been a blood-pumping apparatus lurched in my chest. I wanted to be able to pray right. Lord knows how bad I needed to. She laced her tiny fingers in mine, wanting me to join in her prayer.

I could do this. For her.

"Go on," I encouraged her.

She released my hand once she knew she had me, pulled her knees up under her, and put her tiny hands against her chest, clasping tight to a frayed-edged Bible we got from the Gideon men who were passing them out two shelters back.

Bean started waving his hand across the map as if he was a magician flicking a wand and said in his comedic flair, "Abracadabra, a home is what we're after."

Maize stared at me with expressionless eyes. I had the darkest eyes of them all, with a ring of hazel framing the brown like a field with weeds. Mine was the color of the earth and their eyes were the color of the myriad sky. The colors before a storm. Bell's gray clouds, to Bean's hazel, to Maize's Tarheel blue. Maize got his directly from our white momma. That was about where the resemblance stopped, because our dominant features came from Daddy. I didn't know how my eyes looked to other people, stuck behind a pair of cracked, framed glasses, but the eyes that were looking at me now, they were my world. Those eyes should have still been holding young wonder. At fourteen, Maize should have still held on to the world like someone who can waste away days, playing video games and daydreaming about girls. He was an old man in a frightened, little boy's body.

Bell said, "Dear God and Jesus, too, we about to pick a place. We Joneses are on the move again, Lord, because that's what you would have us do. You would have us to be ramblers for your Word, but Maize is tired, Lord."

Horror filled me as I stared at Maize. I dared him with my dagger-slinging eyes to never, ever give way to his feelings of despair in front of this precious child. Bell had overheard their conversation about him wanting to run away again, and she was sure that girl was sound asleep. Talking about Maize being tired. He looked at me like he needed prayer more than he would ever admit, so I bit my lip again to stop myself from crying at the pain starting to form right behind my eyelids. *Take his tired, Jesus, upon your shoulders.*

Bell patted Maize on the head, her tiny hand sinking into his curls. "He needs a stopping place. So, please, Lord. Give us one. Give us our time. Our place. We been traveling for you long and hard all these ten years. I know we must have paid off our debt by now. Give us a home, God. A real one, this time. Amen."

Bean's little voice came out manly and rich in his echoed amen as Bell closed out her prayer. He believed it, too. The faith of these two combined might take us home.

When I didn't chorus her ending, Bell pinched me hard on the arm. "Say amen, or it won't work, Sweet Potato."

"Amen," I whispered.

In all the emotion of hearing Bell praying, I missed the sound of footsteps. The scraping sound of metal startled us all, and we jumped into each other's arms. Bell cowered between us, and I found myself holding them all up, with Bean holding on to my knees in the huddled position of a tornado drill in progress.

Daddy said, "My, my, what a sight."

When he held up his flashlight, he found what I could only imagine looked like the four of us caught like red-handed thieves.

I wanted to say, *what a smell,* but I kept my thoughts to myself. Daddy had worked a grueling day at that landfill, doing the jobs they couldn't get the salaried workers to undertake. He had one small, brown bag with him, and my stomach growled ferociously at the crinkle of it in his hand, like what I learned from my psychology class on Pavlov's dog reacting to the bell. Never imagined I would give a second thought about my psychology class again, but here I was, comparing myself to Pavlov's dog. I actually missed school, some place to go and feel normal again. I'd forgotten my daily hunger in the midst of Maize's pain.

Bell whispered, "I'm starving, too."

It was so hot since we closed up the shed. Shacks were safer than the main house, because no one would think to go in here to check for people like us. We'd tried staying in the shade of the forest behind the abandoned house to beat the humidity, but the blistering summer heat pure wore us down to the core. We'd been lying down in here for hours to conserve our energy. If it wasn't for the pulled-back, metal roof that must have taken damage from a storm, we would've probably suffocated by now.

Daddy asked, "Who wants some chicken and taters?"

He waved the bag in front of us, and the sight of the grease stains on the paper made my mouth water.

He frowned. "What you doing with that map? You think you

getting a head start without me?"

It was almost as if he could sense Maize's urgency to flee, because as he spoke, he looked directly at him. Maize crossed his arms defiantly, even though he had never once spoken his feelings outright in front of Daddy. He gave them all to me late at night when nobody else was alive to the world to hear it.

I said, "Bell just prayed us into the ceremony. We 'bout to choose. Well, Bell's 'bout to do it for us."

"Without me? That's always been my job. This time I promised we would do it all together, and here I come walking in to find y'all huddled up making plays without the coach." Daddy's shoulders slumped, a tired smile trying to spread across his face but not quite making it.

He handed me the bag to distribute the food, and I suddenly had to push back the bile forming in my throat. His smell came too close to my nostrils, and it mixed in with the scent of the grease wafting through the thin paper. I gave the biggest pieces to the kids and took a leg for myself. I turned to face the wall to eat, trying to block the sight of his body. I knew if I covered my face, it would be disrespectful. I didn't have the heart to tell him I wished he could have at least stopped in at the rest stop and washed up a bit before coming home.

Bean spoke through a mouthful of chicken breast. "We got done praying. That's all you missed."

"Prayin', huh? Well, that's ah right, then." Daddy fidgeted.

We stayed the whole summer out of sight at the edges of civilization. He said he was trying to gather his wits about him and needed time to himself, like Jesus going out to Gethsemane to pray, without stranger church folks trying to help us or give advice or split up us kids and take us away. I knew Bell had been missing the whole church experience, probably mostly for the fresh choir robes and the singing. I was glad for the break, in all honesty. God hadn't done nothing for us, and by now, I figured it was probably too late for him to show up. Why show up for him on some forced Sunday morning with fake smiles and a made-up backstory? I was over it completely.

Bell was a little harp. Whenever and wherever, a song would swell up in her spirit, and she'd release it. Talk about walking guilt strings along the pathways of your heart. Bell could do that to you, and she was starting on a gospel one this time. Daddy hung his head down, and it wasn't long before his baritone voice jumped in on the old-timey chorus.

Take it to the altar, where you are, just stop and pray
Let the spirit move you as you go about your day
Fill me with your promises, Jesus, never let me fall
Take it to the altar, hear the sinner's call

Bean hummed along some, too. I guess you could have called Maize and me the cynical ones. Let them sing for us.

"You already invited Jesus. Now let's get to it." Bean was rubbing his hands together. I could see the sweat beading up all along his forehead as he rocked back and forth in anticipation.

Both flashlights lit the map. Daddy's solemn, deep eyes scanned each of our faces. He had this loving look on him like this was a tender moment for him. Wonder where that had come from? If he loved us enough, wouldn't our lives be different? Even though I hated like all get out to admit it, that look was one that endeared him to me, no matter what our life had measured up to. Daddy didn't have a formal education past high school but wasn't a stupid man. Why did he choose to be this wandering soul, unable to put down roots? Questions left again to the mysteries of life.

He looked around at us as if he could figure out the latitude and longitude of our next living arrangement by the contours of our faces. I hated maps. I knew what they meant. Maps meant moving. Traveling on. Migrating. Still, I couldn't help but wonder.

Bean's hands were clamped firmly over Bell's eyes. He released them, and they all bent over in fascination at where Bell's petite finger had fallen. I was the last to grudgingly look at our fate. No more North Carolina sights for me. We'd never stepped foot out of North Carolina. We had miles to go on this one, all the way to Virginia. Crossing borders this time.

Daddy said, "Well, there we go. Almost to the end of the Earth. Let's get it going first light."

"Already?" My voice sounded more exhausted than I'd ever heard it. Must have been all of this heat and humidity bearing down on me, and the weight of Maize on my soul like a seven-hundred-pound bench press. Maybe it was simply the thought of traveling three hundred country miles.

Daddy said, "No better day than the one before us. Besides, summer's 'bout over, and you know what that means."

Maize's face wore a pained expression.

"Lights out," I said it like we were in a place with an actual switch that connected to current.

I cut off my flashlight and settled back down on the tarp with Bell. Bean decided he was going to stay snuggled up with us, and I minded it so much but couldn't deny him. The sweltering heat was a beast, not to mention the smell now pervading all of my senses. But I didn't have the courage to ask that little boy to move.

Now, despite how I'd managed to get my family through everything we'd endured up to this point without cracking, I had a feeling I was about to get like Maize—tired and fed up.

TWO

Stopping by the Iron Skillet restaurant with all the youngins was usually the free ticket to ride. Daddy had a sense for finding the old truckers who liked picking up hitchhikers with stories to tell, and they'd load us all up in the cab. Sometimes Bean would get to pull on the horn. Bell would always say extra kudos in the nightly prayers for the nice ones who treated us like we were normal human beings. I sure wasn't giving any extra praises for the ones that let Bell Pepper turn the radio station to what she wanted to hear—which was always country music, for Pete's sake. Wasn't our life a walking, talking country song from the minute we were conceived?

On the road, we heard about a homeless shelter in Newport News. Trucker number two told us about another hitcher he'd helped once who had been there, coming back along the road into North Carolina. I almost choked on my water when the trucker said he thought the name of that place was The Home. Funny, that was what Maize wanted and what Bell had prayed for. Goose pimples rose on my arms.

When we arrived in that place of all things new, we hit one city road that merged into another, snaking into the heart of the skyscrapers. The city looked nothing like what I was used to. It was all metal and concrete and iron—no trees or rolling fields of corn as tall as a bus. It was a dull gray. The feeling of loneliness hit me even harder when I realized I wouldn't have trees to hide in.

When we hit that six-mile bridge, I thought I had seen it all. There was nothing like the experience of crossing that monstrosity on truck brakes. My heart drummed as we jolted and inched forward, the brakes screeching. Something told me I wouldn't see the other side of that road. Once I had crossed, one way or the other, we'd either live or die in this place. Living and dying were much the same, so it didn't really matter, in the end.

Newport News was a beautiful sight as you crossed over that James River Bridge. Bean pressed his face to the glass, straining to see all the flashy, fishing boats skimming along the edges of the marsh and the Navy building ports loomed fierce in the distance. Mansions jutted from the shorelines and the tall banks, and I thought of all those folks riding high up there, and how they must have had a fresh view of life every morning as they read their paper and drank cappuccinos in monogrammed coffee cups.

We didn't turn onto those fancy subdivision roads but told Mr. Bill, our nice trucker chauffeur, that we needed a stop near a gas station, if he didn't mind. We had to fill out the lay of the land while Daddy figured out how to get to the closest shelter. The Home, if that was what it was truly called, would just be a temporal thing.

Mrs. Betty Atkins, the director, patted Bell on the shoulder. She said, "You must be one blessed family indeed. A room happened to be made clear for a family. Looks like we've got a family in need."

Daddy said, "You sure do. You mean you've got us a place we can all bunk?"

"The number seven. Usually they don't last a day when the word hits the street that our family unit has an opening."

Bell lit up like a sparkler stick exploding and nudged me in the side. "I told you that prayer was the way to go."

We got twenty weeks here, so Daddy took the little pocket planner Mrs. Betty gave him, and she helped him circle the date. If that wasn't some kind of warning to us all, I don't know what was.

Daddy marked the calendar on the week of Christmas. What a gift that would be—back out on the street like Joseph and Mary, looking for an inn. I couldn't think of that right now. I was a one-day-at-a-time survivor, not a long-term planner with goals and a vision.

Come to find out that our school was a charter called The Dream Academy. Daddy was transported down there to fill out all of our paperwork, and he brought me back a school calendar, all the manuals, and lists. At first, I *knew* that Daddy was telling a fat one, because the thought of us all being side-by-side in K-12 buildings made my heart swell with gratefulness. It was too good to be true. Having Bean and Bell away from me wracked my nerves to the core.

I snuck down to Mrs. Betty's office and asked if she could pull up the school on the internet, so I could see pictures of it myself. When I saw it with my own eyes, I had to ask the good Lord to forgive me for calling Daddy a liar.

Later that night, in my bunk, I visualized the calendar taking human form and sauntering toward me with a smug look of contempt. Calendars were never friends—more like my nemesis. I tried to Jackie Chan it, but it was so much stronger than me, forcing me into submission. I found myself totally spent of all emotion. Could I ever move again? I was so battered and bruised on the inside with the kind of scars that rarely heal on their own. That obnoxious calendar raised its hand in victory, the pages somersaulted by, and I remembered my birthday was coming up in those twenty weeks. I'd be eighteen.

Once, I remembered Momma making me a cake and all the birthday jazz that goes with it, including a balloon tied up on the chair at the head of the table. I had been so blissful then, and now

I couldn't even remember which birthday that was. We didn't have photos or mementos with dates. We didn't have that luxury on the road.

Maize waved his hand in front of my face. "Are you praying out loud?"

I smirked. "Need to be, don't I?"

I didn't realize that what was rambling through my head was coming out of my mouth. Sometimes I had an awful bad habit of that.

He glanced around our tiny room. "It's not the worst place ever."

And he was right. This one had all the other places beat. At least we had a private bathroom. *That* I could be eternally thankful for. Even if I had to share it with five people, at least those people shared my genetic makeup and stink pool.

Bell was lying on her bottom bunk, listening to the iPod her teacher gave her on her birthday this year. Mrs. Betty was lovely enough to recharge it for her. She'd been without her music player all summer, since we didn't have no access to no plugs, and now she was crawling her legs up the wall like an itsy-bitsy spider, sliding back down in time to some unheard melody, probably some kind of musical. She was into that. The whole Dorothy and the Wizard of Oz thing. Let's escape our current situation by making like we could be anywhere else in the world, over some rainbow—but not here. Never here.

Bean was out with Daddy, and I was secretly relieved. Bean was the one who couldn't sit still, and Daddy knew it. He would take him on long walks to wear him out before bringing him back into a cramped-up little space. They were on some kind of adventure that had taken them nearly all day and evening, out looking for restaurants within walking distance of The Home.

Daddy was a cooker. Not a high-priced chef, now. He was just a cook man. He'd always loved that, and with us not actually having our own stove or burners, he liked borrowing other people's. Daddy met Momma like that, going down to the farm to buy some fresh produce for some hotel he used to work at in Johnston. Right after him and Momma married, the restaurant turned into a nightclub, and they went to only serving fruit, yogurts, and them little cereal boxes that you have to peel the lid off. Daddy's days making them fine-dining meals were over.

Momma wanted him to work at the hog plant, but the wages weren't enough to bring home the bacon unless he worked the hours away from us, and he wouldn't compromise the time. He wanted to find new hotels or restaurants to cook some fancy bacon-wrapped scallops in, but Momma never wanted to leave.

Well, now that he'd been traveling around from one place to the next, Daddy seemed to always have a knack for finding some local place that needed an extra hand in the kitchen, even if it meant he had to wash dishes or peel the potatoes for the line cooks. He always kept his eye on the big-money job that he swore to us he would land one day, over some rainbow. Talked to us about his plans for opening his own little diner and calling it Mixed Vegetables. Our little inside joke. Not very funny, huh?

Maybe today would be his day. With Bean at your side for eternal optimism and a sunny disposition, who could fail at finding a perfect job?

Maize was apparently talking to me about how it would be to be in high school, and I was totally lost on everything that he said.

"Sis, seriously. How is it going to be?" He shook my shoulders, almost knocking me off the bed.

"What?" I breathed heavily, trying my best to focus on him. I was staring at the rusted fan making slow circles over my head, taking in little gasps of the coolness that was making its way down to me.

"Freshman here! High school! Girls! You know! Have you even been listening to me for the past hour?" He threw the course schedules onto my lap.

I hadn't even had the energy to glance at mine. With a school called The Impossible Dream or something, what could it be like? Impossible to ever fit in. Impossible to have a chance. Chances didn't happen to the Joneses. Messes did.

"Oh, high school. Well, it's middle school on speed. Does that mean anything to you?"

How could I let him know the truth? How he would be tortured practically every day of his high-school existence for a name like Maize? How the coursework would get harder, and the projects would pile up, and the test demands would be out of this world? How he didn't read like the rest of us or behave the way the teachers expected, he'd fail the second he walked in them doors, and there would be nothing I could do to shelter him from the cruelty of the world? And oh, how I wished I could've been his protector since the minute he was born, but truth be told I'd done nothing for him at all.

"I can run fast if that's what you mean. I've been ready to find me a place with a proper football team. That's my ticket out of Pickville, U.S.A. Get on the team, and nobody will mess with me."

I rolled my eyes. But maybe that was his own way to cope. Sports was never the answer for my sweet, baby brother. It hadn't been in the past. We weren't stable long enough for him to finish out a season, or his grades were never too far away from the D list, and he'd never make it past a progress report. This time, he swore it would be different. Maize vowed he'd be new in Newport News. It had a solid ring to it. What could I be?

Just plain ol' me. There was no point in me trying to even set some kind of New Year's resolution in August, because I knew how those always panned out anyway. I glanced down at my schedule. Daddy had me signed up for Foods, History, Trig, English, Financial Management, and Theater. Wait ... drama class? Was that man crazy?

I shoved my schedule at Maize. "Look at this! He actually signed me up for some drama class!"

A sideways look crossed his face. "He wouldn't have, would he?"

Maize looked down at his paper and fell back on the bed. "Not me, too. With you? Oh, Lordy, I'll be creamed."

"What?" I picked up his schedule.

If it wasn't torture enough, I'd have to endure a dramatic arts class where you would have to do some kind of public speaking or pantomime or actually communicate with another human being, I had to do it with Maize. Sixth period, too? Come on, people. They would say our names back to back, and that wouldn't fly.

"Daddy has lost it this go around." I looked over to the calendar that was forcefully stuck on a too-big nail in the wall. Already, I was wishing my days away.

I'd never done that. Even though Daddy was always on some kind of countdown in his life—to some midlife crisis, by the looks of my course schedule—I never tried to focus too much on the passing days. It was hard enough breathing in the one that God had granted me to try thinking about what the next one might hold. But drama class with Maize in a school called The Dream made the obsession with the calendar a little more understandable. Time to move on.

Daddy burst in with a smile on his face as bright as the stars. That had to be why Momma loved him—a tall, proud, handsome man from a small, farming community on the outskirts of Johnston County. He told me once the families didn't take too much to mixed marriages way back then, but she had to love that smile when he came up on her for the first time. When he smiled at me like that, I forgave him for not having that stable job. I forgave him for not giving me a proper home. I even forgave him for drama class.

The smile didn't fade. It was stuck on him like the Joker. I knew what that meant. He'd landed him a job, and by the looks of it, it fit him to a T. I knew automatically that it wasn't no landfill cleaning crew job or some dumpster duty like he'd done for the summer work, scraping by with enough money to keep us all fed each night on a bag of gas-station delights.

Bean was hiding behind Daddy, thin as a rail. He could very well have disappeared; except I could see the edgings of two brown bags poking out behind Daddy's knees. Not one handheld bag, but two big, brown, grocery bags.

Daddy twisted around, lifting Bean about four inches off the ground, making him almost drop the extra-large brown bags in his hands. I knew the look on Bean's face meant there was food in those bags. My little toothpick of a brother was always on the lookout for food. That boy could eat a whole refrigerator full, maybe even the spare parts and door handle, too. Bean opened up the bag to collards, fatback, a mess of black-eyed peas, hoecakes wrapped up in wax paper, and a thick slab of half a ham that even seemed to look like the shape of a smile. What had Daddy up and done? Held up the store?

Daddy said, "This was an advance on my first paycheck on Friday."

We pulled out Styrofoam plates and little spork packets and went to town. We were all silent, sure the story was coming but too busy gulping down the helpings to worry about all that now. We'd have the whole night for Daddy to illuminate us since we weren't fortunate enough to have cable or satellite systems or those game boxes. All I could focus on was how delicious it was and how on every Friday night, when Daddy brought home the paycheck, he'd been promised a whole 'nother heaping two bags of food.

Daddy's smile was contagious, and I couldn't help but give him a mirror-imaged one right back. He said, "It's good people, Sweet Potato. I'm telling you, good people."

I asked, "What's the name of this place?"

I was always interested in the names and makings of restaurants—the romanticized story of how it all began. Names intrigued me, I guess. I wanted to believe somewhere out there in the universe names meant something other than how Momma named us all by the way she put up the picket signs at the beginning of every summer selling season.

Sweet Potatoes
Maize
Beans
Bell Peppers

Bean yelled, "Soul Food!" He made that funny, little snort-laugh I adored.

Bean kept cutting in anytime Daddy would try to tell us the story, but I did learn that the owner of the restaurant, Mrs. Sunshine Patterson, was a godly woman who believed in the spirit of helping others. Since we were in a world of need, she'd held out her hand to Daddy. I loved that name, *Sunshine*, and I couldn't wait to see what her face looked like. I imagined her being a white lady with golden-orange hair colored from a box and a plump figure as round as the sun, wearing those flowered-up housedresses and bedroom slippers.

Daddy said that Mr. Patterson was the head cook, with Mrs. Patterson running the front. They had a son who bussed the tables and helped on the line when needed and a niece who was a waitress. So, it was a family-owned-and-operated business. Letting Daddy in was something she said that they had never done, but something in her spirit told her it was right. That let me know that it was religious type place. Maybe seeing Daddy like this every day, feeling the tiny twinge of hope inside me, staying in this room and sleeping on this actual cot … maybe God was coming to visit me.

Some Soul Food was just what we were about to need, and I didn't even know how bad.

THREE

Loving your family should be the easiest thing to do, besides breathing. But sometimes, for me, it took effort. And I'm not talking about the energy it took to break sweat. I'm talking about full-out exertion that causes me to almost faint with exhaustion. It's actually just a little too difficult to gulp down, like castor oil. Love should be there, as part of the natural flow of creation. Something just springs out of us when we are born and makes us snap right into the missing pieces of the other half.

That's how I imagined it should be, anyway. Maybe it was, for other folks. But for me, I didn't quite know yet. I knew it was mighty hard to love.

That rule applied to Momma especially. And not for being a user, which was number one on my list for hating her. But a mighty close second was for calling me Sweet Potato Jones. What on God's green Earth did she think when she sprouted us out? I mean, come on. Who names their youngins after blessed vegetables? Daddy had never been able to give me a proper history of it, so it never settled right with me. The names. I mean, really, Momma. At least once a day I looked up to the sky and asked Momma why would she have done such a thing to us poor youngins? And she never answered me, and I'm sure God's still laughing about it. Think about that page in the Book of Life waiting for us. Sweet Potato Jones, Maize Jones, Bell Pepper Jones, and still-up-for-grabs Bean Jones. Why, God?

Daddy said that Momma wasn't right in the head. He told us once she was born that way, and he loved her all the same, because there was something about the way she smelled, and her name to him was like a spring day. Momma's name was Marigold. So, one might guess she'd name all us kids after flowers, not food. My name would have been so much better as "Rose" or "Violet." The possibilities of smell-good names were endless. I even Googled them once when we were at the library, to read down the list of what she could have called us. Bell Pepper would have definitely been "Lily." Maybe Bean would have been named "Cactus Jack." Didn't that sound like a Wild West showdown kid? That's Bean to a T. Maize—well, I found "Cornus." Even went to see what a picture of a cornus looked like, and the way the sprigs all jump out at you kinda looked like Maize's hair. He begged Daddy to let him get cornrows once, said he would take care of it and Daddy wouldn't have to pay anybody to help him keep it up. Daddy gave him the boy-you-must-be-crazy look, and that was the end of it.

Without Daddy knowing it, we'd overheard him the last time we'd gone down to the Tabernacle Faith Church. He was in the pastor's study, but the door was cracked. We had all been fitted for our choir robes because we were going to be having a fundraising service for the building fund, and the church was chaotic. I guessed Daddy thought we were off being taken care of. Instead, we all lined up at the door to patiently wait for him to take us back to the old train depot where we'd found an empty room to lie a spell. He said something to that preacher man that he'd never spoken aloud to any of us youngins. He said he'd blamed himself for years on end for

Momma's trip to Heaven. He said if he had stayed in Smithfield like she wanted and worked at the hog plant, it wouldn't have been this way. With her being right down the road from her own folks, she wouldn't have left that farm for nothing, not even for a loaf of bread. But Daddy said that was why he forced her to move on and branch out in the world. That branching out wasn't Momma's style, I guess. Her limbs weren't strong enough for a mighty wind, so she snapped right to pieces.

As soon as I shut my eyes, at least a couple nights out of the week, those words would come to haunt me, and I'd hear the cry in his throat as he confessed. Daddy never did the drugs like Momma. If he did, he sure didn't show the signs of it. He was the one taking care of us when she'd go out to have her fix or go downstairs to *check the pipes*. Now, I got the meaning behind the pipe inspections, and I hated how she thought we were all naïve to her lifestyle choices. Her destructive path to what? To lie in a grave while I took care of her youngins for her? Bell was a baby. Bean, too. I was up to Daddy's belt buckle then. I remember the force of the hug he gave me after she went on. His silver belt buckle left a mark on the corner of my eye that will always be there to remind me of the day my world stopped turning.

Even after a night of restlessness, I still had my duties. Daddy went off to throw out some biscuits and gravy at Soul Food at an early six o'clock a.m. That left me there with the kids all day long. At least Bell was a complete angel, and I never once had to worry about what she might get into. Bean and Maize—well, a whole 'notha story.

The Home had a small backyard for the kids of the establishment, and there were about three other families that had kids around Bell's and Bean's ages. No one was as old as me. I was the one that always had to carry the torch and watch out for the little ones, but I guess it could've been worse. I might have had cleaning the urinals or some other menial task like that. They had a small sandbox in the corner by old piles of Chiquita banana boxes lining the chain-link fence, and a basketball court where the net was gone off the rim. At least it would keep Bean and Maize busy all day long. Give those boys a ball, and that was it.

Bell was listening to her music again, singing quietly in the corner, and I was reading, as usual. Right now, I was into trying to memorize a poem from a collection book, one of those fancy, gold-letter anthologies I was fortunate to find on the dusty bookshelf. The worn books always caught my attention, because if someone loved them enough to hold them until they were ragged, then they must have been worth it.

I found a treasure when I caught on to a poem written by an Anonymous. Now, there was a name I could identify with in this great big world. They wrote "The Kissing Trees." I needed to start to let things matter to me. I didn't quite know how I could accomplish it, but I had to start somewhere.

Hope has wings
when Freedom sings,
finding peace in the
purest of things like
the joy of a morning
under the kissing trees.
Hope has wings
and other things like
you

Maize stuck out his tongue, sweat beading all on his forehead.

"What are you doing, you weirdo? Come play." He threw the ball at me, knocking the book clear out of my hands. Copying down stanza one was as far as I got.

"That hurt! And I don't want to play today. I'm at peace right now."

I couldn't help but stick out my tongue right back at him, as immature as it might have been. I could play a mess of ball with them, but I didn't feel up to having Bean hanging onto my pants with all of these other kids around. They picked at my height, because I was right at six feet. Another attribute I got from Daddy, I guess. Bean always begged me to dunk. Even though I knew I couldn't, he still thought I was as tall as the blue sky.

Maize's eyes grew misty. "I know you loved our adventures in the woods. Do you remember that time when you made us a treehouse? How we didn't topple out of that thing, I will never know. Now we are away from anything growing green except Daddy's paycheck. I get that you miss the pines to hide in, but this flat dirt makes a savage court. Suit yourself, sis."

He grabbed Bean by the arm, and they had at it for another round of Horse.

I closed my eyes, feeling the warmth of the sun on my face. The slight nudging of Bell's black Converse against my own let me know she was right by my side. It came to me. Peace that felt like a quieting somewhere in my soul. I folded the first stanza and placed it in my pocket. If hope had wings, I sure did wish that I could fly.

Mrs. Betty Atkins called us in for some lunch after a while, but I couldn't find a way to eat. All I could feel was that yearning to fly like a free bird on wings of hope. Instead, I was the bird trapped with a broken wing for so long that I'd forgotten how to fly. Always behind the bars of another person's cage, accepting a little piece of bread.

Bell graciously accepted the wrapped sandwich and apple, curtsying as she went through the line. I held out my hand robotically, trying not to give away all the thoughts I'd been collecting from poetry and memories.

Mrs. Betty Atkins smiled at me, but her face was pensive. Drawn lines etched her eyes. Seems like in her line of work the pitying eyes would have worn off by now. She'd been the director for twenty-three years, for goodness' sake.

"Hey, sweetheart, are you okay?"

I could say, "Yes," and really mean it, but somehow the words would not come. They stirred right below the surface.

Because why wouldn't I be okay? It would have been ungrateful for me not to be. I wasn't in an abandoned train depot or one of those renter shacks by the field that were so scary at night. We had our very own private bathroom, and Daddy was a cooker man, not a HAZMAT worker with a wage under the table. We had brown bags of food in our hands that included BLTs, apples, and Jesus Saves tracts. That meant Bean, Bell, and Maize would be okay. That had to be enough for me.

As the other residents chatted and talked about their transitional opportunities or upcoming job interviews, or how they had settled themselves with a new community service project, I couldn't stomach the thought of having to hear all those endless possibilities. I pointed upstairs, and we trekked off to our room to eat in privacy.

Daddy popped in around nine-thirty, and to my surprise, he had each of us a small bag of candy from Mrs. Sunshine. I split all of mine between Bell and Bean, who now believed that Mrs. Sunshine must be a pure angel. From collard greens to cotton-candy bubblegum—enough to earn a place right next to Jesus. Daddy wanted to talk to me, too. And this time, it was up on the roof. He'd found a way to get up there from a pull-down staircase that Mrs. Atkins had had him climb to look for some extra light bulbs in an upstairs closet. She'd told him that the roof was a place where families could sometimes congregate to get away from the noise.

It was strange on the roof like I was sitting over creation, and I couldn't help but hum that old Carpenters song that Momma used to sing on good days, "Top of the World." The stars were starting to come out, and the longer I looked the more they seemed to materialize for my very own show. I could almost touch them. It was too personal, and the beauty of it made me sit back and wonder how things in this world could be so messed up and so perfect at the same time.

Daddy was pacing back and forth, rubbing his mustache sideways—the tic he had when he was nervous.

"Go ahead, Daddy. Spill the beans."

He said, "Well, see, there's this thing I need to talk to you about."

He hesitated, and the silence was deafening. Were we about to talk about how he wished that things could be different, that I could have a Momma and I wouldn't have to pretend to be one? All those words he should've been able to say to me, but never could. So many words between us unspoken as we tried to manage this life we led.

"Go on." He needed the urging, because now he wasn't budging, propped up against the industrial ducted fan unit.

He asked, "You gonna take care of the kids for me or not?"

Why ask me that? Of course, I would. They were the only reason for my existing and staying here.

"Do I have a choice?" Choices were for rich people. Not for a girl who owned one bag of clothes and borrowed everything else, including other people's poetry books.

"Yes. You do." He crossed and uncrossed his arms, looking down at his scruffy boots the whole time.

The ever-fear crept in. This time, it might be out of my control. "What is this? You giving me away?"

I was eighteen soon. Wasn't there some law where I could choose not to go into foster care, because I was so close? Even though we had the prior threats from when school personnel had turned us over to social services, I'd never had to go to foster before. Why now? I was too old for this. And Bell, she was too young.

Daddy said, "No, child, good heavens, no, baby. I wouldn't give you away, just like the man in the moon wouldn't give away his change. I meant an arrangement."

So, I wasn't given away. That was a relief. If I had to leave my little cage, for all it was worth, to fly to another one, I'd rather be shot down in dove season than endure that kind of heart-wrenching pain.

"Arrangement? I'm listening." But was I? My mind kept going back to that word. *Choice.*

"You workin'. How about that arrangement?" He was still looking at his shoes.

"You sending me off to work?"

I knew once when a family had gotten too big on the road, this momma farmed off her kids like pure slaves. Never knew they did that anymore, and I was sure it wasn't legal, but she put her boy with a group of workers and left him there on the side of the road. The girl had gone on a long dirt-road walk to where I never knew and couldn't imagine.

We'd been staying in an abandoned tobacco barn nearby, and we'd witnessed the whole thing. Sometimes it still gave Maize nightmares, and honestly, me too. My heart stopped cold. He wouldn't. He wouldn't think of that. I fell on my knees right then and there and began to pray aloud for my Father in Heaven to take me away from this choice. I'd make the decision to go to Mrs. Betty Atkins. I loved Daddy, but I loved my Bell enough to know that what he was saying was not going to pass with me. 'Cause if it was me, then it might be her, too. Daddy had lost it.

He shook me, tears streaming down his face. "Stop praying out loud, child! I'm telling you to work with me at Soul Food, taking shifts. If you want to stay home and take care of the kids at night, or I can work breakfast and lunches and you can work dinner shifts, either way on weekends. What is wrong with you, girl? I'm your Daddy."

Even when it was simply a normal kind of part-time work arrangement that could be discussed between two adults, I still imagined a day would come when he would split us and give us away. Overreacting wasn't my typical style, but this time I lost it. *Composure, return.* I lassoed my fear back in.

I hugged him fierce. "I'm sorry, Daddy. I'm sorry. I let my imagination run wild for a second, that's all."

"I'm your Daddy." He kept repeating it over and over. "I'm giving you a choice."

It only took me a second to decide. "Shifts sound great, Daddy. I'll do the after schoolwork and the weekends. It will do me good to have some kind of ... work to keep me busy." I desperately wanted to say, "Some kind of money for when I take the kids on my own to support them the right way."

I'd never had the opportunity to hold down a part-time job before. I could buy Maize his own ball, Bell needed some new bows. Bean needed manners and hyper pills, but I'm sure I couldn't go down and buy those at the Five and Below.

"One stipulation. Your wages go to helping us buy stuff for us, like clothes and school supplies for the kids, and whatever left is put up in the piggy for the calendar day."

The trip. He was already figuring on leaving this place before we were settled. Typical.

"Deal. I can handle that."

Immediately, my mind went to my school wardrobe for my senior year. My jeans were classics, fine. But we needed hoodies, because the sling bags were never big enough to carry jackets. We always had to ditch those and grab new ones when they could be worn, not packed. And I positively needed a couple of new t-shirts for school. I was a collector of graphic tees, like a wearable scrapbook of my life. It was the closest thing I had to mementos.

Before we headed back down the staircase, Daddy grabbed my arm. "They are mighty good people, Sweet Potato. I feel it. You'll like it, I'm sure."

"Sure, Daddy. Give me a break from Bean, and I'll be a five-star cooker, for sure." I couldn't help but share in his laughter.

"Oh, you won't be a cooker, but a waitress. Their niece is going off to college, and they needed somebody to take her place. I showed them our old family picture I carry in my wallet, and for some reason, Mrs. Sunshine waved her hand in front of her face like a fan. She started having heart malformations or palpitations or something like that. She said you had to come down and help out." He swung open the door wide and pushed me forward.

"Daddy, I don't like these rooftop conversations. Something about the heights had my head all loopy. Maybe we can stick to the room next time."

"Okay, child." He chuckled. "You actually thought I'd do something like give you away, or worse?"

I gulped down the fear that rose again at the thought. "Sorry, Daddy. If not the roof, maybe it's this Virginia heat. It's worse here, I think."

He was emphatic. "No way! I sure don't think so. You up to doing breakfast and lunch times tomorrow, and I'll be here to keep a steady eye on the youngins? I'll stick to the evening shifts for the time being, then I'll do the morning shifts when you start up school. You can let the bus drop you off there in the afternoons if you want."

I grimaced. Only four days left to sleep in late, but that was gone now, too. "Sure, Daddy. Whatever way I can help, I will."

He sighed. "That's my girl. You are the sweetest, you know that. My Sweet Potato Pie."

"Daddy, that's old."

He told the kids I'd be early and out in the morning, and I needed my beauty rest. Bell was the disappointed one, but she would be okay with her iPod, probably wouldn't even realize I was gone. The boys couldn't have cared less, and that was okay, too. They'd be out in the back every chance they got, now that they discovered the basketball court. Daddy would even like to get him some exercise. He'd be out there playing with them; I was sure of that.

Bell broke my train of thought and said, "Let's say our prayers to bless this place."

We stopped our ritual of the flashlight theater show tonight because of my getting up early. I was sure it was my round to be the storyteller or solo artist for the evening, and I was grateful Daddy let me have my peace tonight. Daddy led us into our nightly prayers, and usually right after the amen round the whole room would soon be in snore mode. But not for us, not tonight. We kept whispering in the dark about the new adventure waiting for me. I didn't know if talking it out eased my nervousness or built up my anticipation. I would wake up at five o'clock and get ready for my first job. What would it be like? Would I get orders all mixed up? *Lordy, no.* Would I have to wear a nametag? *Lordy, no.* Would they make me wear one of those checkered uniforms with the short skirts? *Lordy, no.* Would I have to say, "Kiss my grits," to get a tip? *Lordy, no.* We all went back and forth on those for a while before we could settle in.

FOUR

Five o'clock, Daddy was my rooster. I splashed water over my face for about the twenty-fifth time, then fixed my hair. I looked decent enough for an early-morning wake-up call. I was never one to wear makeup—wouldn't have been able to afford it even if I'd needed it. Thank God for my clear complexion, free of the blemishes and pimples other kids my age had. I stared out at my almost-adult self, with my fixed-up hair and dark eyes.

I guessed if I had to choose one quality, I had that was worth looking at, it was my eyes. It seemed like when I looked at myself in the mirror, I always saw Momma's eyes staring back at me, as if she was trying to tell me something from the grave. An urgency was always behind them. All the way down to the Soul Food place, I kept wondering what people saw when they looked into my eyes. Mrs. Betty Atkins asked yesterday if I was well. Did I look sick? Lost? Hopeless? Or like a wounded bird on a cracked sidewalk? Definitely not the kind that deserved a kissing tree.

I pulled out the torn-out notebook sheet where I'd copied my newest poem to memorize and tried to busy my mind with the words to get the thoughts of the new job out of my dizzy head. I was at the part where Anonymous said that hope came in *the joy of morning* when I reached the door to the place where our family had found a helping hand.

The words were scrolled in deep violet lettering on the door, some of them worn with age and peeling a little. "A Daily Dose for the Soul ..."

The closed sign was still posted. It was about five forty-five. Daddy must have taken a long safari walk with Bean yesterday, because it had only taken me about four minutes to get here.

I was about to rap on the glass when he stepped into view. He was staring at me quizzically, his head turned sideways, his brow furrowed deep in concentration. He turned and yelled something behind his shoulder. He had on a simple, white t-shirt, with a purple apron draped across his muscular chest. His eyes were a deep brown with golden flecks, and I could tell right away his face was the kindest face of any boy that I'd seen in my entire life. Not a boy, though. He was a man, top-to-bottom solid.

How old was he? Who was he? And I was sure to find out, because the door timidly opened. His voice was of a lyrical kind. That was it. Like the lyrics of the sweetest song. It reminded me straight away of Bell and the way she could captivate me with her voice.

He said, "Are you her?"

I stammered, "Am ... am I?"

He smiled a full smile, his teeth perfect in alignment. "Well, if you don't know, then I sure don't know, so we both are at an impasse. We don't open for customers for about fifteen minutes."

Girl, pull it together. "I'm not a customer."

He smiled again. This time, I felt like I could melt straight on down. "A food critic at five forty-five?"

I grinned back at him, then forced myself to hold it, because he seemed to sidestep me. Did I do something? Did I have something stuck in my teeth? *Oh, Lordy!*

"I'm Sweet ..." I stopped myself, reined it in, and began again. "I'm supposed to start today. The waitress job."

He opened the door wider, swept his hand out in a grand fashion, and hollered, "Momma, the girl is here."

The girl. I was *the girl*. He picked up a bucket from one of the violet booths and turned back to work, wiping down the already pristine table.

The sunshine white woman in my imagination was far from what Mrs. Sunshine Patterson was in person. She had a commanding presence about her, a strong-looking Black woman with proud eyes and a swagger to her hips like none I'd ever seen. She wore the same white t-shirt, same violet apron with a Bible verse scrolled across it in fancy, gold lettering. *My soul will be satisfied as with the richest of foods; with singing lips my mouth will praise you.*

I didn't have time to notice if Mr. Door-Opener's apron said anything important, because when I looked back at him, I was too busy staring at those eyes of his. He was beyond fine, and that was all I could think of.

Instead of shaking my hand or smiling at me, Mrs. Patterson embraced me straight on, taking me in her arms like I was the long-lost prodigal daughter come home. "Well, my ... my ... lookie here, will you, Joe? Joe! Joe!"

Her husband's chubby face peeked from the service window. "What is it? What now? Too early to get my blood pressure working into a tizzy. What's the matter?"

"Lookie here! It's Sweet Potato Jones, come to work for us today!"

I froze solid at the sound of my name being called out that loud. It echoed around me, and I knew the boy was looking at me from one of the corner booths. No hope for a proper introduction, or even time to think up a lie like "Rose Jones" or something that had a nice, catchy ring to it. Lordy, no! She had to go hollering it out.

The soon-off-to-college niece came up to me then, holding

out my nametag. It had been printed out with one of those inkjet printers, with little, lilac flowers embroidering the sides. "Jones" was written out in the middle. These were godly people, after all.

Denise smiled bright at me as she fastened the tag. "Your Daddy told us you'd like it simple like that. Is that okay?"

She could probably tell it was just from the look of relief flooding my features.

I nodded, still too disoriented to speak. This whole being present without the kids in tow made me feel discombobulated—bashful, even.

"Come on and be my shadow this morning. By lunch shift, you'll have it all together. It's so simple, I'm sure even Bean could handle it."

I let loose a grin then, imagining him taking customers' orders. The spelling alone would cause a catastrophe in the kitchen.

"Thanks," I muttered.

And thankfully the customers all welcomed me the same as the family did. Come to find out that the locals 'bout came here every single day and had been doing so for at least the past twenty years, since Soul Food had first opened its doors for business. I ghost-walked behind Denise all morning long and watched as she openly confessed Jesus to the customers, right down to breaking into a song from the gospel radio station blaring out of the old speakers. Mrs. Sunshine would occasionally come by me and offer me a word of encouragement or a compliment, or break out singing a duet with Denise, spinning her around on her heels to another apparent favorite: "There's a harvest, souls a-plenty ..."

All I could do was conjure up my public smile behind Denise, and that was enough for the morning. She was right, at least: it was simple enough. The menu was as plain as the day was long—another blessing under the Soul Food tin roof. And one more was the pair of pecan eyes that kept watch over me. Even when I least expected it, he'd be there. Once, he accidentally touched my arm as he walked past, carrying his gray bucket piled high with flapjack remains. My cheeks prickled, and I wondered if he felt this strange sensation, too, because he stumbled a bit but caught his footing and carried on about his business, trying to brush it off. Could that mean we both felt something going on? It wasn't nothing. It was something, and whatever it was, made my heart flutter.

When the rush settled down, around eleven, Denise took me to the corner booth reserved for the family.

She eyed me curiously. "You don't have a lot of words about you, do you?"

I shrugged. "I'm a little nervous, that's all. It's my first job."

Denise leaned in and said, "You have found the best place, just saying. Maybe I'm biased, but it's hard for me to imagine myself any other place than here. I'm nervous about leaving for college, between us."

College. I didn't know how to respond. That had never been a blip on my radar. I had never even imagined myself staying in one place, period. There was no place that held roots for me. Nothing really for me to miss, except a porch swing.

Mr. Joe was out from the back, dipping into some blueberry pie that Mrs. Sunshine brought out from under the large cake stands. I watched them exchange loving glances, and then Mr. Joe swatted Mrs. Sunshine playfully as she swished by him flirtatiously.

It took attention to detail and strong focus for me to be around people—without the kids, that is. I wasn't used to standing on my own two feet unless I was in a school situation, and then I could busy myself or have a book in front of my face for cover. Here, it was different. I was expected to perform tasks that required communicating. I was expected to smile, to engage, to converse with others. It wasn't about filling customers' bellies. Denise and Mrs. Sunshine worked with an intensity and care like it mattered.

Mr. Door-Opener remained in the back most of the time. He would jog out to do his duty, to disappear yet again. I peered through the diamond-shaped cutout in the silver, swinging door to see if I could catch a glimpse of him, but all I could see was his back against the line of sinks. He was taller than me, which was a relief since I was like the Jolly ol' Giant. His nose seemed to come right at my eyes when we faced each other at the door this morning. I tried to calculate it—maybe six feet three?

Denise waved her hand in front of my face, and I knew that I blushed cayenne. "Life to S.P. You better eat up quick, because the lunch crowd will hit in the next few minutes. This will be our only break until after three."

I did as she instructed, listening to her rattle off about going to Virginia University of Lynchburg to study seminary. She already had the makings of a fine youth minister, Mrs. Sunshine reported as she slid in the booth, cradling Denise protectively under her arm.

Then she fired a question at me. "What is it that you want to be when you graduate, Sweet Potato?"

She threw my name out there like it was "Linda" or "Cindy." Not a root vegetable.

"A free bird." My rambling was embarrassing.

Mrs. Sunshine beamed. "A free bird leaping full on the coattails of the Virginia wind, my … my … I love it. I love it. You've ridden those gusts right to our door, sweet girl. All those miles led you right where you were meant to nest. I think that the gusts in your life have quit a-blowing, and God has set you in the right place. It's there in my very soul—the whole nature of you. I want you to know that I get you, girl. And now you are one of the Soul Food's finest ladies. The best in town."

I didn't quite know how to take that speech. Was this woman for real? Did she spout out wisdom in daily doses for the soul like the letters on the door said? The name of this place fit her like a model's dress, and with a name like Sunshine, she was a fashionista for sure.

He emerged from the swinging, silver door, hands free of buckets and rags. I was trying to listen to Mrs. Sunshine as she turned back to Denise, but I couldn't quite make out the words. There was something about that boy that made me stop and see only him. The world and all its problems seemed to fade away into white noise and backdrop. Never once had I paid one ounce of attention to boys. I didn't even care I hadn't been kissed, been on a date, had a boyfriend, or even talked openly to a boy unless forced to in some group at school. The point was that no boy in the entire geographic area of North Carolina ever got my attention. Move to Virginia—bam, a different story all together.

His strong hands came up from behind, draping over the violet booth right beside me. Those hands that cleaned fascinated me so. My eyes could not leave them. They looked so soft, not cracked as I'd expect from years of scrubbing. He had long fingers that reminded me of those jazz men with the guitars on the covers of the old albums we once owned. I could only imagine what it would be like to feel those fingers intertwined with mine.

Oh, Lordy! Lasso that back in, girl. Get your head ship-shape to the here and now.

He reached over to Denise's plate and swiped a fry. I couldn't help but watch the way his muscles flexed and danced beside me.

Denise giggled, cupping her mouth with her hand. She could probably see that my face was as red as beet juice. Regardless of how bad I wanted to hide the feelings that were rushing through me like a violent thunderstorm, I could not do it. I was an open book, and Mrs. Sunshine knew it, too.

She pursed her lips and said, "I knew it, and I tell you I did. As soon as I saw that portrait of your family he carries around in his wallet, I told your Daddy, 'Bring that girl right on up here to work for Denise.' I'm sure glad that the Spirit does the talking around this place. We'd miss out on the world, otherwise."

I exhaled heavily, not fully understanding a word that she was saying. Denise seemed to be right in alignment with her thoughts, though, and she winked at me.

Mrs. Sunshine cooed, "Ray, why don't you sit down with us?"
Ray. His name was Ray. Sunshine. A ray of light in my darkness. My Ray. *Oh, Lordy!* What was wrong with me?

He stretched back. "I can't right now, Momma. I've got to go down to the library really quick to check out that ASVAB study guide."

My mind raced to a catalog of acronyms I'd seen once. I'd heard of the ASVAB in a counseling lecture at my second-to-last high school.

Denise frowned. "I thought that you weren't going into the military until after college, Ray? Please consider going to Lynchburg with me. You've already got your acceptance letter. You have to send them the confirmation. You still have time."

Joe hollered from behind the counter, a piece of the pie spitting out of his mouth in the process. "Let him follow in the old man's footsteps. Army strong, I am."

I sat solid as a stone figure in a museum. Army. Guns. Fighting. Overseas. War. Temporal. He was just like everything else in my life. My heart sank right down like it had been hit with a submarine missile, right to the bottom of the Atlantic Ocean. Ray Patterson, Army man. Gone. Moving on before my thoughts of him had even settled. Typical.

Mrs. Sunshine stood up. "I guess I've got to go on and accept this, huh?"

Ray stepped beside me and put his arms around his momma. "It's right. Trust me on this. It's something God is leading me to do."

Her lips pursed tightly. "Then follow. Who am I to interfere with the plans of the Almighty? Go on, but hurry back. I'll need you shortly."

He pecked her on the cheek, and for a split-pea second, his eyes met mine, and the world seemed to stand still even as he spun far away from me. He was gone with the clanking of the little bell at the door, the wind was carrying him MIA, and my hopes of being a free bird with wings spread in flight were ridiculous yet again. Back to the cage.

FIVE

Daddy was pleased when I reported an easy, breezy shift. It had been quite pleasant, besides my nervousness, my foolishness, and my infatuation with a soon-to-be military man. I left that last note out of my rundown. Daddy was ready to leave to take the four o'clock shift, and it was my turn with the kids. I looked at Bean's face, saddened by the rain clouds that had appeared out of nowhere, and decided right then and there that I would step in and make another choice, since I had been given some leeway lately.

"Daddy, until I start school, I'll stay down at Soul Food, if you'd like. I can do the all-day stuff. You've got to go down to the Social Services building anyway. Remember? Go ahead and sign them up for their insurance and all and look into some of the programs they might have. Like maybe the Y or the Boys and Girls Club to help with Bean's and Maize's tutoring and stuff, since I'll be working at the restaurant in the afternoons."

I was used to the system. I knew we could get on the list and actually get us a place of our own, if we could hold tight instead of rolling on. I knew we could get a credit card for the grocery store, and Daddy could whip us up some of his very own magic, if Mrs. Betty Atkins approved us some use of the kitchen equipment. I knew that the kids would go somewhere other than the shelter for the afternoons, like the YMCA or the Boys and Girls Club.

I didn't know if it was hearing about the Spirit talking, but deep down in my heart, I knew this place somehow had a different glow. It might be worth holding on to. And maybe, just maybe, Daddy would see that, too.

He'd say, "Newport News, what fine people. What a fine place. I think we'll stay awhile."

That would get him looking for us some kind of place that was available on the income he'd be able to provide, and with my help, too, we might do okay. Daddy couldn't be expected to work six to nine every day. That would be like fifteen hours' time seven, and that would be way more than any man should have to do for his family. I was older now. I could pitch in joyfully, and maybe that would get us a chance at permanence like the kids prayed for.

Daddy agreed with me, surprised by my enthusiasm for working. I overheard him talking to Mrs. Betty about setting up some transportation to take them all down to Social Services tomorrow while I would be at work. Daddy knew about all that stuff, but sometimes he needed a sticky-note reminder.

I kissed Bell on the head and promised her I'd tell her a special bedtime story tonight, the one about the red birds. Speaking of birds, I'd memorized most of the stanza—my fancy move to plant poetry in my soul. I still needed to memorize the last part, and I pulled out the paper from my pocket for a quick glance. *Hope has wings and other things like you.*

The paper was almost blown out of my hand by the wind as I walked back toward Soul Food. My mind was in a million places at once. Could I look at Ray straight on? His eyes were of the purest of things, and there was peace in his presence. Was he too bright for me to hold? Could I claim him, as my heart wanted to claim hope and so many other things?

Mrs. Sunshine smiled when she saw me back and ready for duty. "Forget something, Sweet Potato?"

I shrugged, pulling the apron back on and fastening it. "I gave Daddy a break, I guess."

She laughed heartily; her hands wrapped to her sides. "You took one look at Bean and decided that you needed the break with the impending storm brewing, huh? Coming to work to get away from work? Girl, you are a trip and a half and then some."

I smiled back. "I guess you had your very own experience with Bean to be able to read me like that."

"You, my child, are what I call a special reading, an open book. I can see the emotions clear across you at every point and turn. I also saw something else today, and so did he."

She pointed through the swinging silver doors. Mr. Joe? What had he seen me do? Did I mess up an order? They were going to fire me, for sure.

"I'm talking about Ray, honey, not my feisty, old man." She put her arm around me and whispered softly in my hair, "I saw you and Ray."

Me and Ray. She used us in a sentence. I frowned. What could she see? How when I walked away from them today, I prayed for a way to find my way right back to them, so I could be in the same vicinity as Ray? That man was going off somewhere to enlist in a war, and I'd never see him again, because Daddy was sure to have other plans for us before he could make it back home. We'd have twenty weeks here; would he leave before me? I was tired of all these temporals, and the heaviness engulfed me at once. Couldn't she see how tired I was? That's probably all she saw: this worn-out, old soul I wore around like a ragged outfit.

He came out from the back and stopped short. "Momma, did you call me?"

A puzzled look crossed his face, and the smile returned. He was beautiful, for sure. As mouth-watering as an unwrapped candy bar to a poor girl like me, and more golden than the ticket.

Mrs. Sunshine picked the order pad up off the counter, passed it my way, and put her arm around Ray. "Come on, boy. We've got some talking to do."

Oh, Lordy, no! Would she be talking to him about me? I prayed not. What would she say? "I see the way Sweet Potato looks at you, all with love on her like a new song."

I didn't have too much time to think about it, because a customer was rattling an empty glass of ice at me, mouthing for some more sweet tea. I was off, trying my best to keep busy and not think about what they could be conversing about. Surely it couldn't be me.

Ray didn't seem the least bit put off when he came back out to clear and put away. He did see me looking, and for the first time, I didn't turn my gaze. I leaned up against the swivel stool and stared at him. *I dare you. I dare you to claim me. Come on. You can. Just put one foot in front of the other and find your way to me. I can't do it, Ray. You seem like the kind that can.*

Head talk, that's all that was. Denise nudged me on the arm, making me lose my balance on the stool, and I thought I'd topple right down like a Jack on them fool cards. That was me, Joker Jack, for looking at that Ray. I should have been right ashamed. Thank heavens I didn't let on.

A bushel and a peck—I'd done it this time, because Denise said, "He doesn't have a girlfriend. Broke up with a girl a little while ago. So, he's a free bird like you. Why don't you fly over there and ask him out?"

"I ... I don't know what you're talking about."

I tore off the order, stuck it up on the silver spinner for Mr. Joe, and hit the little bell.

Denise rolled her eyes as she took me to the booth for a break. I was sure the way she wore her hair, flat tight in a clip at the base of her neck, was pulling all her brain cells out of order. Did she really think I could ask Ray out? It went to show how far this girl was from knowing me. I couldn't even talk to him.

She leaned over and whispered, "He's really a great guy. I promise. I wouldn't steer you wrong, sista. He's worth asking."

"I ... I couldn't." I couldn't even begin to imagine what I would start to say to him. "I live at The Home."

Lordy, no! Why did I say that out loud like that—putting it out there on that corner table like it was a normal piece of news? A homeless girl couldn't be asking no boys out. That wouldn't be right. They'd be supposed to walk home holding hands and kiss under a porch light. Not stand by ugly, steel double-doors, where the bug light zapped the night away, gathering the dead as a sign of all the hopelessness on the inside.

She put her arm through mine. "The Home? So what? What does that have to do with who you like?"

I frowned. She wouldn't understand what it did to a girl—to be sheltered or abandoned or boarded up most of her life. What that did to me, to the core of me. It changed me. It changed who I was, fundamental. I wasn't good enough to expect greatness, and Ray was the sky.

I ignored her and went off to help a new couple that had come in. I could fake a smile, even after all of that. Fake smiling came easy. It was the real ones that hurt the most.

I did my duty for the rest of the night. Denise dropped the whole pushing-me thing, and I was glad.

When the last customer was out the door, Mrs. Sunshine flipped the sign and let out a prayer to Jesus, thanking Him for another glorious day of spreading His word. I stared at her exuberance. Where all of that came from, I could not figure it out. I had never met anyone close to the likes of Mrs. Sunshine, that was for sure.

Ray came out, the apron gone and packed away. He came right up to me with the boldness I knew was within him and grinned. I thought I would fall over like a blown leaf on a March day from the sheer force of it.

His voice was low and deep. "Are you ready?"

"Mmm …" Ready? For my first boyfriend? For the first love of my entire life? *Yep. You bet.*

"To go? You weren't planning on spending the night with us, were you?" He snickered at me.

It was adorable, the way his dimples creased the corners of that perfect, full mouth. He had a straight nose and a hard jawline that twitched with a hint of apprehension. Perfectly set eyes that crinkled in the corners. I imagined him as old as Joe and all of the crinkle-cut-fry lines framing those eyes from years of smiling.

"I'm sorry." I took off the apron and hung it up on the coat rack by the door. "Goodbye, Mrs. Sunshine, Denise, Mr. Joe. I'll see you in the morning."

They all waved as Mrs. Sunshine turned off the lights. "Sleep well, dear. Thank you for the helping hand."

"You, too." She was the one needing the Medal of Honor for her service.

Ray opened the door wide. "Come on. I'm walking you home."

I spoke a little too forcefully. "No!"

He smiled, assuring me. "I know where you live."

Panic began to rise. "No!"

I was determined on this one. I walked right out of the door and tried to close him inside with the force of my body. I pushed with all my might but to no avail. He was stronger than me.

He laughed, one of those purest of things. "Stop it, Sweet Potato."

At the way he said my name, with this gentle urging, I released the door, letting the bell jingle wildly.

Ray leaned in close to me. I could feel his breath on my cheek. He whispered, "What? What is it?"

He wasn't going to listen to me. So he was that kind of stubborn.

"I don't want you to see."

I leaned up against the corner bricks, letting the rough edges remind me that I wasn't dreaming, but I was still too afraid to move. His hand found mine in this ridiculous moment of fear and acceptance. It felt right like I knew it would, fingers lacing together, his long ones sliding down mine, sending a shiver right through me. New. Exciting. Had to be the release of adrenaline.

He spoke softly. "Don't you worry. I know."

The tears wanted to fall so badly that my eyes stung, like a force of a thousand yellow jackets pricking my eyelids. "What do you think you know?"

"I know. That's all. Now come on and stop being so silly."

He pulled my arm, and I fell in step beside him. I couldn't have let go of him even if I wanted to. And the four minutes seemed to be about four seconds, because there we were. The Home. Some stragglers hung out by the doorsteps, which would be against Mrs. Betty's approval. She liked to close shop early so the vultures who liked to take advantage of us would think operating hours were over. We lingered by the fence, not stepping over the line—the boundary between my world and his. Ironically, a perfectly paved, gray sidewalk led up to broken stones, rubble, and white rocks scattered around the entryway.

I couldn't think of anything to say. I stared down at our hands, still joined. Ray Patterson. He had the makings of a good man, and he was right here, holding my hand.

He asked, "See you in the morning?"

I sighed. "Until school on Monday."

"How old are you, anyway?" He let go of my hand.

"I'll be eighteen next month." Saying "seventeen" made me sound too much like a baby.

He seemed pleased. "Okay. Bye, then."

His hand came out in a short wave as he turned and walked away.

Daddy was at the steps, boots finishing off those helpless moths that hadn't quite met their end by the zap of the bug light.

He exaggerated an extra-loud cough. "Well, I guess that was nice—Ray walking you home. To be honest, I was getting a little worried."

He eyed the travelers moving from the stoop to the side of the yard. "In fact, I don't know how comfortable I feel about you traveling between here and there by yourself at night."

I hurried up the cracked walk, wondering if one of the cracks would swallow me up whole and send me straight down to hell like I deserved.

"Hey, Daddy."

He frowned but didn't say much more—only that he felt a little guilty making me work the entire day through. I reminded him it was my choice, and that seemed to settle fine with him. Just like it was my choice to do it all over again the next day.

One more day with Ray. I'd take every single one of them that I could get my hands on.

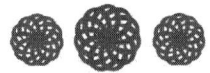

Five forty-five on the dot, and he was there at the door, as I knew he would be, with the same smile spread across his face. "Are you her?"

If you mean the girl of your dreams, I hope so. In all my dreams the night before, I could only see his eyes and his hands. Now I was standing right in front of him, and I couldn't find my words again. He didn't even wait for me to respond this time, opened the door, and went on back to his business.

I grabbed the apron from the peg and started to put it on when Mrs. Sunshine busted in. "Uh-uh-uh ... hold up a second. That's the wrong apron. Drop it."

I let it slide out of my fingers. *Oh, no. Here it comes. I'm a bad influence here. I'm canned, for sure.* Had I lost my job? Had I done another thing wrong, like show up? Not until I saw her holding up a new apron with gold lettering from an iron-on transfer, adjusting it right to me, did I understand what she was up to.

"This is your apron, child. Put it on." She made it sound so regal like an angelic host was ready to celebrate.

I held the apron out in front of me and read the fancy lettering. *Look at the birds of the air; they do not sow or reap or stow away in barns, and yet your Heavenly Father feeds them. Are you not much more valuable than they?*

I couldn't speak, even to say a thank-you. I tied the apron up around my waist and let my hand fall across the lettering one more time. A walking testament. That was what we all were: walking servants of the Lord in this place. I would be the one representing those who didn't have a place to lay their head—valuable children of God, like me, even though in all the past moments of my life I only felt worthless and useless. I was more valuable to God than the free birds of the sky, and I was already freed by the blood of Jesus ... that was what she was trying to say to me. Or maybe it was the Spirit talking in this place.

It was imperative that I find Ray. It hit me with a fierce urgency—to read the words his Momma had picked out for him. When my eyes finally rested on him, I was surprised to see his apron was blank, turned inside out with the seams showing. Funny how you didn't notice the smallest things when you were so concerned about the bigger ones. What was he hiding?

Denise had already gone to freshman orientation. She was starting her new life today, so her apron was to remain a mystery. It should have said something about playing matchmaker for the hopeless.

Around eleven, like clockwork, Mr. Joe came out looking for desserts. His apron was downright hilarious, and I wondered how many times he had to testify to it night and day. It surely was a message of Mrs. Sunshine's own conniving: *Husbands ought to love their wives as their own bodies. He who loves his wife loves himself.*

Mrs. Sunshine was hollering at him about his cholesterol while singing another hymn from the radio. She'd go back and forth between speaking the Lord's praises and blasting Mr. Joe about the crumbs on the side of his lip. I was sitting by myself, enjoying a whopper plate of the breakfast special Mr. Joe whipped up for me, quietly praising Jesus for letting me fall right into a place like this. If there was a place patterned after my own heart, this had to be it.

Ray sat down, a plate of fries drowned in ketchup in front of him. He went to his business, flipping through the ASVAB book. I stopped eating as he looked at me. I couldn't chew and look at him at the same time. My mouth felt like a bag of marbles had filled my cheeks to maximum capacity.

"I should have asked could I sit here."

He went back to eating, without properly asking. I tried to focus on my plate, not wanting to even glance at the book, because I knew what the study guide meant. I was trying not to stare at his hands, either, because mine twitched wanting to hold his.

Finally, he stood up, leaving the book behind, and going behind the counter with his plate. I figured he'd be back, so I took the rest of my plate down with style before he could come watch me eat. When he popped back out, he took my plate and disappeared again, coming quick so I wouldn't have a chance to flee. The bell jingled, and I was about to rise, but it was just the mail carrier, so I sat back down.

"Do you like working here?" He folded his arms across his chest and leaned back in the booth.

I nodded, biting my lip. His folded arms were some dangerous business, because I could see the outline of his muscles. I looked at Mrs. Sunshine, and she eyed me over the bills, sticking them in her apron pocket before swishing away.

"You seem to fit right in—except with the singing and the dancing and the talking and the joking and the loud hollering. I could go on." He laughed again, and I knew I loved him.

"I love that." *You.*

He raised an eyebrow. "What?"

"Your laugh." I knew it sounded ridiculous, but I couldn't help myself. What was wrong with me? Was I coming down with something?

Claim him. You can. He's single. You are definitely single. You can be bold. You can walk in the sight of the Lord in this place and not be ashamed. Not here, anyway, not where food for the soul came in daily doses or something like that.

"I love your eyes." He was still smiling, seeming to enjoy the banter. And what he said seemed so genuine. Like he truly meant it.

I rolled them, shaking my head, which was a mistake because it made my glasses slide a little down my nose. I quickly pushed them back up and turned away. "What do you see when you look at them?"

His eyes widened. "What do you mean?"

I shrugged. "I don't know. When I look in them, I see them wanting to say something, and it's just a mystery."

That sounded ludicrous, and I was flooded with relief when I heard the jingle of the bell—my cue to get up and escape from looking like a reject. *Too late.* I let my rambling mouth open. Mistake number one. No, mistake number one was thinking I could claim the sky. Number two was actually trying to.

Throughout the day, Ray had a puzzled look on his face every time he looked at me. Maybe he was trying to figure out what I'd been trying to say. His momma kept calling him, and he kept disappearing. So, I went to the task at hand, taking orders, smiling, trying to lose myself in the gospel singing on the radio. It all seemed to swing into gear for me, like a well-oiled machine, like I was meant to be in this place. Like it was the natural order of things. Maybe this was as close to normal as I was ever allowed to get.

It was soon a Friday, and Mrs. Sunshine prided herself on paying me, even though we hadn't worked an entire week. She said that didn't matter one bit, and she sent me home with a more-than-generous paycheck, together with two full bags of food that Mr. Joe packed up for us. He gave us enough to last us an entire weekend, not a Friday-night, end-of-the-workweek kinda celebration. They didn't know how scarcely we ate, or how sometimes in the past we'd tell Bell we were fasting for the Lord when in fact we didn't have anything. I had a feeling being four minutes from this place would guarantee we'd never go hungry again, and it wasn't all about the belly. It was more about the soul. The name sure did fit the place.

Ray walked me home. He held the two large, brown bags easily in his hands and still managed to open the door for me. Carrying the bags meant he couldn't hold my hand, and I was aching for it. I wondered if this was going to be a nightly occurrence for twenty weeks, and if so, what that would do to me on twenty-weeks-plus-one-day. Him walking me home, holding my hand, could eventually mean an arm around me, a stolen kiss, a promise. It could. I could dream, couldn't I? But even dreams end. I knew that.

"Do you ever feel the need to talk? I want to hear your voice." He couldn't help but smile again.

I wondered if that was all he ever did. If I had his life, I'd probably only smile, too. A stable family, a working family. A future. He was free.

"Where is your home?" I'd seen them escape two nights in a row through the swinging, silver doors after Mrs. Sunshine switched off the light.

"Behind the restaurant, like an attached place. It's nice enough, though. All we need." He walked a little slower.

The four minutes might drag tonight. I closed my eyes and imagined myself as a box turtle, taking my very own sweet time.

"Let me guess. It's purple?" I could imagine how Mrs. Sunshine's flair for decorations carried over into her home if it was anything like the restaurant.

But it would be a beautiful place, one that I'd never want to leave once I'd entered. Kinda like Soul Food. For some reason—and it was more than Ray—I felt like I had a connection to the physicality of the place like it was already an extension of me, and I spiritually lived among those Bible verses and warm, caring people.

He laughed. "How did you know?"

"Lucky guess. Can you take that off?" I pulled on the apron strings, and he stopped short, the bags tipping.

He put the bags down on a bench behind him. "What are you trying to do, Sweet Potato? Pull off my clothes? I tell you, I'm not that kind of—"

I interrupted him. "I want to read your apron. I have to read it."

He glanced down at the front of the apron as if expecting to be already able to see what was written—like it was a gold etching of his very soul. For some reason, I had a feeling that it was.

"Why? Why would that matter to you?"

I shrugged. "I don't rightly know. It just does."

I put my hand around my waist, holding in my own words of Scripture. God valued me even when I didn't feel good enough. That was what she meant when she gave me that verse—like she knew the self-loathing that was stitched along my heart. What would his say? I thought of the old song, "You Are My Sunshine." His momma would have gotten a kick out of typing that in her gold lettering. I was sure he was her morning sun.

He stared into my eyes under the dim streetlamp, searching me out. "I see what is there." His voice was low, almost a whisper.

And all at once I knew what he meant. It got real super quick. *Oh, Lordy.* I loved Ray. It was all-consuming love that rushed through me like a violent storm, wrecking me and making me shiver.

"I can't hide it very well, can I? Trust me, I'm trying mighty hard."

I bit my lip, scared to go any further. I broke from his gaze to stare down at the apron, wanting to pull it off and uncover his hidden secret. He had already discovered mine.

"Is it true, then?"

He reached out a hand to mine, and our fingertips brushed together. He slid those fingers down to hold my hand firmly in his.

I whispered, "You said that you can see it, so it must be true. As crazy as it all is, it must be."

I could feel it. Even though I'd never felt love for a boy, I was as sure about this as I ever could be. I knew that I loved him. Strange as it was, I knew right down to the very core of my being. He was to be my Ray. *Thank you, Jesus.*

He stepped closer. "I need to hear it, too."

I could smell the sweetness of him right there so close to me, and I felt the tears beginning to creep forward. I couldn't tell him I loved him. I couldn't say that out loud.

He would have to wait. "Show me your apron."

I found myself stepping around him to pull the strings apart, my hands shaking. He lifted the apron off and handed it to me.

"Momma gave me my apron when I was twelve. I never knew the full meaning of those words until Monday, when I saw you."

Even though it was too dark to make out the words, my eyes scanned the lettering as he spoke them softly against my cheek. *Let the morning bring me word of your unfailing love, for I have put my trust in you. Show me the way I should go, for to you I lift my soul. Rescue me from my enemies, O LORD, for I hide myself in you.*

"Me? What do I have to do with these words from the Lord?"

"I've put my trust in the Lord every day since then, trusting in God to lead me. I've served him patiently, waiting for the day when He would reveal my life's purpose. God's proof of His love came to me the morning you walked into my life. And I knew the second that you smiled at me God had yet again shown me a purpose more than myself, and that was to love you and take care of you. I love you, Sweet Potato Jones."

With every part of me screaming with joy and complete elation,

I wanted so badly to say it aloud. To let the words flow out of me like they had done for him. Instead of stepping back, he moved one more step in and rested his cheek against mine. So close to my first kiss, yet so far away. It was intimate. It was right. And that was enough for my Ray Patterson. That was enough for me.

SIX

Daddy was waiting by the fence this time, not the stoop. He had that look on his face like I'd been caught with my hand in a big, off-limits cookie jar, and since Ray was all sweet and brown sugar I couldn't resist. I'd stolen him, and now he was mine. He was a part of my very being now, because he'd told me he loved me, and I'd believed it. Ray wasn't no player. He didn't have that way about him. Ray was pure light. A godly man, and from a strong, stable family. *Oh, Lordy!* How could Ray love a homeless girl? Was this just a handout mission to him? Some outreach community service project that he'd been forced into by his youth group?

"Mr. Jones. Nice to see you, sir."

Ray handed the food bags to Daddy, and Daddy nodded back slowly. I could tell he was about to put on his conductor hat and pull rank, and that train was going to collide right into us any second. *Bam.*

He huffed. "Ray. Sweet Potato, it takes four minutes to come home. I expected you home around five after nine, with a minute to spare for tying a shoe, if need be. It's fifteen after, and I was about to leave them youngins up there to come after you. And you know I can't leave them up there more than a minute."

"I'm sorry, really, Daddy. I didn't mean for you to get all worried. We had to wait on the food, and Ray walked me home."

He eyed Ray and me with this beady-eyed suspicion. It was like the world must know everything about me as if I could broadcast news across the features of my face. Now that the love was between us, Daddy's eyes changed. And they didn't have any light in them, only dark.

"Ray?" It came out like a question—an accusation, even.

Ray squared his shoulders, taking a battle stance. "Yes, sir."

Daddy pointed up to the steps. "You want to come in for a spell?"

I thought that I'd fall out right there and start having my own heart palpitations. "No, Daddy. No!"

Tears formed behind my eyelids. It usually took a lot to make me cry, but this was a category five hurricane. Heavy rain predicted.

Ray said, "Maybe tomorrow night, Mr. Jones. Momma will be looking at the clock, just like you. She's probably already pulled out the shotgun and started the walk on her own."

Daddy nodded. "Okay, then, young man. Go on back, but I expect me and you to do some talking tomorrow night. Let your momma in on the plans I've established."

Ray smiled at Daddy and at me. "I'm looking forward to it, sir. I'd like to meet the rest of your family."

I couldn't return his smile. Daddy was punishing me for loving him. Why? Why would Daddy be so vindictive? He didn't operate like that.

In our room, Daddy set the bags down, and the kids jumped in on them like a pack of wolves, devouring the burgers almost without getting the wrappers off first. Daddy eyed me with a trepidatious look and muttered under his breath, "Roof."

I didn't want to follow him, but I had no choice. I heard the way his breathing was abnormal as he made it up them clackety stairs. He was laboring over this talk before it began, and in all honesty, we might as well have it now.

He went right back to the vent and leaned against it. I stood holding onto the iron railing, as far away from him as I could possibly get. Daddy wouldn't physically hit me. I knew that. But sometimes words could be just as hurtful, and this was my way of bracing myself for the pain.

He laced his tired-to-the-bone fingers on top of his head, leaning forward, trying to gulf the space between us. "Sweet Potato, what have you up and done?"

I shrugged, not really knowing what I'd done. I was innocent. No crime committed here, or I didn't think so. I didn't do anything to make him ashamed of me—around here, or at Soul Food, or in front of anybody, ever. There were many roads I could've diverged down many times before. But I kept the straight and narrow, and I didn't need or deserve this kinda talk from him. Especially after all the weight I carried for him.

His deep voice bellowed across the distance. "I never would have thought that it would have happened to you. And now here we are, and they are some good people. I tell you; they are good people. What have you up and done? No need to go up solid on me now. Talk to me, Sweet Potato, right now."

He took two strides and was right there in front of me. I wasn't afraid of him, but from the way he was looking at me I couldn't help but feel intimidation.

"They are good people, Daddy. I agree."

They truly were. Among all the folks we'd called acquaintances and friends, this family was like the top, prize-winning crop at the state fair—worthy of the ribbon and fame to go with it.

"I know that. I've done told you that. That's why you can't go messing this up." His voice was soft, but his eyes were still all contorted.

"I'm not planning on messing nothing up, Daddy."

But I knew full well about plans and how they could sometimes change, and this meant a new move down a dirt road out of sight might come quicker than I'd even thought possible.

"But you love him, Sweet Potato?" He searched me out and then sighed. "Did you tell him so?"

"No."

He shrugged again and leaned up against the brick wall, hanging on the same iron bar as me. "Maybe you should keep it that way. It will be easier on the both of you when you go."

He paused, looking up at the stars. "But he told you he loved you, didn't he?"

I nodded, still not wanting to speak about all that out loud. It was like my secret was now going to be on the bestseller list. *I Love Sweet Potato Pie*—a recipe book for all the ways you could make sweet potatoes melt. And every single person in the universe would see me, immediately ask for an autographed copy, and ask me questions like, "How does it feel to love for the first time? Sugar and spice and everything nice?" Or something stupid like that.

"He's Mr. and Mrs. Patterson's boy. And he's nineteen and you're sixteen, and you are not even thinking about going out with him." He nodded matter-of-factly.

"I'm almost eighteen, Daddy, remember? And I know who his momma and daddy are, and they are fine people. I don't have to go out with him, if that's what you think is best. But I do, well, you know ... I do love him."

Daddy started to cry. I hadn't seen him cry in a long time. After years on the road, you accepted the life you walked in, and the crying stopped—unless it was for big-time things, like Momma getting swept away playing spoons. Since then, not much rain in our forecast. Was this one of those big-time things for Daddy?

"I wished that you had your momma to talk to about these things. Loving a boy means you and I have to talk about some particulars."

Oh, no.

"No way, Daddy. I'm not having them buzzing bee talks with you. Don't you go off worrying about me none. I have not once never even kissed no boy, and even though I love this one, I ain't planning on making no honey in no beehives with him. No, siree."

He laughed nervously. "Okay, calm down, child. I trust you. You are good people, Sweet Potato. I find it hard to stomach that you'd be after a guy, that's all. You ain't no little seedling no more, just a big old bushel of a plant."

"Thanks, Daddy. I guess that's supposed to be a compliment. At least you recognize I'm grown. Do me a favor. Don't talk to him, Daddy. Please."

He was already patting his stomach. I was sure he was wanting to get one of those burgers before Bean devoured them all.

"Already been done, Sweet Potato. I expect a young man on this roof with me tomorrow night at nine-oh-seven, approximate. It'll take us about three minutes to walk in, pull down the step ladder, and climb on up here before me and him talk about a few things."

"No! Now, I've got to draw the line right here." I was totally beyond freaking out now.

He passed me by. "Come on. Don't you worry your pretty, little head over nothing. I'm going to find out what his intentions are."

"Oh, Lordy, no!"

"I almost forgot. Thanks to the Lions Club, you can get you a new pair of frames after you visit the bus a corner down."

There was so much to be thankful for in this place.

I prayed as we made our way back to the kids. *Lord, please don't let Daddy scare off Ray. Please don't let this place scare off Ray. We are just your people trying to do the best we can. Doesn't it say I'm a worth-it person because I'm yours? Don't I deserve to love? Can't I love in a normal way? Lord, don't let this place scare off Ray. Amen.*

In the room, everybody was already settled in the bunks, waiting for the story of the evening. Daddy turned on the flashlight and pointed it at me. "Go ahead, Sweet Potato. Time to work the night shift."

I closed my eyes and let a song come.

Lord, there's a harvest, souls a-plenty
Lord, can't you hear them crying out to you?
Falling at your feet, begging for your mercy
Lord, why don't you come see about me? I am a part of your harvest, too.
Fill me up, Lord, and I'll be a laborer for you.

Everybody clapped, and Daddy said that should be added to our prayers each night, and would I teach it to them? I told him not to worry. He'd soon hear it blaring from the speakers at Soul Food.

I told Bell the story about the red bird family that helped a whole flock of geese fly south for the winter. But as soon as the story left my mouth, I regretted it. Why had I given Daddy the idea to fly again?

I took the folded-up, notebook paper out of my back pocket and stuck it down in my clothes bag, to the very bottom. No thoughts of kissing trees, or I would never sleep. I rubbed my hand against my cheek. I could still feel the warmth of Ray there pressed beside me.

SEVEN

Saturday morning sleep-ins were things of the past. It was five forty a.m., and I didn't care if I had to wait five more minutes outside to have Ray swing open that jingling door for me. I hadn't slept a single wink the night before, and there was no point in me trying to keep myself in that room. Daddy frowned at me and pulled the tan cover back over his head, letting his feet pop out in the process. Blankets and cots at temporals didn't fit us tall people all too well. I did hear him grumble out a thank-you before I crept out of that room of snoring, little warthogs. I wanted to holler, *"No, Daddy, thank you!"* I would have meant it from the bottom of my grateful, loving heart, but I refrained out of respect for the sleeping.

All the short way there, I was repeatedly thanking Jesus for this, all of this. The walk in the early morning, right before the sun decided to wake up and show itself. The way I could feel him right there waiting for me, even though I was a tad bit early.

He was there, like I predicted. Maybe I could believe the feelings starting to form. Maybe it wasn't all too bad. Daddy recognized I was good people. Ray had to realize I was good people, if he could confess his love to me in front of the Lord last night. I did feel the Lord was there. And here. And right now. *Welcome home, Lord. It's about time you showed up.*

Ray smiled at me through the window, and I wanted to reach out my hand and put it up to the glass, touching those violet letters. He didn't open the door just yet and let his hand come right on up and touch my fingertips with his. Even with thick glass between us, a current of emotion coursed through me.

He had a knockout smile that made me want to jump for joy. "Are you mine?"

The "her" changed to "mine." I loved that.

I returned his smile and couldn't help but notice the way he stepped back again. He must have felt me shining. He was a ray of sunshine to me, warming me to the very part of my soul that had been popsicle-frozen for so long. Thawing out was so wonderful I wanted to curl up my toes.

When I stepped through the door, he was standing like a pillar, not backing down or backing away. I loved that, too.

I whispered, "Always yours," and I watched as his eyes closed for a second.

Mrs. Sunshine was right there, breaking up our exchange. "Come on. To me, now. Come on."

She waved at me from the counter. I pulled my apron on and looked back at Ray. He winked at me, and I couldn't help but beam to see him with that apron turned right side out. He was wearing it—and proud, by the way he kept pressing it down firmly with his hand.

He followed my gaze. "You noticed, huh?"

Mrs. Sunshine clapped out a beat. "Come on, come here."

I was trying my hardest to read the moment. Her voice wasn't resonating disappointment. But it was a no-nonsense kinda tone that made me either want to take two steps in the opposite direction or hide behind Ray.

Her strong arm came around my waist and tugged. I couldn't help but look over my shoulder as she dragged me through the swinging, silver doors. Ray was only laughing and shaking his head, sauntering to pick up his gray bucket. I wasn't amused one bit.

Mr. Joe was pouring that something-special-about-that-batter pancake mix onto the oversized griddle when we pushed through.

"Hold up, wait a minute! Don't mess with my flow, woman." He frowned. "Sweet Potato, what you doing back here in my personal space? Y'all women are gonna drive me mad up in here."

Mrs. Sunshine shushed him. "Go on back to what you know best and leave me to what I do."

We went out the back door and stepped right into a living room. When Ray said it was like an extension of the restaurant, he wasn't kidding. It was as I imagined it to be—perfect.

My eyes went right to an enormous, framed picture of Jesus hanging over the dark green, leather couch. The picture showed the disciples on the storm-tossed boat and Jesus stretching out his arms over the sea. Mrs. Sunshine followed my gaze.

"That's a right massive work of art right there, and one of my special moments with Jesus, if I must tell the truth. And I must."

I wondered what the story was—why it mattered so much she'd let that picture take up about ninety percent of her wall space.

"Okay, I'll wind up with Jesus, throw it back to where this was supposed to start, then hit it out of the park with Jesus again. In that order. Sit on down. Coffee?"

"No, thank you."

She sat me down on the couch and went to the little kitchen. I found it kind of comical that there was a kitchen beside the actual kitchen. She leaned against the counter as she poured herself a large cup. She stirred in three packs of sugar and two helpings of vanilla cream before coming back to me.

"Jesus woke on up, you see, and those fishermen were a mess. They were in hysterics, crying and all, saying what in the world was wrong with Jesus—how could he be asleep in a storm like this? I think of them crab-fishing shows where the boat is a rocking and the waves are crashing onto the decks, and those deckhands look like they are about to disappear into the abyss. That's what I see Simon Peter like, with John shaking in his big, fishermen boots. Anyway, I'm dragging. Sorry. Look at Jesus. Look at the expression on his face, the peace in his eyes. He says, 'Why are you so afraid? How is it you have no faith?' And then they still were so confused, those blind men, questioning who was Jesus to have even the sea obey his command? If I was on that boat, I'd have me a party up on top, knowing my Savior had my back even in the roughest of weather."

She watched me and must have known I needed another connection. "So, I know that Jesus takes my storms for me. He is my pillow where I rest my head, and no matter what else comes, I've got the protection of my Savior. No matter your storm, Sweet Potato—and I mean life's storms, not just the rain, baby. I mean poverty, disillusionment, heartache, homelessness, Momma gone. Jesus restores us if we only have faith. So, I have faith."

I whispered, afraid that she might swallow me up whole like Jonah and the whale if I spoke too loudly. She was that big of a woman—not big physically, but big in life. She made me feel, and that was something new about me in Newport News. Never would I have thought I would change, or I could change. That I could believe in something. My insides were shaking like a leaf in a storm, but with this place and these people around me, maybe this would be my foundation to start something. To be something real and substantial. So, I said it and meant it. For the first time in a long time, I felt my spirit stirring up in a mighty way.

"I have faith, too."

"I know you do, child. And my boy, he has faith in you. He told me all about the goings-on between the two of you, and I'm mighty pleased." She patted my arm.

"Pleased your son loves a temporal?" I couldn't understand this woman from beginning to end.

She laughed, throwing her head back. "A temporal? What is that?"

"Me."

She'd done me the favor of extra explaining; I could go on, I guessed.

"Temporal means to have a migratory position on this planet. We live in The Home twenty weeks. Daddy either decides to give it a go and we try to establish, or we move right on to the next 'let's point our finger on a map and go there.' He's already told me about wanting to move forward again. It's temporary. There's not one thing about me that's permanent. There is nothing about me that's worthy of Ray, if you want to know the truth of it."

She frowned, sighing heavily against my arm. "You are so wrong about that, honey. You have the permanent spirit of the Lord shining within you. You are a strong, rooted woman on this planet, because God deemed you so to be. Ray loves you, and I know it. Question on the table right now is do you love him?"

She slapped the coffee table like a judge pounding a gavel.

She pulled back, looked at me square, and answered for me. "I know the answer to that, too. Okay, my conversation about you is over. Now I'm finishing it up with Jesus."

It was my turn to sigh heavily. That wasn't so bad after all. But I could tell she didn't believe me about our way of life. Probably because she had never met anybody like our family. But I had never met anybody like hers, either. Maybe theirs could be the beacon calling us home.

"Ray walked in with that apron turned around, and I knew right then he was no able to testify." She finished the rest of her coffee and reached for a Kleenex. So, it might turn into one of those kinds of moments.

"Why was he ashamed to wear it before?"

"He wasn't ashamed, honey, no. Ray has never once been ashamed about the workings and sayings of the Lord. He's a good boy, a good Christian warrior. The Spirit speaks to me about others, and that was what it spoke to me about my own son. And I might not have known the magnitude of it until your family came along, but I do now. And now, he knows."

She dabbed her eyes, and I turned away, standing up to go look at their family pictures on the mantelpiece. That was one thing we never did—have pictures made. Daddy had one portrait of us taken at the fire department.

"Well, why did he wear it backward? I don't get it."

I picked up a picture of Ray when he was probably around the age of twelve, around the time she would have given him his apron

"If somebody stops me in Soul Food, I can sing my praises to the Lord, and they will know what I speak is true. I am a walking testament to the Word. We all are. And I'm not afraid to share the gift he bestowed upon me. Those words we bear are sacred. Think of Ray's words. Funny how God doesn't reveal everything all at once. Sometimes it's seven years in the making."

She blew her nose and wrapped her comforting arms around me. It was a motherly hug, and the scent of her perfume filled my senses. Special-like.

"He's trusted the Lord. He's waited to hear the direction. The morning brought you in, the Spirit spoke to him and told him you were the way he should go. He would be able to provide and care for you, and no matter what he says, I know that gets to the heart of it. Now he's dedicating his life to the service of the Lord in Joe's military. And those enemies will have no chance against my Ray because he will hide himself in the Lord and be saved."

I heard the words. I understood them, but I couldn't understand how I fit into it.

"I know what I feel for your son. I've never in my life even dared to look at a boy, but when I saw Ray, I knew."

She grabbed my hand and led me toward the door to the other

kitchen. "I knew the second your Daddy pulled out that picture of your family and your eyes were staring back at me from that gloss."

My eyes. There it was again. I'd asked Ray, and he said he saw that he was there. He knew my love for him for real. What had Mrs. Sunshine seen there?

I was enthralled by this revelation. "What did you see?"

"I saw the peace of Jesus, child. Faith in the unseen, belief even in the darkest of places. I saw a hope in you that you probably didn't even know you had, and that was enough for me."

I sighed with a prayer on my lips. "Thank God the Spirit does the talking around here."

She swung open the door to the heat of the kitchen, and the smell of frying bacon brought me back from one world to the other. I could get lost here and never want to venture out in the storms of life again.

Mr. Joe fumed and waved his spatula. "Got enough of that woman talk? Ready for work, are we?"

Mrs. Sunshine waved her Kleenex at him. "One break in the last twenty years. I think I deserve it!"

He winked at her. "You sure do, baby. Ray, come on in here and flip these jacks, and let me take your momma around there for another break."

I giggled, and Mrs. Sunshine pushed me through the door before kissing on Mr. Joe. Ray was holding an order ticket in his hand, talking to the customers, and showing off his apron. I got it now. He couldn't wear it until he could confess it with a full understanding of his calling, and he seemed ready to spread the good news.

Two older men who seemed to only come here for the corner checkers game called out to me. "Jones, coffee?"

Ray handed me the pad. "I see you survived the lion's den."

I smiled. "She's a sweet, old cat. What do you mean?"

He laughed. "Don't let her hear you say 'old' in a sentence about her. She might show you a claw or two. Is my fate going to be about the same?"

"What? Your momma gonna grill you, too?"

He shook his head. "No, your daddy. Remember? I have plans tonight."

I bit my lip. *Lordy, no!* I'd forgotten all about the rendezvous on the roof at nine-oh-seven. "Verdict's not out yet."

"The Lord has told us, 'I am the Lord, the God of all mankind. Is anything too hard for me?'" He winked at me before grabbing his bucket again. "I trust in the Lord, remember?"

I replied, "Since you were twelve. I got it."

"I'm glad. Now get to work, Sweet Potato Jones. And don't be ashamed to wear that name. It is the one I love, after all."

He wasn't being quiet today, and some of the customers heard the word "love" and my name. I pulled off my nametag, took my purple, Bic pen from deep down in my apron, scrawled "Sweet Potato" on top of the "Jones" in my best handwriting, and stuck it back on.

Mrs. Sunshine clapped in victory. "Joe, she's got her name back! She is no longer MIA."

I yelled back, surprising her. "I never knew I was lost!"

She laughed. "That's my girl! Welcome home, Sweet Potato."

"Glad to be home, Mrs. Sunshine."

And the rest of the day went like they all seemed to—too doggone fast for my liking.

EIGHT

This time there was no bag to carry. Our hands found each other as soon as he closed the door behind us. Ray draped his arm around my waist, bringing me up close to him. My heart quickened with each second. This was a dream, but my eyes were wide open.

"Did you forget something?" He stared down at me, and I swore it wasn't just the sun that could shine in his eyes, but the moon, too.

"You put your arm around me." I couldn't help but feel the wonder in everything.

"Is that okay? I know we've worked all day. I don't stink or anything, do I?" He sniffed his underarms.

I closed my eyes. *No.* His cologne was still as present as ever. "Can I tell you something you'll just have to believe?"

He put his arm back around me, and we started walking again, faster than I would have liked. He wouldn't want Daddy out on the front stoop, pacing as he waited.

"I will tell you this now, Sweet Potato, and this is the truth: I believe every word that comes from you, because I have this feeling you don't lie. It's almost like you *can't* lie. You are like a fresh new way of looking at the world, and I love it."

"I've never had a boyfriend. Not a crush. Not a like. Not a … a … boy, period."

Ray squinted. "I said I would believe anything you say, but that one is hard to take in. No one?"

He squeezed me, and I melted right into his side.

"Just you." *My Ray.*

We reached the chain-link fence, and his arm dropped. "I'll make you proud of me, Sweet Potato. And I promise you I'll always do what is right by you. I love you."

Daddy wasn't at the gate, but he was standing under the bug light right there at the entrance, waiting. I would have to wait for another night to confess my feelings to Ray.

Daddy said, "Hey, how was work? You are looking right rested up, Sweet Potato."

He didn't know that being at Soul Food was the easiest thing I'd ever had to do in my life.

"Good evening, sir."

Ray reached out to shake Daddy's hand, and I could tell Daddy wasn't convinced yet, like a big, old question mark at the end of the million-dollar question: *Are you going to hurt my daughter or not? Because I've got something for you, if you are.*

"Be nice, Daddy."

Please, Lord. Let Daddy be the man that I know he is. Don't disappoint me now, Daddy. Don't run now, Ray. Have faith, Sweet Potato. There. I'd made all the prayers that needed to be made.

I wished I would have asked Ray if he'd ever set foot in The Home before. I figured that he hadn't. Most people hadn't. Why would they?

On the grand tour, we passed the kitchen and the first-floor rooms, which were for the "ins and outs." Our rooms were on the second floor, along with most of the other families with children.

We were what they called the "hopeful transitionals," the ones they could try to remediate—like we were some school assignment or sustainable housing project.

We didn't speak during the jaunt through The Home. I couldn't look at him, either. I couldn't imagine the thoughts running through his mind. I thought I'd spoken all the prayers I needed to make, but I forgot the most important one. *Don't let Ray pity me after this, Lord*—and again, for good measure, *don't let him run.*

We reached our door, and my heart flailed around in my chest like a ping-pong ball knocking against paddles. A plain, white door, no violet lettering, no golden words of wisdom. Just a number on it, like at one of those roadside motels—a crooked, scratched, brass number seven, that was us.

They were in their bunks when I came in. Daddy had already conversed with them about me having a boy over. I was sure the whole lot of them was going to dive right into this mess with all they had, like U.S. Olympic swimmers. Bell was the first to jump off her bunk. She eyed Ray curiously. He smiled at her, she smiled back, and I knew it was love at first sight for her, too. She held out her hand like I'd guessed she'd seen in some old movie.

She curtsied. "I'm Bell Pepper Jones. Nice to meet you."

He turned to me inquisitively at the sound of her voice. People did that. It was the same with his voice. That sing-song quality was rare.

"Ray Patterson. Charmed, my dear." He bowed low to her, and she giggled.

Maize came up to him—couldn't stand the thought of him being so big and tall, I was sure. "I'm Sweet Potato's brother."

I sighed. "It's okay, Maize. He won't laugh. Ray, this is Maize."

Ray didn't laugh, only kept that same smile on his face. "Hey, Maize. Ray."

Maize nodded and plopped back down on the bottom bunk. Bean was already asleep. I laughed softly. "What did you do to that one?"

Maize gave his short, little laugh in return. "Daddy worn him out all day on the court. He was asleep by eight. I think we've figured out the fix for Bean."

"Maybe he don't need any hyper pills, after all. He might need some ball playing and good ol' exercise. Let's make him a pro, Maize. You think?"

Daddy huffed. "Sports ain't the answer. I've been telling Maize about this since he's been obsessed with the whole football fascination."

Ray's interest was now piqued. "You play football?"

Maize shot up from the bunk. "Want to. I'm going to be a freshman. I figure I'll try out for the JV or something."

"You going to The Dream, right?" Ray looked at me, and I nodded. "I don't see your uniforms hanging." No closets here. He had already quickly done an inspection of our room and assessed the lone clothes bag beside the bunks.

I gawked. "Uniforms? Daddy, you ain't said one thing about uniforms. School's on Monday!"

Why did we always end up with last-minute disasters? The money we'd made this week was already spent.

Daddy said, "Calm down, child. Calm down. I had to wait for the check anyway, and I didn't want you to go about dreading the school, knowing about a uniform. We'll go tomorrow, then."

He picked his head up, motioning to Ray. *Come on now, and let's go talk.*

I wasn't ready for that yet. I'd postpone it if I could. "I love the uniform idea. Nobody will know." I couldn't sit down on the bunk, because there wasn't a place to offer Ray to sit. I couldn't even offer him something to drink. That was the way you were supposed to invite people into your home, judging by the way Mrs. Sunshine had treated me this morning.

Ray frowned. "Know what?"

I nudged my bag with my foot. "That's me in the bag. And that's

Maize, and Bell, and Bean. Uniforms are safe. We ain't never once been to a school that was safe for us, so we would always stand out like a sore thumb. Recycling the same clothes gets noticed, this day and age."

Bell giggled when Daddy stepped between us. "That's enough in here. Sweet Potato, go on to bed. You got early-morning work ahead of you. One more day of it before the school week begins."

Ray said, "No, Mr. Jones. We wouldn't hear of working on the Lord's day. We are closed on Sunday. It's church and eating, usually with the church, and more church after that. Just the way I like a day to go."

It was like I'd been slapped. "I won't see …"

You. I let it drop when Daddy gave me the hush-up eye, and I realized he was right. I was probably about to sound a little desperate.

Daddy was already escorting Ray out the door. Ray turned to me and winked, not a care in the world. Not even a fear about walking up those tiny, creaking steps to his doom.

"I'll be here to pick you up at nine, Sweet Potato. Don't worry about what is in that bag. We will stop by Momma's before church service, if you need to."

Bell squealed, waking Bean up. Little moaning noises escaped from him. "Can I come? Can I go?"

The last words I heard from Ray were, "Sure. All of you are welcome."

And I fell to my knees when the door slammed. "I'm thankful to have him, God. I'm welcoming them rays of light you are shining down on us. Thank you, Jesus."

I broke into our newly added prayer song, and the kids sang right along with me—even tired-out Bean, with a yawn on his lips.

NINE

Maize was waiting to strike, like I'd expected. "What do you think Daddy's up there doing to him? It's been twenty-six minutes already. Just enough time to cut him up and grill us some Ray kebabs."

Bell giggled. "Them would be some good tasting Ray-babs, Sweet Potato. He's mighty juicy."

I frowned. "You are too young to be calling boys juicy. Don't let me hear that from you again. You hear me, girl?"

She sighed, exasperated. "I've already had a boyfriend, remember?"

In second grade, she'd rushed home to tell us how some boy wrote her a "Do you like me? Yes or no" letter and she'd pushed him down into an anthill. I guessed to youngins that constituted a boyfriend-girlfriend kinda relationship. Me and my Ray, we were the Declaration of Independence. With him, maybe I could feel that freedom I longed for.

Finally, the door creaked open, as if Daddy didn't want to disturb us. Like we could have gotten any sleep with the FBI investigation going on up top. Bean had gone on to sleep after our prayers, but the rest of us were waiting impatiently for the verdict.

He cleared his throat. "All right, go on to bed. We got church in the morning."

Bell clapped with a *hallelujah*. She loved church. And when I say the word "love," I'm really putting it mildly. That was the only place in the world where she ever truly felt like she belonged. I had to admit there was something peaceful about sitting in a pew together, side by side, praising the Lord with a song coming from all of us in unison. Now, I had two other places where I had a peace that passed all understanding: Soul Food and walking beside Ray.

Daddy grumbled, "Well, you got you some makings of a fine man, Sweet Potato. I see the two of you now. I get it. And I'll let you be, for now. Just let me trust you, that's all I'm saying about the birds and the—"

I yelled out, "Uh-uh!"

Bell was in the room, and there would be no talk like this. Maize made little bumblebee sounds, and I swatted him on the head with my pillow. The pest.

"Thank you, Daddy, for believing in me."

He pulled the tan cover up to his chin and turned to me. "Why should I not, Sweet Potato Pie? You've always believed in me."

"You are right about that, Daddy. Through it all, I believe. For the most part."

But I'd always wondered about something. Was it the belief I had in him, or was it that I'd learned not to question him? Those were two completely different concepts I didn't want to spend my energy on debating, but they were always there in the corners of my mind.

We all settled down in our bunks. I held the flashlight out to Maize and waved the light to get his attention.

I whispered, "Uniforms? Ain't that great!"

He smiled in the darkness. "At least that's one good thing about this place."

"There's more than just one thing, Maize. You've got to open your heart to it. Open your eyes tomorrow and really see the good. It's staring right at you, Maize. I'm starting to take off them dark shades and see the world for clear skies. You can do that, too."

He turned to face the wall, but I felt the despair in every syllable he spoke. "Whatever, Sweet Potato. Whatever you say."

The morning saw us all rummaging through our bag for our Sunday finest. We all had one set apiece. That was all we needed. No one should go to church worrying about what you wore, no way. God was the one all clothed in shining white light. How could anybody compete with that?

When I heard the knock on the door, I knew it was him. It was eight fifty-seven. Three minutes early. I was finishing up twirling Bell's hair when Bean opened the door. He eyed Ray curiously and decided to give him an anaconda hug instead of a handshake. Gotta love that Bean for everything he was.

Daddy picked up our family Bible off his cot, straightened his tie, and held out his hand for Ray to shake. He wouldn't tell me any of what they'd discussed the night before, and I wasn't fortunate enough to have some texting machine or cellphone to find out from Ray. And I wasn't expecting to get that far in our conversing on the walk to the church, with the family all crowded around our heels, Bell holding on to Ray's arm and Maize talking his ear off about what he needed to know about football at The Dream—the physical requirements and such.

It was another six minutes past Soul Food down the avenue to the Assembly Revival Church. This whole block was an inspiring walk, from the chain-link fence around The Home, to the taste of heaven that was Soul Food, to the whole divine kingdom of worshippers that would leave me changed forever. To the Lions Club center, where glasses could be passed along for free at the other end, making the corners a mighty place to help anyone in need. Four corners of freedom.

The ladies streamed in with them fancy hats and those gold-beaded necklaces that looked like they weighed about twenty-five pounds, and that meant nothing more to the Lord than my straight, black skirt and white, button-up, high-collar shirt. We had them colors because at our last church we were all choir members, and the church bought everybody in the choir matching clothes. Me and Bell loved to look alike, and Maize looked so nice in his black-and-white striped tie. Bean, too. And Daddy didn't own no coat, but he was a sharp man. Impressive by his stance, I tell you.

Mr. Joe and Mrs. Sunshine were right where I was expecting them: in that choir vestibule, shining like bright twinkle lights. All the choir members were dressed in the fanciest white robes and were welcoming in the congregants with the radiant voices of those in harmony with the Lord. Bell could barely contain herself when she saw it all up there, and by the way that she moved in that red pew, she might as well have been up there with them. She didn't miss a beat. Mrs. Sunshine pointed at us a time or two, leaning over some of the elders—to tell them about us, must have been. But I wasn't the least bit ashamed, because I knew she wouldn't introduce us as "them homeless folks." All she would say is that there is Ray's girl and those good people we got working for us now—something like that, I was sure.

The Rev and First Lady were like a peaceful, warm wind blowing against my face. All the Word, hallelujahs, and hymns of praise somehow seemed to be heightened here, like they were on an electrical charge. Ray didn't hold my hand or put his arm around me in the service. But just him sitting right there beside me, every now and then beating his hand down against his knee, rattling out a "Go ahead and tell it" or an "Amen," told me that Ray was that way when it came to me and the Lord—letting it come fully without a care in the world. He was just Ray. And I loved that.

The two hours of the service flew by. Ray stood up to testify during the final call. With my heart laid out on those red, velvet pews, I looked down at the carpet instead of up at him. He was dedicating his life to the Lord in the U.S. Army. He was going to be a chaplain assistant and preach the word of the Lord. The calling had been placed upon his heart for a long time, and he could not deny it any longer.

As soon as the words came out of his mouth, that whole church was on him like beetles to a rose garden—praising the Lord, laying hands on him, and putting him right up there at that beautifully crafted, wooden pulpit so the whole place could worship the Lord in celebration of one of their own. And I couldn't help the tears of joy streaming down my face. I was not ashamed to cry, because this time it was a mighty big thing. It meant that much.

Mrs. Sunshine called us up to the front, next, and introduced us all as the newest members of her family. We were enlisted in the Patterson family, and I was proud to serve. Everybody welcomed us with open arms. Many of the faces I knew from Soul Food. Instead of the service ending, Mr. Joe hollered out for everybody to traipse on down to the restaurant, and if they could wait a minute, he would conjure up a Sunday after-service meal on the house in honor of his boy's Army celebration testimony. Everybody seemed to warm up to that idea super quick, because we were all traveling down the sidewalk for the walk to Soul Food, clapping and singing like we were in our own little, Christian-soldier parade.

They didn't flip that open sign. We were closed for business that day. Mrs. Sunshine blared the gospel music on the old radio, and when our song finally hit, Bell let it out in front of all them strangers, and what a let-out it was.

The place became deathly silent, and Bell stood up on the booth and wailed out that song about the harvest. Since it was the first time she'd heard it with the music, she had no other way but to go with it. And I knew God truly blessed this place, because it allowed my Bell to ring and shine brass like she had always deserved. The choir director was right fast to our table, and when Daddy told them the whole lot of us could sing, they shooed us up front on that purple-and-white checker-tiled floor—right in the middle, to Mrs. Sunshine's beckoning.

She whipped that finger out at me. "You didn't let on to us that you could sing, Sweet Potato."

This was apparently a no-no in her book, because I knew how much singing meant to that woman. But my voice was always something I kept to myself. The sudden attention was uncomfortable, like the thought of lice crawling on you when there really weren't none.

I shrugged. "Not much. It's not good, really."

Daddy sighed. "She don't see nothing she does as good, but she is good, people, I'm telling you."

Pastor applauded and said, "Go ahead, child. Let your family sing us something."

Daddy wouldn't say no to the preacher man, so he pushed us all forward and lined us up. We sang what Daddy said was always Momma's favorite, "Amazing Grace." He always said that we could honor her memory by singing it, so I went along with it. But we gave Bell all the solo parts. The rest of us sang the backup, until I was needed to hit the high notes with her. The whole time I sang, I looked straight at Ray, hoping I wouldn't embarrass him none in front of this special congregation of people that he'd been raised in the Spirit with. But the way he looked back at me let me know there was no shame there, only pride. He was glowing love for me in front of this whole place, and I especially loved that.

Mrs. Sunshine was wiping them streaming kinda tears, the kind that seem to have no end.

She whispered to me, "God has given your family a gift, child. He's given you gifts, and you don't even let them out. God wants you to shine, baby. We gonna make it to where you shine bright."

Ray held out his hand to me. I took it and smiled at them both. "That's all I seem to want to do since we found this place."

The First Lady put her arms around Bell and the rest of us individually and told us how we were now members of the Assembly Choir if we so chose to be. Daddy wouldn't say no to a First Lady, and when she said God had chosen that for us, and we had to walk His way, Daddy accepted the call. So we all followed suit, nodded, and found out that our dress would be taken care of week after week, because the black pants, skirts, and white shirts applied to this church, too. On occasion, we'd get to wear matching, fancied-up choir robes. God was good! All the time. He had clothed us, and there it was again for my apron to testify.

TEN

Later that afternoon, when the dinner had been all devoured, Mrs. Sunshine offered to take me on into town to pick up the uniforms and supplies we needed for school. Daddy stayed behind to help Mr. Joe and Ray clean up the place, with the kids in full-swing clean-up mode, too. I'd never had this kinda time with a lady, and even though it was only a Wal-Mart run, it sure felt like we were going someplace fancy.

Ray had printed up the different grade-level lists of required supplies, and they were each a page long. I didn't know how I was going to buy all them expensive three-ring binders with all them dividers. They could be like five dollars apiece. And then the uniforms, too. *Lordy, no!*

Mrs. Sunshine pulled out a church envelope and handed it to me as she hummed "Amazing Grace."

"What's this?" I peeked inside, and it was a big ol' wad of greenbacks.

"After that performance at Soul Food, the church members felt the Spirit hit them to give us up a collection. They've all had kids or grandkids going to The Dream and know about the uniforms and the likes of all you'd need, so they all wanted to help out."

Mrs. Sunshine turned on the radio, still humming. She must have worked better with the background noise of the Lord's words. I could fully understand that about her, even if other things about her didn't make sense—like how she could take me in and see me for more than I really was. That was still the biggest mystery of them all.

"We can't take no money from strangers." It took enough of the world's resources to eat and sleep and go to a doctor, let alone to buy glue sticks and uniforms.

"Strangers? Strangers? That hurts me, Sweet Potato. I ain't no stranger to you. Them are my people back there. We take care of our kind."

She frowned, glancing at the rearview mirror, and turning into some heavy traffic a little too sharply. She spit out a couple of improper words, which surprised me. She wasn't the type I would have pegged for road rage. People have a way of surprising me every day.

"You are my sister in Christ, child. You are my son's future. You are our hope. You ain't no stranger to me. You are after my own heart. Now, you will take the good deeds of others and use them for good doings. You can't not accept this gift of love. If the Spirit moves, then you must obey."

She shook her head matter-of-factly. Something else I'd come to recognize in Mrs. Sunshine was that she meant what she said. I loved that and vowed I'd try to be more like her, at least in that sense.

"It's hard for us in schools due to the fact of how much Daddy moves us around, Mrs. Sunshine. This here money could be all for nothing, and then those uniforms would be all worn out for no more use."

I folded the money and set it down in the console tray. Like the seats, the console of the pearl Escalade was fancy leather. Mrs. Sunshine also didn't seem the type to have such a nice ride. This car must have been parked behind the house, because it would have probably never survived out in the open street.

"The Dream is different. You know that practically every single person who goes to that school either joins the military or goes on to college. I'm not talking about a little bit of them. The success rate is phenomenal, because everyone there believes in the dream."

She nodded again as if to encourage me to be one of those believers. How could I make her understand?

"Maize is different. He's not like me. I worry about him most of all—even more than Bean."

School was always so hard for Maize—the grades and all the social experiments that his peers always challenged him to partake in. It would always scar him deeper, make him a little rougher. This time, I was really scared for Maize, because he sounded more lost by the minute. Desperate, even. The storm clouds were seeming to hover over him and break clear over me. It wasn't fair. I'd take all them dark clouds to get them away from my best friend.

Mrs. Sunshine asked, "What are your grades like?"

She swerved into the Wal-Mart parking lot, tires squealing, and found a space near the front.

"A's, mostly. Maybe a C in English, every now and then, if my teachers can understand my way. Maize, it's more than the D list for him. He can't take the punishment like me. I guess I must have thicker skin."

For the first time in my life, I might have been onto something. "That might be why Daddy always refers to me as the root vegetable of the family. I seem to be more rooted down, firmly planted. The storms don't get to me, because I have them roots already spread out—enough to get what I need and keep going. And then—here I go again—that might be why Maize is different."

Mrs. Sunshine laughed. "I love the way that you can explain yourself. You fascinate me, you do. How is Maize different, tell me?"

She pulled the four lists out of her purse and started down the school aisle, practically doing the shopping for me as we talked.

"Maize is like the tall stalks of corn in the field, swaying in a strong wind at drying time. He's fragile, like the brittle kind left in the field. I don't know how much more he can take before he snaps."

Mrs. Sunshine grinned. "Well, then, we have us a new prayer request. We'll just have to see about Maize, won't we? We'll take a special interest in him. Let him see the way Jesus can make a weak plant strong. Jesus is the one that builds us up in a time of trouble. You don't let Maize trouble you no more. Jesus has got him. You hear me? Jesus has all of you. It's not about what you have. It's what God is. Remember that."

I nodded. "I will."

But even as I said it, I knew I was losing him.

She stopped by the beauty product aisle and bought some extras that weren't on the lists, like butterfly glitter clips for Bell's hair. They even sold The Dream t-shirts on a special rack by the bookbag section, and we each got one a different color. Mine was burgundy, because Mrs. Sunshine thought that would be most complementary to my coloring. We all got khaki pants, since we already owned the black pair of dress-ups. And we each got a polo shirt, too. Classy, if I did say so myself. I told Mrs. Sunshine how difficult it had always been to be in school with no wardrobe, and how uniforms were the next best thing to bologna-and-cheese sandwiches.

She pulled up to another storefront on the way home: Maria's Discount, a secondhand place. The neighborhood made me a little nervous; the people here eyed Mrs. Sunshine's ride suspiciously. But I loved this kind of store the best, because there was no telling what kind of treasure t-shirts you could find here. Mrs. Sunshine hollered at Maria like they were the best of friends, waved a hand at her, and took me right over to the section with The Dream uniforms. This place must have had the leftovers of graduates who had all went on to better themselves in the world and get out of this neighborhood.

One of the goons from the street was peering in through the

window at us, and I didn't like it one bit. Mrs. Sunshine didn't even seem to notice, but he noticed us, and I felt the hairs rise on the back of my neck. Danger was lurking around every corner. The Devil was on the loose.

Mrs. Sunshine held up two more sets of clothes with dollar tags on them.

"But we got a set from Wal-Mart," I protested. "We should have come here first."

She insisted. "Something old and something new ... that one suit won't do."

She snapped her fingers and kept moving on a mission.

I bit my lip. I'd hate to get all them sets of clothes and not be able to wear them again. But she insisted, and the register counter was piled with clothes. I saw a brown box out of the corner of my eye and asked if I could buy that, too.

Mrs. Sunshine chided. "Honey, you don't need to buy no box. What for? I've got plenty of boxes back in the storeroom from the leftover shipments."

She gave me something better than a box when we got back to her house: a solid, rubber tote with a purple top. I rubbed my hand across it. "You sure do like purple, Mrs. Sunshine. Why is that?"

"Purple is the color of the King, robed in majesty. That was the color of the robe they placed on Jesus while he was on trial. I go to the color purple to remind the world what sacrifice was made for us that day. We can share the good news of grace by the colors we show the world." She transferred the clothes to the purple-lid box and tucked the bags in the trashcan.

I could hear the commotion still going on through the walls. Faint sounds of the kids singing made me smile. Mrs. Sunshine caught it.

"What is it, Sweet Potato?"

I pointed. "It's my family."

She laughed. "Seems to fit right in here, huh? I think so, anyway.

God sure does know what He is doing, I tell you. I never doubted Him for a minute, mind you. But He sure knows His people."

Ray shuffled out of his room, barefoot and wearing the jeans I loved to see him in. He was wearing his white shirt again. I found it refreshing he didn't worry about what he wore or feel the need to be flashy. He was a t-shirt-and-jeans guy, and he was perfectly fine with that.

He smiled, a light in his eyes. "Hey."

I was emotionally spent but had enough in me to whisper back, "Hey."

Mrs. Sunshine patted the seat beside me and motioned for Ray to sit on down.

He kissed his momma on the cheek and gingerly took my hand in his, resting it on the pillow between us. His momma started right on.

"Ray, what is this plan of yours for the future? I'm sure wanting to know more details about it."

He turned to me. "I am going to the Army, Momma. God needs me there now, not four years from now after a college degree. I'll work on that later—while I'm in, even. They allow that with the chaplaincy program. I have to be there now."

Mrs. Sunshine chided again. "Why the urgency? I thought you were settling yourself with the idea of going on up with Denise and starting on the seminary classes with her, first. Then you mentioned that ASVAB, and I knew your plans had gone straight in the opposite direction."

"Sweet Potato changed all of that." He wasn't backing down, only staring right at me.

I bit my lip, and my insides started to boil. He didn't need to bring my name into anything, as if I was worth mentioning. "Don't join the Army because of me."

He turned to his momma and winked. "I'm joining the Army because of her. I was going to eventually end up there anyway,

Momma. You knew that. Now, I can support her and her family and still do what God is leading me to do. I'll be a Chaplain Assistant. That will be an opportunity for me to learn firsthand."

She kept her poise, her hands crossed in her lap, but I knew she wasn't one-hundred percent convinced. "But you'd be an officer if you wait."

He was solemn. "It's not about what I would have. It is what God is, Momma. God is leading me to this now. I feel that."

I laughed softly. He listened to every word his momma said and knew how to remind her of them. How many times had Mrs. Sunshine used that line?

She relented. "Okay, I support you, but Sweet Potato is still in school. How do you think you're going to support her? You are talking about whisking her away with you to some base, but she's still in school and has her family to think of."

He turned to me. His voice was soft and sweet, reminding me of the rush after tasting the best candy you'd ever had. The kind that made your cheeks tingle.

"I love you, Sweet Potato."

His eyes were shining, almost like tears were framing his thick lashes. It was my turn. He deserved to be told what was in my intimate heart. He'd told me in front of his momma; he'd probably told Daddy, too. This was the moment he needed me to confirm it.

I held my breath, looked straight at him, and got up the courage to begin this race with him. *On your mark, get set, go.*

"I love you, too, Ray."

ELEVEN

Mr. Joe stepped in, along with Daddy and the youngins, as soon as I said it. This was a completely unplanned moment. Why did it have to be so dramatic?

Ray continued. "I want you to know when I go to basic training, I'll only be gone for ten weeks. I'm waiting until the spring to enlist and timing it around you. When I finish that up, the recruiter has already let me know I'm going to an AIT school—an Advanced Individual Training school for chaplain assistants. I'll be in Fort Jackson, South Carolina for that. Soon enough, I'm going to get down on my knee in front of God and our families, and I'm going to ask you to be my wife. And if you say yes to me, I'll take care of you and love you for the rest of your life."

Daddy huffed. "She ain't but a baby. You are moving too fast here, Ray."

Mrs. Sunshine got up, and I scooted in closer to Ray. He squeezed my hand, and I blinked back the tears. I stared intently at the picture of Jesus taking control of the sea, so I could remove myself from the moment and get on that boat with him. *Take this whirlpool in my soul and ease it, Lord.* In my peripheral, I could see Daddy calculating. Knowing him, we were probably gonna flee with the youngins before the stroke of midnight. Talk about a Cinderella story about to happen to a poor sista. I wondered if I should make my Converse somehow fall off now, but the laces were too dang tight for me to try to pull it off without making a scene.

"God had a way of bringing you here to our family," Mrs. Sunshine said. "Ray is a good man. He will take care of your baby, and we will take care of each other."

I interrupted. "Stop while you're ahead, Mrs. Sunshine. I know you mean well and all, but—"

Bean shouted, "Your baby will probably be ended up called Asparagus, because Daddy is gonna to whip your—"

Daddy bellowed, startling me. "Bean, hush it now."

I cried, "He's not asking me to marry him because I'm having a baby for him. I haven't kissed this boy yet, and he loves me. Daddy, he's saying all this to let me know that I have a future with him."

We all had a chance to make it here. I knew it was our time. I felt it in the new song bursting forth right from my inner spring.

Daddy held out his arm. "We best be going now to The Home, Mrs. Sunshine."

He emphasized those words like he thought I needed a refresher course on where I came from. He was going to go and mess this up for me, for us. After all our years on the road, we could finally be who we were without condemnation or fear, and here he was going to pull that map out anyway. Now the veil was lifted, and I recognized a good thing when it held my hand. I had to fight this one out.

Daddy's eyes were suddenly bloodshot, as if he was trying to hold in his blood pressure. I wondered if eyeballs could actually pop out of a person's head?

He signaled us. "The kids have an early morning. Thank you again for everything today. I'll see you bright and early, too. I have to get used to all this growing-up stuff. Thanks again."

Mrs. Sunshine and Mr. Joe said their goodbyes to Maize, Bell, and Bean. I could see how much Mr. Joe and Mrs. Sunshine had taken to them, and I knew somehow, we would have to make it here, regardless of Daddy's bad attitude or closed-up sensibilities. We could make it fine—even without him, if we had to.

I pointed to the Wal-Mart bags of school supplies and the purple-lid tote. Each one of us got a bag, including Ray. We left out the back way, through the big, wooden fence, to circle back around the block to the place we called home. The way Daddy had said it to Mrs. Sunshine still rang in my ears like a clanging cymbal.

Was he going to tear us down when we were starting to build up? He could have said something like, "Let's mosey on down to the home place, youngins," or, "We best be getting to our house that we pay bills for." Maybe even, "Let's go home." Not with a capital *The* in front of it.

Maize would crack under this. I felt his emptiness resonating off him like humidity. Why couldn't Daddy sense it? If Daddy hadn't figured it out, Maize had my back, and right about now he was about to jump over it and get to Daddy for embarrassing me like that in front of Ray and his people. The kids couldn't contain themselves, peeking through bags, already claiming folder colors. Ray and I didn't speak, just stole glances at each other when we could. Maize held my hand all the way back. He was on the verge of falling without a net. *Maize, please hold on. Please, a little more. We've got this. God's got you.*

When we made it back, Daddy ordered all bags dropped in a pile in the center of the floor. He grabbed my hand in one of his hands, Ray's arm in the other, and shut the door. I knew what this meant: another showdown on the rooftop. I could hope and pray. And God did answer them prayers—even from me.

Once we were on the rooftop, Daddy growled, "You're talking about a future with a family that ain't got no roots, no foundation, and no present. You stop filling up Sweet Potato's head like that. She doesn't deserve to be hearing that. You go running off, and the next pretty thing you see you be all in love with *that*, too."

Ray stood strong. He found my hand and did not let it go. "Don't worry about me, Mr. Jones. I will do right by your daughter. I will do right by your family."

"Doing right by my daughter will be leaving us right alone."

He turned to me, and I knew. I got the shuddering in my system, the blinds dropping straight down with a loud thud and a lock. "We gonna be moving on soon. You know that. You know the date."

Ray spoke life into a hopeless situation. "It doesn't have to be like that this time, sir."

Daddy's voice was grave. "We've got twenty weeks here, Ray. Well, we've got eighteen now, since we've already stayed on here a full two. You need to know that. You are talking about a spring planting season, and we ain't making it to then. We'll be out by the first frost."

"They are good people, Daddy," I said. "We can make it here, if you would just try. Those kids deserve more than uprooting all the time. It takes time for us to till, to cultivate. We need some patience. Maize's drying up, Daddy. This is it for him. I'm telling you now, and you better listen."

He frowned. "What you mean is *you* need some time. You need some time with this boy. Well, somehow this boy has it fancy in his head that he's gonna take care of you. That's my job is to take care of you, and you might not always have agreed with my decisions, but I've done my best."

I bit my tongue until it was bleeding. Not once had I ever gone against Daddy. Fundamentally, he was a good man. He was fair to us kids, always there for us. He'd kept us together when he could have very easily given us over to Mr. and Mrs. Foster. But then again, he dragged us around like little sacks of potatoes and couldn't seem to see what he had done to us, to the very core of us.

It was taking a mighty hard toll on us, especially on Maize. He was the youngest of us all, inside—even compared to Bell, who had an old, singing soul. Bean was probably falling right in step with Maize, poor kid, but Bell and me, we'd survive. Bell had that internal voice, a ringing that would save her spirit. I had the Lord all rooted up and down in me, and now that I found Ray, I knew without a doubt I'd survive. But wasn't life more than just surviving? I felt that now. I'd had a little taste of some good food, and I knew there was more than the gruel we'd been fed. A whole bushel and a peck of opportunity was waiting for me. I could taste it right on the tip of my bleeding tongue.

This was a perfect place to become a garden. Daddy had to believe it. I had to make Daddy see. If Mrs. Sunshine said she could look into my eyes and see the peace and faith of Jesus, I could somehow make Daddy see that Newport News was the place where he'd finally claim his own home sweet home.

My eyes dried up. I squeezed Ray's hand to let him know that I had my composure back. I was ready to do this thing.

"I believe in you, Daddy. I believe God will sort us all out. Don't go worrying about me. We've been living in a mighty hurricane with the winds a-blowing us in all different directions, but I feel the hand of Jesus stretching right over our heads and calming us right down to where we can breathe. That wind won't take my breath anymore. I don't give it power to do so."

Daddy usually heard me. I hoped he comprehended me properly, this time.

He exhaled deeply, and his shoulders relaxed. "Go on ahead, Ray. I'll see you in the morning, hear?"

"Yes, sir. See you in the morning."

He turned to me. "I'll see you after school, Sweet Potato. I'll be praying you have a good day."

"We're gonna need all the prayers we can get."

Ray said, "We'll start calling the Assembly for a prayer chain."

Ray turned to Daddy and told him about the Monday men's group and how it would be a good time for Maize and Bean, too.

Bell could come with me to the restaurant on those evenings and we could care for her there, or she could join the choir practice that was always going on at the church. Ray had seen this place, and he didn't want them kids here no longer than necessary, either.

It wasn't just about me, after all. He truly was thinking about my little ones. I so didn't deserve this.

Daddy nodded once. He'd be there. Daddy was raised to never turn down a church invitation. Thank God for his rest-in-peace momma for teaching him that one good thing and passing it to us youngins, because that was something we had to look forward to along our broken-up roads. We could seem to always find us a church to call our own, even if it was only for a spell. And the Assembly Revival could be more than church for us. One day at a time, I could fight for this life.

I remembered the tiny, scrolled writing on the bottom of the Soul Food menu as clearly as I could feel the touch of Ray's fingertips circling my palms. I whispered to Ray, "'This is the day that the Lord hath made …'"

Daddy exhaled deeply. "I know this one. 'Let us rejoice and be glad in it.'"

Ray grinned that special way when the talk turned to the Lord. "I'll seek the Lord, and the Lord will not fail us. Even in all of this."

Daddy clapped Ray on the back as we made our way down the hallway, stopping him before our room. "So, you really going to be a preacher one day?"

He smiled. "I knew it from a boy of twelve that I was called by the Lord, sir. I've been waiting on Him to get me there."

Daddy laughed. "To see 'First Lady Sweet Potato' on that billboard …" He sighed deep again. "I guess that could make a daddy proud. Just would have never thought it to be so."

When Ray left us, and the kids were all packed up right proper, layered up and color-coordinated with their uniforms neatly folded beside the bags, I prayed aloud in thanksgiving for the giving hearts of the Assembly and Mrs. Sunshine. I took the flashlight and shone it right on Bell.

She jumped off the bunk, clapping her hands and shaking her little head. Her bare feet shuffled across the cool, tiled floor in a tap-dance frenzy. "My turn?"

Daddy settled down in his cot, and the rest of us gathered on the floor at his feet. We could get a front row with Bell, and it was a special occasion. We found joy and comfort in church. We held each other up in the times of pain and hurtful rejection that society threw at us. And we loved the sound of that girl's voice more than any other sound on the face of God's green earth. When Bell sang, we heard it with all the layers of a symphony in the background. The way she would start soft, then build it up—we'd be on top of a mountain somewhere, soaring. Not in The Home. Not in poverty. Just soaring. As we would hum along or softly sing her backup, we all knew that Bell would be famous one day, on a stage with bright lights. We were sure of that. One day, when it came to pass, it would be a special occasion, indeed.

TWELVE

Just like on any other first day of school, Bell and Bean were excited. Me and Maize were ill to the point of throwing up in the shared bathroom. Our nerves were all bundled up, like a live wire waiting to electrocute the innocent passerby—which happened to be the bus driver.

We had to wait down by the corner for the bus. The line didn't run right up to The Home—for good reasons, I supposed. They didn't want to draw attention to where we came from. They decided it would be best for us kids to walk four minutes in the opposite direction from the chain-link fence and broken sidewalk.

The only problem with the four-minute walk was that it wasn't the one that took me to Soul Food. It would have been right fine by me if it was, because I would have had the opportunity to see Ray through the window. Maybe he would come out and hold my hand while I waited for the bus. Maybe he'd even hug me and wish me a blessed day. That would be a great way to start off any morning, even a dreadful first day of school.

But the four minutes took me to another world—a world that was a deep-space black hole. Knowing I'd have to walk that way every single morning for however many calendar days we had left here scared the living daylights out of me, because in the forefront of my mind I kept seeing Maize being sucked right into a spiraling great void, to be lost forever.

This place reminded me of the kinds of places we'd go with Momma while she was looking for snow—boarded-up shops, shiny cars popping by with dark tinted windows, flags hanging out on white clips, waving in the wind. Doors hung open on the houses across the street, and the sidewalk was a lot more broken even than it was by The Home. It wasn't the street signs gave the name of the street, but the spray paint tagged along the broken sidewalks and abandoned buildings.

Bell stepped in closer to me, and Maize stepped two steps in the opposite direction. *Oh, Lordy.* Here it was. The great divide. There were a couple of shady creatures hanging by the bus stop, and I knew they weren't there for a ride to school. Instead, they were passing to the exploited pushers—Class A stuff, yellow pills or blue ones or powder. Whatever the kick was, these days.

Thank heavens to mercy we were never really exposed to this kinda life. Daddy might have taken us to a run-down hotel a time or two, or even to shacks in fields, but nothing had been like this. The tiny, little hairs rose on the back of my neck and on my arms. Something was not right about this place. It was a four-minute trip to hell, and this was a pretty hot corner.

The bus rolled on up, taking its time. The driver opened the swinging door. "Jones family? The Dream Academy chauffeur, at your service."

He shook all of our hands and smiled at us with genuine warmth. I'd never had anybody from transportation treat me like I was a VIP. He sat us down behind him on the front-row seats, saying we got special treatment, being new and all. He wanted to get to show us everything up close on our first ride. It was weird, I tell you.

I watched in silence as uniformed kids walked up from the projects and loaded onto the bus, leaving behind scenes of despair and tragedy. I kept my eyes dry, not wanting to show my fears, but inside I prayed, *Lord, keep our heads up regardless of our circumstances—each and every one of us on this yellow ride.*

"Just stay close to the little ones on the corner in the morning. I'll be there as soon as I can. We can't control who stands by the stops."

The driver said it a couple of times to some of the older ones, the ones like me who were looking after younger kids. Lots of us had that "Momma" look—not because of how many diapers we'd changed, but because of how many hands we'd held or hearts we'd tried our best to mold, even with our own hearts cracked and bleeding.

He had a caring heart, that man with the blue tie and white dress shirt. He was different from any of the school people I'd had in the past. He almost seemed like he wanted to pick us all up and keep driving—to give us the world, if only he could.

I was bold. "Can you not pick us up at that corner anymore?"

He frowned. "That's your scheduled stop."

I frowned right back. "But it's not a nice place for us to wait."

I heard a couple of people behind me tell the others to hush so they could hear. It wasn't loud on the bus anyway. Usually, we'd be getting slapped all in the head by now, or a shoe would be thrown at the front, missing the driver by a thinning hair. This bus had order. Had to be first day.

"But I have the route mapped. You must live near there." He kept his eyes on the road, but he did seem interested.

Maize pushed me on the leg to stop me talking, but I couldn't help myself.

"We are staying at The Home; four minutes' walk the other way. Could you pick us up at our fence in the morning, please? I couldn't risk having the kids down on the corner ... I saw ..."

He cut me off right quick with a look. "Hmm-mmm ..."

I should've thought about what these kids saw every day. Maybe that was even one of these kids' family members, exchanging money for little bags of colored stuff.

"No problem, Jones. I'll be at The Home starting this afternoon."

Maize had leaned over in his seat, and I wasn't quite sure if he was breathing. He pressed his face against the window, letting the silver frame press against his skin. Bean and Bell were protectively holding on to their bookbags, missing what had just occurred. Maize's eyes were brimming with tears.

"Thanks, Sweet Potato. Thanks for making my first day of high school memorable for me. I'm sure it will be all I dreamed of and more, now."

I shook it off. It would only take one kid overhearing what I'd said, and by the end of first period everybody would know about the homeless kids. But I was tired of living like it mattered. It wasn't what I had. It was who God was. And I still had to look after Maize. Something told me that corner wasn't right, and if we went down there another morning, we would find out why. I had to listen to that something. Maize would have to get over it.

I grabbed his shoulder as we walked to the fenced-in school. "We can't go to the Devil's playground or allow the temptation to suck us in."

The school was pristine. It had this almost otherworldly feel to it, like it was some fancy college or private school—all gleaming, white paint and glass. Teachers in swagged-up clothes were welcoming us onto the grounds, holding doors for us. I wondered where the sniffing dogs and metal detectors were. At our last school, uniformed officers had been the ones patrolling the grounds and guarding the doors.

People called out names and shook hands like everybody in this place knew everybody. There had to be a catch. I shivered, waiting for somebody to come popping out of some bushes and start hacking away at us. Maize stayed closer to me now, hitting the side of my shoe with each step he took. Bell and Bean had to separate from us, and I kissed Bell on the head. I wished Bean a blessed day and made him promise to pay attention and get in no trouble, not even one bit.

An elderly woman caught my arm. "Hello, sweetheart. Welcome to The Dream."

She was good people, too. I could sum her up right away by her tone, all pleasant and reassuring. In fact, everybody seemed to be good people. We found Maize's first-period class, and as we separated, I whispered encouragement in his ear. No matter what happened today, we would survive it like we always did.

First period was an unexpected turn of events, to say the least. When roll was called, I clenched my teeth until I could almost hear them creaking and rattling.

Mrs. Barrington called out, "Sweet Potato Jones?"

No one snickered. Some glances came my way, but nothing else. I feebly raised my arm. "Here."

She pushed her pencil into her soft, black, bunned-up hair. The typical English-teacher move. "Nice to have a new face this year. Welcome, dear."

I bit my lip. Nothing? Nobody whispering or pointing? Clock chimed. Bell rang. I moved and went to class number two. Same thing. Number three. Ditto. Number four was AP Biology, split into two sections with a lunch break in the middle. I was dreading lunch more than the name-calling. Having to walk into that open place with fifteen hundred faces all staring up at me, some flicking food, or others laughing right out in my face and never letting me be. As Mrs. Wethington was going over the syllabus, I was privately praying for Maize to be strong. For Maize to be able to make it through lunch. That he'd survive it with minimal scars.

Thank God, He heard what I didn't pray for. I was too busy fretting over Maize's adjustment to pray for myself. God still provided.

A girl named Chanel came up to me right as we were standing up from our seats. "You want to come hang with us today?"

She pointed at a group by the doorway, all wearing happy smiles.

I nodded and tried to smile my nervousness away. Embarrassingly enough, I was not able to find my voice.

Chanel introduced me with this elaborate drawl. "This is Sweet Potato Jones. She's new here, and she's with us."

Dorothy, a strikingly beautiful girl with dark hair, put her arm right through mine as if she'd known me my whole life, and they started chatting as if I was already their trusted companion. As we moved down the hall, I couldn't help but peek through each window, hoping to get a glimpse of Maize. I needed to see his face. That would be all it would take. Just a quick glance, and I would know the entire story from beginning to end.

The lunch period was actually not eventful. Everyone seemed to be talking about the community basketball game over the weekend or what they'd done over the break or making plans to go to the movies downtown—safe stuff. None of the nastiness or foul language that I was so used to hearing at lunch tables at my old schools. We were at a place that seemed to be on another planet altogether, or at least a different continent. Did places like this truly exist for people with pasts like mine?

Sixth was drama class, and that meant I would finally get to see Maize. I guessed Daddy knew what he was doing, putting us together like that. I'd have to somehow pull him aside and thank him for it. It dawned on me that I would get to go with Maize to meet Bell and Bean, afterward. Maize wouldn't have to be alone when most of the dirty, after-school action would take place. Either Daddy planned it, or God did. I'd thank them both, just in case.

I waited at the door for him, to get a glance before he could notice me. He was walking with five other guys. A couple of them were shorter than him: he'd found the freshmen. All of them had goofy, childish grins plastered on their faces. They gave each other side punches —*oh, no, here goes a fight*. I wanted to scream to the nearest officer, but the punches turned to laughter. They were horseplaying around. I breathed a sigh of relief, the fresh taste of tears right on my tongue. I turned to the doorframe, so he wouldn't see me looking at him, and then quietly stepped into the room, finding a seat at the back, knowing that was where he would go. I was always a front-seat kinda girl, but not with Maize around. I'd sacrifice my place for him.

He came in, straight-faced, and sat down beside me, amazingly enough. He wasn't going to separate from me, so maybe that meant he forgave me for the bus-ride announcement. *Praise Jesus.*

I whispered right before the teacher took to the podium, "You okay?"

He nodded, a little look of bewilderment crossing those handsome features of his. "This is high school, Sweet Potato? Is it real?"

I wondered that, too. I was beginning to feel like this was some sick joke, and right before the final bell rang the devils and demons would start to pop out. My fears were cut off by our drama teacher, this lanky guy with a goofy attitude. He had us all get in a line and do a silly skit about checking times at a bus stop. Ridiculous, yet fun, all at the same time. Daddy signed us up for some stress relief at the end of the day, because all of that pent-up anxiety between me and Maize somehow seemed to vanish inside this safe theater classroom, and I prayed to the Lord as I heard the last bell ring that this was real, that it wasn't a dream. I couldn't go back to the nightmare, not after I'd had this taste of pure, one-hundred-percent heaven. That would be the cruelest joke of all.

THIRTEEN

Back at The Home, the kids sprawled out on their bunks with their homework, which gave me a chance to change out of my school uniform and into my work t-shirt and jeans. I was completely down for the count, plain floored. Leaning against the sink, I glanced up at the ceiling and wondered if it was going to fall on me because we'd all had one nice day. It was astounding—downright spectacular. Bell had smooth sailing and made a new friend in gym class. Bean even got a smiley-face sticker on his little report sheet. We even stopped by the Lions Club since Daddy had made me an appointment, and I got fitted for a brand-new pair of glasses right then and there. With Maize's help, he found me the perfect pair that I called "studious" and he called "fly." Either way, they suited me fine.

Daddy paused at the door when he got back. I was sure he was expecting wailing. The typical scene would be Maize and Bean pouting, with me trying to soothe it all over with sweet balm. Bean would usually come home from school ill-tempered, because he had so much pent-up anger and energy. Honestly, this weird peacefulness made me more exhausted. Strange, but that was it: right down to my toes tired.

Daddy frowned. "What happened? Who died? You don't like your glasses?"

I sighed heavily. "No, that's not it. I love them. They had a great day."

"And you? You didn't? I hear that tone." He patted me on the shoulder, trying to console me.

I shrugged. "No. I had a good day, too."

"Well, then. What's with the long face?"

I whispered, not wanting to spoil the tranquility. "It was too good to be true, I guess, Daddy."

I couldn't get my hopes up. I was already doing that with Ray, and it was dangerous, I tell you. I couldn't do it with school, too. Too much to handle all at once, and I felt it chipping away at my core.

"I had a good day, too. I got my own work apron today."

I'd told Daddy about the importance of the apron and what it meant for Ray and for me. He seemed mightily proud that he was now in on the heavenly secret.

"What did it say?"

I eagerly waved at him, but he didn't respond. Instead, he passed out little, smiley-face notes from Mrs. Sunshine, wishing the kids good luck for the school week. There were suckers taped on with invisible tape.

"I'll show you later. Go on and get to work. They've had a mess of people, and they need you. Mrs. Sunshine is worn out running them orders and that register."

I hadn't thought about how my school day would affect the runnings of that place, and I hated I'd left them short-changed. "What you been doing in there?"

He smiled—beamed, even. I almost had to shield my eyes. "I been cooking me up a mess of food today, Missy."

I was astounded. "Cooking? Mr. Joe let you back there?"

"Mr. Joe was diving into them glass pie containers and enjoying the break, it seemed."

I rolled my eyes. "Mrs. Sunshine liked that, I bet."

He went over to peek at the goings-on of the homework. "Sure did. She seemed to get a kick out of what I could fix up. And she seemed mightily pleased that Mr. Joe had a break. Something about Mr. Joe hadn't had a break in —"

I said, "Twenty years. Yeah, I'd heard that the other day, too." I kissed him on the cheek. "I want to talk to you a second, Daddy. We ain't got to go up on no roof, though. Just let's pile in the hall."

He patted the kids all on the head and shuffled out with me. "You okay, honey? I see the world on you. Did something happen today? Was it bad for Maize?"

"No, Daddy. I wanted to thank you for putting me and Maize together at the end of the day in that drama class. And I wanted to thank you for letting Bell's finger fall, because I've been thinking about that, too."

I paused for a split second, because I wasn't sure how to explain. "You know, you have always thought it was by chance where your finger would hit the map. But, Daddy, I've come to a revelation of my own. An angel, Jesus, Momma ... whatever it was, it was something extra this time. Maybe it was all of them looking out for me, for us, because we are here. We are in this place, and God is all in it. One hundred percent, this time. I am going to let myself believe it. For the first time, I am going to believe it all, and you have to, too. We need the faith of a family, and you are the one supposed to be leading us, not leaving us behind."

Daddy sighed heavily.

"Calendar, Sweet Potato."

He was sending me a signal that I wasn't ready to receive, not yet. I believed. That meant I could call in for miracles, too.

"Hand of Jesus over me, over you, Daddy."

My finger twirled around his face, and he smiled an enduring, sad smile. He was such a fine-looking man. I wondered how Daddy had managed all these years to have never brought a woman home to us—but then again, never once had we really had a home for him to bring her to. Eli Jones must be one sad and lonely creature, roaming without that kind of companionship and care. He was missing out on something mighty special. I'd never even thought about the emotional needs Daddy might have. Until now. And the feelings rushing toward my pounding heart to know I'd see Ray again in about five more minutes, if I got a move on, made me hurt for Daddy who had no one to rush to but us.

"Speaking of Jesus. Your boy has invited me to church tonight for the men's meeting. We're all going, it seems. First Lady Anderson wants to meet with Bell for the choir spotlight. Seems like they have choir practice religiously there." And you could tell it, too, because they all sounded like a beautiful host of angels.

"Me, too? To a men's meeting?" Ray. Soul Food. *Oh, Lordy, no!*

"No. You workin', child. Go on, too, before we both get fired." He opened the door again as I hurried on down the hallway. He didn't have to tell me twice.

I hollered behind me, "Remember what I said, Daddy."

He yelled back, "I never forget the words that come out of your mouth, Sweet Potato Pie. It's like butter covering my veggie-loving soul."

Ray's eager face popped out through the silver cut-out when I came in. His smile was radiant, a bright light at the end of my dark tunnel.

He announced, "Sweet Potato is here."

Mrs. Sunshine burst through the doors. "Thank heavens!" She put her arm around me and squeezed. "How was it? I've got to hear it. Every single detail, now."

I didn't know how to explain it to them. "Different."

Ray was there now, and my heart was soaring higher, about to reach the tin ceiling. "I told you The Dream was a safe place." He took my hand, smiling at me in a way that told me I was truly his. "You don't have to worry no more."

I was still trying to figure out how to describe our day. "We didn't get picked on none." That was the best I could do.

Mr. Jackson, one of the regulars, was right behind us, nosey as ever. "If you would've got picked on, I'd have to go out to that school in the morning and show them my muscles." He held out his at least seventy-year-old wrinkled and skinny arm, and I couldn't help but grin back at his broken-toothed smile.

"I told you. The Dream is a model school. It's a place to be safe and to learn. That's what it's all about. You have a future there." He squeezed my hand.

Here. A future here. Maize is going to make it out all right.

My eyes filled with tears. They fell on down uncontrollably. It was like a dam had burst after a hundred years, and now the rushing water was going to swallow the world up whole.

Mrs. Sunshine tugged on my apron strings. "What is it, child?"

I shook my head, trying to clear my eyes. "It's okay. Just give me a minute."

I took off to the bathroom to wash my face. These youngins were the heart of me, and they'd had a good day. It was too hard to try to put that kinda feeling into words for people to understand ... normal people like the Pattersons, that is. Days were good for them more than they were bad. That was the difference between me and them.

Ray was waiting by the bathroom door. I regained my composure. "Get that frown off your face now. I'm fine, really."

He wasn't convinced. "What are you not telling me?"

"Just how much I love the kids. It's about them. It's not about me." I took his hand this time, and he tried to smile, but he still didn't seem sure. "I had a good day. I had to let out the good."

He laughed quietly, his voice refreshing like a summer rain. "That was good. What happens when I try to kiss you? You gonna cry on me about that, too?"

I bit my lip. The kiss. "I don't know. I haven't bridged that one yet. And it might not be good, so I don't know. Don't go thinking too highly of yourself, Ray Patterson."

He moved in a little closer, and I got a smell of him. Not a disinfecting table cleaning smell—more like a spice, like cinnamon and brown sugar. "I'm about to do some construction and start building that bridge. I'll show you good."

My eyes lit up with love for him. "Well, this ain't no place for no first kiss."

He nodded. "I'm working on that, too. See, my blueprints for the bridge are all working out in my brain. And it's called our first date."

He pointed up to his head, knocking his temple, and I laughed.

"Don't overwork yourself. The foreman ain't gonna agree to nothing like that, no way."

Me on a date! Please. I couldn't even imagine that conversation between Daddy and Ray. Daddy might try to throw Ray off that rooftop.

Ray spoke with the courage of a lion. "Don't you worry about your Daddy."

He grabbed my hand and spun me around toward his momma. She picked up my arm and started swinging me to an upbeat gospel tune on the radio that had the whole place clapping or popping the silver tables. Mrs. Sunshine belted out some fancy notes, and I let it out with her.

Ray was rocking by my side, humming along, and praising the Lord. Mr. Joe was throwing up the spatula, and the Lord was letting that rainbow shine right over me as the music played on. Nothing could touch me or my family here. We might be safe. Our emotions were a trampled-up stampede of a million African elephants, but the best thing to do in cases like this was to sing and move on.

But how long would these feel-good moments last if that lovely boy was going to the church meeting tonight and asking Daddy about a date night? When it was his time to leave, I wished him good luck as he was walking out the door.

He smiled at me—that precious smile that had my heart on fire. "Call me Irish, blessed, whatever you like, but I don't need luck when I have the love of the Lord—" He winked at me. "—and you."

The little bell rang, reminding me somebody up there might have earned a new set of wings. Maybe it was even Momma, and she was the one guiding us right to this place. Maybe they'd let her into heaven, after all.

Mrs. Sunshine watched me as the night went on. She fanned my face. "Is it too hot in here, child? You're right sweating."

I hadn't even noticed, but when she brought it to my attention, I realized my brow was soaked with beaded dew. "Sorry, Mrs. Sunshine. I can't stand this pressure, that's all."

"Pressure? Child, you go and worry yourself into a tizzy over trivial things. That's a habit-forming thing. You need to pray that away." She waved the menu at me, whooshing my hair.

"Like Ray getting mutilated in the church yard? That's not a little thing."

She laughed heartily, but I was dead serious. I hoped Ray would make it through this night with all his teeth.

"Well, it seems like they made it out all just fine." She pointed out through the glass windows. And there was my family, right around Ray, circling him like he was a king and they were his subjects.

He was smiling, and right away I saw that his teeth were all in place. I mouthed, "Are you okay?"

He winked at me again. Bean jumped on his back while they were coming through the door, and Ray spun him around. Daddy waved and smiled at me. Maize was already picking up the little dessert menu by the silver napkin holders.

He bellowed, "Ray said we could pick out any dessert we wanted tonight. That we're celebrating something. Some kind of surprise!"

I held my breath. Could it be true? Mrs. Sunshine welcomed my family all in and ushered them into the corner booth. Daddy pulled his neatly folded apron out from behind the counter drawer and put it over his only pair of church-going clothes, heading to the back. I didn't get a glimpse of the apron front. What could it say? *Stay here, my son. No more trifling or strife. No more twenty weeks for you here ... just the rest of your life.* But knowing Mrs. Sunshine it was another Bible verse, and I didn't think the Lord had my specifics worked out in minute details that could be embroidered.

Ray slid out of the booth and came to stand beside me, still laughing at Bell. She was talking about how at choir practice one lady got right happy when she was singing and fell over the front pew. Ray nodded at Mrs. Sunshine.

"They've compared her to Mahalia Jackson down at the church, Momma."

I frowned. "Who is that? Does she sing there?"

Mrs. Sunshine screamed right out, almost scaring the pants right off me. "Mahalia Jackson? Sweet, singing-gospel, enchantress Mahalia Jackson?"

I guessed she was famous, after that reaction. Mrs. Sunshine took off like she was on some personal mission to uncover a secret treasure. In a minute, she was back, carrying a case of CDs and an old portable CD player that showed years of love.

She pointed to Bell's iPod. "What you got playing on that thing all the time, child?"

Bell held it up preciously, like it was worth a million to her. "My Broadway stuff. I like to hear the musicals, like *Phantom of the Opera* or *The Wiz*. Music like that."

Mrs. Sunshine pointed to the CD, raising it high and praising the Lord as her foot stomped to an invisible rhythm. "Gospel, baby. That's your gift from God. You listen once to Mahalia Jackson, and then you'll see. Hook, line, and sinker. Just listen."

There was still some chitter-chatter from some of the customers eating a late dinner. But once Mahalia started, that all stopped. Even Daddy and Mr. Joe came out from the back. She was singing "His Eye is on the Sparrow," and my heart stopped right in its cage.

Those words, *I sing because I am the one who is free ...*

The power behind the voice was not of a woman, but of angels singing like how I felt when I heard Bell sing. And I knew whoever thought of Bell this way knew the feeling, too.

Bell had tears streaming down her face at the end of the song, and Mrs. Sunshine was wiping hers with the back of her sleeve. Bell broke the silence, her tiny voice filled with wonderment.

"Can I have some of those songs on my iPod?"

She handed the iPod to Ray, and he took it gingerly in his hands. "I'll take care of it for you, Bell. I'll download you all kinds of music I think will inspire you, and I'll have it for you tomorrow after school."

Her eyes lit up with the brilliance of a thousand stars. She squealed with pure joy, "Would you really do that for me, Ray? Did you hear that, Sweet Potato? He's gonna get me some new songs!"

Ray looked at Daddy more than at Bell. "I'd do whatever I could for your family. Whatever it takes."

Daddy must've received the message, and he nodded a *yes* to him. "Go on, son. You can take her out like you asked, but with our discussed conditions, and on one condition more."

My heart hadn't started beating yet, and I told my nervous system to wait a second more before sending the beat signal.

When Ray spoke, I closed my eyes. "Yes, sir?"

Ray held my hand, and I felt the release of my heart and breath and blood pumping all in such a rush that I was lightheaded.

Daddy went on back through the silver doors, letting them swing closed behind him. Mahalia was still around us, Mrs. Sunshine was winking at me, and the hand of the man I loved was resting firmly in mine.

Maize clapped. "That pie? Where's my pie, people? Promises, promises."

Ray closed the distance to me and said, "You and I have the building permit. The inspection's approved. Friday night is the ribbon-cutting."

I was still confused in all the commotion. "Does that mean Daddy actually agreed to us going out?"

Bean hollered out, "Yeah, Sweet Potato. You and Ray get to go out smooching on a date because I heard him ask Daddy at the church corner, which I must say was the proper place to build up courage, and after a few choice words I ain't allowed to repeat on the case of getting popped, Daddy agreed. And that's what Ray's called a 'celebration night,' and that's why we're getting us some pie. You go out on as many dates as you want. You've got my blessing. Order up!"

Ray laughed. "Now, Bean ..."

I turned to Bean, then to Bell, who knew the secret even before me.

Bell nodded. "We all get to go on your date with you, Sweet Potato. Like official chaperones. Mrs. Sunshine, do you think you could make us up some fancy nametags?"

I sighed, understanding the catch—that condition had been previously discussed and recorded. A family date and my first date combined all up into one. How typical *Jones*. But what did I mind, honestly? Those kids were mine. Ray was mine. The world was mine. I had claimed the sky and it wasn't falling on top of me yet. I couldn't complain. Not one bit.

I went to taking orders, and Ray went stealing over to his momma, who seemed delighted in the role that she was now taking as planning committee chairperson for the Jones Family Date Night Special. After the orders were in, I grabbed Bell and led her outside.

"Okay, spill it. I can't wait till this is over." My eyes scanned to see if Daddy was watching, but he was busy in the back.

She told it all. "Ray was bold, Sweet Potato. You would have been right proud of him, and when Daddy said no, he shook his hand anyway and said, 'I appreciate the chance to discuss this with you, sir, and I will be again in the future.'" The way that she tried to sound like Ray was hilarious, and I couldn't help but hug her and laugh.

I sighed. "So, Daddy did say no."

"No, then yes. After Maize got to him."

Her gaze hit my goofy, little brother, my best friend, sitting right there in that booth gobbling down pie and licking the fork clean.

"Maize? Go ahead. Tell it now before I lose it."

She squeezed my hand, delighted that she had a story of her own to tell and one of such importance. "Maize told Daddy all how you deserved to be happy on the account of you taking care of us our whole life, and now it was time for somebody else to take care of you."

She nodded, tears framing her lashes. I was so choked up I couldn't even begin to talk, to breathe again. She smiled softly, her beautiful, long curls framing her face.

"And he was right, you know. And Daddy couldn't deny the truth, not in that churchyard. Not after that mighty big singing practice where that lady flipped over the pew and that time when Ray went to testifying joy in the men's church meeting. It was all too overwhelming for Daddy, and the spirit of the Lord was resting upon his heart. He knew this was right, that Ray was right. So, he came up with the conditions."

I wanted to ask her what conditions, but I bit my lip, afraid if I spoke, I wouldn't be able to stop the tears. I would've never thought my youngins would've fought for me like that.

She knew I needed the whole gravy spill anyway, and she listed them right out for me like a shopping list. "First condition, to The Home by ten. Second condition, we all get to go, even Bean … sorry, that one wasn't negotiable. I tried. Third, no kissing, just handholding, and we have to report back, and I can't lie. So, you better not be kissing on that boy with me there responsible, even though he is fine and all."

I nodded, scared to even think of it right now, anyway. "So, all this is really happening." My head hit the glass, leaning up against the faded lettering of the door.

"All of it and more. Sweet Potato, for some reason, this is all straight out of some storybook, you know. I doubted about them fairy tales, you know. But now, I don't know. I think I might just be starting to believe that …"

I pulled her in my arms and gave her a sweet, big hug. "Don't *start*. Believe it right now, Bell. I need your faith with mine."

"Okay, okay. I believe, too. Now let me go in and eat my pie before Maize gets to my plate next."

I nodded, watching as she went back into the restaurant just as my man was exiting. He smiled, spinning me on the pavement right there under the streetlight.

"Well, did you hear the full-out story?"

I nodded, shy all of a sudden.

"And … you aren't upset, are you?"

I nodded again, this time biting my lip, scared to speak but too afraid not to. "I know Daddy said I couldn't kiss you on our date on Friday night, so come here. It's Monday. That doesn't count."

He laughed softly, bringing me closer to him.

"I love you, Sweet Potato Jones."

His lips fell tenderly against mine as his arms circled around my back. He pulled away, eyes gleaming. Love pouring out and spilling over. The sweetest of first kisses—it had to be. The one that was meant to be.

I whispered, "I'm glad you do, Ray Patterson."

And I kissed him right back. This time, I let go. Letting my arms find his neck, feeling him close to me. Feeling every ounce of emotion that was in me and him, all together in that one kiss.

When he finally pulled back, he nodded. "Mmm … mmm … mmm … I might need to go and renegotiate my contract for Friday night. To know that I'll have to go a whole night without kissing you, after this ... it would hurt me. Devastate me."

I smiled. "Rules are rules. Now come on before the foreman cancels the contract."

He grabbed my hand and pulled me in close to him as we walked the couple of steps back to the door. "Momma's got some architectural blueprints of her own."

That piqued my interest. "What do you mean?"

He raised his hands acting like he was innocent, but I knew there was more to this than he was letting on.

The bell jingled, and the singing was in full force. Mrs. Sunshine had Bell singing about pie, shimmying like they were in a Motown group, and the whole crowd was laughing. Ray never had a chance to tell me what his momma was up to on the sidelines.

When my crew was out the door and my night shift was over, I told Ray in front of them all, including Daddy.

"I love you, Ray. Goodnight."

Ray was still riding the rainbow after our kiss. I could see it on his face. "I love you, too." He held out his hand to Daddy and said, "And thanks again, sir, for letting us all go out on a date."

Daddy laughed softly, pinching my arm. "I guess I need to change the conditions about the kissing. Just don't do it in front of the kids, okay? Don't want them getting ideas of wanting dates of their own."

FOURTEEN

I blushed like Red Hots. "Daddy!"
Ray laughed. "Sorry, sir. She kinda …"
Daddy shrugged. "Knew it was coming anyway. She's right around the corner to being an adult, but I'm still wanting her to be a baby, I guess."
Mrs. Sunshine ushered us out. "Birthday coming up, Sweet Potato? We do those right around here, now."
"No need to worry about me and birthdays. We don't do those at all, where I'm from."
This eighteenth year of mine would mark ten years of us being the "Rambling Jones and the Motherless Children" circus show. Ten years of never knowing what was next or where our next meal would come from. How much more of that could I take, after having this piece of heaven served up to me on a purple-rimmed plate? I didn't know.
"Well, you don't seem excited about this one, Sweet Potato. We'll have to get those plans a-going. When is it?"

I couldn't find my voice, so Maize answered her, his eyebrows rising a little at my inconsideration. I couldn't help myself.

"It's September 24th. The day that started us all down the vegetable stand." He rolled his eyes.

How many times had we heard Daddy say it like that? At least seventeen times before, and still ridiculous as the first time.

"Well, we'll have to mark that on our calendar, won't we, Ray? Sounds like a perfect day to me."

She winked at Ray, and I knew the planning committee was going to swing into gear not only for my first date but for my birthday, as well.

I walked quietly behind my chatter bug family all the way back to The Home, and when we made it safe inside, locked behind our door number seven, Daddy turned the flashlight on me. But I didn't feel like it tonight. Instead, I opted out and turned the flashlight on Maize. After what he had done for me, he deserved a night in the spotlight, and he could really sock one to us. So, we all listened animatedly as he told us a scary ghost story about a girl about to be eighteen who'd lost her golden arm. As he neared the end of his tale, the girl's corpse found the grave robbers who stole her birthday arm. Maize would jerk at the last second and shriek, "Give me back my golden arm!"

He would get Bean right at the end every single time, regardless of how many times we'd heard the story, and Bean would about jump clear out his skin. Supernatural storytelling was Maize's specialty. As he closed out the nightly variety show, he flicked off the flashlight. Before long, a hush fell over the room, letting me know the others were out.

The bunk mattress creaked as Maize turned so his voice could carry closer to me. He whispered, "What's gotten into you, Sweet Potato?"

I loved him, and by my soul I wouldn't drag him down to where my mind was brooding. He never talked about Momma. In fact, none of us ever talked about Momma anymore, period. We did for a long time after she had first gone, but it seemed to only make Bell and Daddy cry, so me and Maize learned not to bring it up in conversations that involved the rest of the family. We kept it secretly going until it didn't matter whether we remembered her. She had abandoned us, so we gave up on her, even her memories.

"Sweet Potato? Is it Ray? You don't like him?"

He leaned over the side of the bunk and balled his fist up, as if his little ninth-grade self could go against what Ray had—and what he had was a lot, I tell you.

"No. I love Ray. Just let me be already."

I could do this. *Don't hide anymore. Let it all go.* I couldn't let the world stay inside me, like I'd done for all these years. I had to let the world spin on its own, because honestly, some things were out of my control.

"Well, if this ain't about Ray, you worried that school was a dream today?"

He chuckled, letting me know his own fears. Maize never had it so good.

"No. Ray promises me that this place is different, and we won't get it bad here. Regardless of our name, our skin color, or our family situation, even." Homelessness, motherless, brokenhearted.

"Well, when Mrs. Sunshine brought up your birthday, it was like she was talking about your funeral."

The words took a second to settle before sinking right down to the bottom of the ocean.

"Oh," Maize said.

That was all he could say, but it was enough.

I turned over, facing the wall, tracing Ray's name in a heart on the peeling, pale green paint. "We don't celebrate it for a reason, Maize. And this year, above all years—no. How could we say it to normal people?"

The distinction was clear. They were normal, and we were not.

Nothing about us was ordinary. Our looks, our names, our birthdays, our past. It all was a blur of confusion, all messy and stitched together from rags. To bring Ray, a wonderful, God-fearing man, into my abnormal life was not fair to him, not right. Ray was right, and I was not.

"You are too quiet, Sweet Potato. Don't do this."

He knew I was done with cultivating and tilling. I was tired of this.

"I can't drag him into our life."

Plain as that. No frills, no more promises or tomorrows or dates or birthdays. I pulled myself up and off the bunk, shaking Daddy.

"Daddy, get up. Daddy."

Bell stirred at my voice. "What's wrong, Sweet Potato? Is something wrong?"

Daddy got it. The words were short. And for the first time, it was my turn to say it. "Map."

He stretched his arms above his head and yawned. The faker. "Not tonight, Sweet Potato. Go to sleep."

I stomped my foot, not even caring it was something I'd never done before or how childish it looked. I was done with playing grown-up for this family. Those days were over.

"No fair. When you say 'map,' we all line up behind and follow the leader. I'm saying our calendar is all crossed off, and we are ready to ship out. I mean it. I can't do this anymore."

"Yes, you can. And no, you don't know what you are saying. You are just being your Daddy, and you are being a scaredy-cat. That's all. Your feet are touching the oil in the fryer. Stop being chicken and go back to sleep."

What was this, reverse-psychology mumbo-jumbo? "Chicken? You're the selfish chicken!"

I couldn't help but wonder who was talking inside my body, because I'd never once disrespected Daddy. The tone I was using was insolent on a whole other level. But I couldn't stop.

"How dare you question me? I've done everything I could to help keep this family together, to keep the kids preoccupied so they wouldn't fall into despair, to try to give them some kind of existence in this screwed-up world you've dragged us up, under, and through. But no more. I'm calling the shots now, and I say map."

He got up then, stood with his massive build over me. Part of me wanted to cower, to hide my face from him in shame. I wanted to cringe, in case he reached out and slapped me. I sure did deserve it. But I just stood there, my arms dangling at my sides like a lifeless rag doll. Years of crying from the inside had rusted me to the core, and now I was with corroded wheels turning, staring at a man who had been on E for so long I didn't know how he could survive only on the fumes.

"What happened to you believing? Having faith even enough for the both of us?"

He was solid. Eyes different somehow. Now that I was standing up to him, he seemed to get some life into him. I should have done this years ago. Was it my own weakness that had kept us on the road?

It was time to say it. "Do you think we like being homeless?"

Bell's feet hit the floor. "What's happening, Sweet Potato?" Her face was already starting to lose its composure, and her lip was shaking. "We ain't never been homeless. We are the home."

"Look at us, Daddy. Have you ever really looked at us? We're just kids. You've dragged us from one mill house to shelter to ragged-out shack to the next. Years of having nothing but me trying to hold them together with what little we could find. Days on end in starvation and dirtiness. The filth of it. The shame of it. And now, I tell you to go, and you tell me to go to back to sleep!"

Tears fell, and I wasn't close to stopping. Maize and Bell were now crouched together on the bottom bunk, but I could see the pride welling up in Maize's eyes. Bean was awake with the cover pulled right up to his chin. I couldn't even regret what I was saying, because it needed to be said. It was about time.

"I'll forgive you for this, Sweet Potato. And when I say calendar, then it'll be time." Daddy crossed his arms in that defiant way, but I could do it, too. I crossed mine right back.

"Don't you see? That's the thing. It's not about you anymore. We've dragged Mrs. Sunshine, Mr. Joe, and ... and ..."

I couldn't say his name, because I would probably internally combust and char up right there. "And ... you are letting them think that I can have a date or a birthday, and they'll go to all that trouble planning, and for what? For you to say 'calendar' and we leave? So, then, let's just leave. Let's go. Tonight."

I pulled my one bag together and draw-stringed it shut, slinging it over my shoulder.

His hand came firm on my arm. "Sweet Potato. It's okay. It's going to be okay. Kids, go on back to sleep. She's having a moment, but this too will pass. Sweet Potato, I love you." His voice was soft, almost a whisper.

"I love you, too, Daddy. But this is where it stops. This place is too good. It's too good to be messing it up, so we've got to go."

He frowned, a tear escaping his own grief-stricken eyes. "You trying to say that this place is too good for you, that those people don't deserve you, but that's where you're wrong. That's where I've been wrong all these years, running and mourning and not knowing which way to turn, when I always knew the road sign that I should've followed but couldn't bring myself to do it."

He sank down on the cot, creaking the old springs, his hands covering his face. It was more than one tear now, and I had caused all of this mess. Was Daddy trying to soften me up with this pity party?

"I can't let him into this. It's not fair to him."

Ray was the only thing outside of God and my family that meant anything to me, and if I had to walk away to protect him, then I could do it.

"Let him into this? I don't think you have a choice in what he gets into. I believe the boy really loves you, and you love him, Sweet Potato. Even though you're just a youngin yourself, you've seen the world from a different view. You've led a life that's growed you up faster than Miracle Gro on a potted plant, and that's my fault. I should've stopped long ago. I've had many an opportunity. I've been hiding behind revelations that could change our lives, and I've not been able to face it. It ain't right, what I've done. To the whole lot of you. I'm sorry."

"I'm not right, Daddy. Don't you see? If I wouldn't have cried to Momma that day to take Rambo on a walk—you remember that day. He was only a puppy, and we needed to take him out, and I was going to train him. If I wouldn't have wanted that dog, then we wouldn't have needed to take that walk, and she wouldn't have got that dime bag laced with crystal meth."

He put his hand over my mouth, covering the words that were still coming.

"Don't bring that up, Sweet Potato. Not now." His eyes pierced hot, like a fire poker.

"It's my fault, Daddy. I've done this to all of us. And tonight is where I'm stopping it. If you don't leave with me, then I'm taking the kids and going off on my own. I can take care of them, and I am the only one that can stop us from dragging these good people down."

I passed Daddy on the cot and made it to the door. Maize was already gathering his things and grabbing Bell by the hand. Bean was balling up his fist on the corner of Maize's shirt. It was time to take control of this.

Daddy blocked the door. "Up them stairs now, Sweet Potato, and don't be fussing with me about it."

When we made it up them rickety stairs, I wailed at him. "I ain't no good for Ray, Daddy. These kids can't take this anymore, because they've found something good. You know we are a messed-up lot. Look at all of us—ridiculous, right down to our names."

"That's it, Sweet Potato. You get so caught up."

He put his arms around me, and it was a warm place to be. No matter how much I was hurting, he was still my shelter. No matter how much I wanted to punch him, he was still Daddy.

"My name is stupid, Daddy. Right mad Momma was at the world to name me that. You are trying to distract me."

I always pictured Momma as the lonely one, the wishing-well one who was always trying to penny-pinch her way back to that farm but never could. That was why I wasn't that wisher kinda girl. Wishing was for losers.

"Marigold knew what she was doing when she named you all. Have you thought about it? Even once tried to get her message to you?"

He was shaking, and I stepped back. Hearing Daddy speak of Momma was making him about to fly away, Sweet Jesus, and I was scared he might carry me with him.

"If you only knew how much I've thought of our names."

He rolled his big eyes. "Tell me what Sweet Potato means to you."

I gave a big shrug, then put my hands on my hips. "It's orange, and bumpy, and hard, and dirty. Even at the grocer, it still has some dirt on it when you pick it up. It takes a long time to cook before you can get in the insides of it."

He stopped me. "But with some butter and some cinnamon and brown sugar, man, you can't get nothing better … can't get nothing better than you, child. It's more than the taste. Think of the whole process."

I had already studied up on the plant. He didn't know how many times I'd done this very same thing with all our names. "It's a root vegetable with all kinds of fibrous roots all sticking out."

"No, Sweet Potato. Go on."

I did it again, hands on hips. "Daddy, what else is there? It's a dirty vegetable? You are distracting me from leaving. You think you slick, huh?"

He leaned up against the wall, placing his hands across his chest. His eyes welled up at whatever memories he'd stirred up in his old, black cooking pot. Oh, Daddy.

"Marigold named you Sweet Potato because of the morning glories."

"The what?"

What was this rambling? I heard how he sucked his breath in, and I knew that this was killing him. He had never told us much about Momma—nothing except her not wanting to leave Johnston and her "Amazing Grace" story. And all other stories had been forgotten, the good ones along with the bad. So, this was a whole new experience for the both of us.

"Morning glories were your momma's favorite flower, you see. She thought right hard about naming you that, but she didn't want you to end up like her, so she couldn't do the flower naming. Scared you would pick up on her genes. She wouldn't listen to me one bit when I told her the name didn't do that to somebody, and your name as Morning Glory Jones would have worked out just fine."

He let out some laughter as the tears rolled down his face. "I tried to tell her that you'd get that genetic makeup of the both of us, but she didn't understand that biology stuff. Thinking that the name was more important than the stuffing inside them cells. So, she did the next best thing after her morning glories: the plant that produced it. Not a flower, but a vegetable. So, there you go. You were named after a flowering vegetable."

"A morning glory? I've never seen a sweet potato flower. You're making this junk up, Daddy."

I couldn't say, "You're lying about this," because I knew that was one thing Daddy didn't do. Could the flashlight be on him right now, and he was spinning me a spider tale?

"It was on them fields at her daddy's place. Them special-looking sweet potatoes grew them morning glories, cascading on the vines like a waterfall of blue and violet waves. She'd walk with them in her hair, looking mightily fine. She was a blue-eyed girl with a purple flower stuck behind her tiny ear."

Tears dried up on his face, but I knew he was carrying on his crying on the inside.

My voice was thick. "I always wanted to be named after a flower … Morning Glory, huh?"

"Yeah, Morning Glory. Never be ashamed of who you are. No more of this, Sweet Potato, my girl with the thickest roots, the stable one. The one that helped shape us all into who we are right now. I've messed up mighty bad with you. I've stuffed you in that draw-string bag and slung you around with the rest of them, and you still have been the one to carry us through. Oh, God. How can I ever ask you to even forgive me? I'm going to find a way to make you forgive me."

He covered his face with his hands, ashamed as Momma circled him now with her memories. Ashamed and more alone now than I would have ever imagined one could be.

"Stop it, Daddy. None of us has been perfect. We got a lot of life in us yet. And we can't go back. And we can't run. And we can't move forward until you lead us."

I always felt like we tried to make the best of times, looking back over our mixed-up years, but those years created the memories and we owned them. The years were what made us.

He stood up tall. He shook his head, as if he was shaking off the past. He put his foot forward and spoke loudly.

"Well, let's follow the leader, then. This time, we're not counting down to an end, but to a beginning. I say no more map. We done with that living. Time to settle down."

He put his arms firm around me, and the love there made me feel all toasty and perfectly safe, in our own messed-up way. He pulled away. "Don't tell them youngins yet that I'm trying to make this a stomping-ground for us. I don't want them getting their hopes up too high if I can't follow it through."

I frowned. "I bet Mrs. Betty Atkins can help you out in a mighty way. Maybe you should talk to Mr. Joe and Mrs. Sunshine, or the pastor."

"Not yet. Tell that Ray nothing about that calendar. You don't worry your head over none of that now. I'm going to take care of this here family the right way." He led me on down the stairs.

The whole thought of my name was tinkering with my heart, clinking away at it with a tiny, little hammer and oil stick, making it beat a little stronger. I was to have been named after a beautiful, purple flower, a morning glory. The color of Mrs. Sunshine's world. The morning of Ray's revelation. God planned for me to end up here. What had Daddy said? He had me planted right before we even knew?

When I walked in, they were all huddled on the floor by my bunk. Maize caught my eye and then nodded. He pushed his bag under the bedframe and loosened Bean's arms from around his neck.

Bell started to sing the song she'd heard tonight, the one by Mahalia Jackson, and I stood still, my hand resting on the tarnished knob. She sang the sparrow song, and my heart sprouted wings again.

Maize's hand was now laced in mine, and I felt the panic from him like a heatwave. Bell was at my other hand now, pulling me back toward the bunk.

Daddy spoke softly as I slid down beside the kids and kissed them all on the forehead.

He said, "It's okay, Sweet Potato. This time, I think you're right. This place is the one. Angels are watching over us here. We're here for a reason. I believe it. So, if you've lost that running faith, I guess I'm the daddy, and I'm going to have it for the both of us."

I couldn't argue anymore. Hearing Momma's story coming from Daddy had deflated me, but Bell sang the fear right out of me. Years of pent-up, angry words had finally been said, but the air was still sweet between us all, and the love was stronger than ever. I finally fell asleep to Bean's soft snoring and Bell's gentle humming.

The last thing I remembered was praying to God to forgive me for what I had done ten years ago—for wanting something I didn't need—and for what I had done tonight by threatening to take the kids and move on. And to go ahead and forgive me for what I was about to do tomorrow. Because now, with Ray here with me, things were going to have to change.

FIFTEEN

School passed by again with an A plus. Flying colors, smiling faces, no attacks, just friendliness and belonging. It all was confirmed at the end of sixth period, when Maize told me a girl gave him her number. Okay, where were we? On some alien planet, about to have our brains sucked out for testing?

He punched me while I was doing homework on the bus, making a long pencil mark on my paper. "What got into you last night?"

"Life. Truth." A slap in the face was needed—across Daddy's face, not mine.

"We are starting something here, Sweet Potato. Don't go and mess it up for me."

He waved the tiny slip of paper in front of my face for the fiftieth time—the proof that a girl was bold enough to endure teasing for liking a boy named Maize Pile Jones with an address like The Home.

I asked, "Do you think Daddy is going to change his mind and take us all away from here?"

"Well, then, we've got to change Daddy." He was nodding, his lips pursed out.

I laughed, despite the hurt coursing through me. "Change Daddy? Go change the weather, Maize. Let me see some Southern snow in August. You'd have a better chance doing that than rewiring Daddy."

It was sad, but it was truth, and I was beyond hiding behind misconceptions and cloudy days.

He leaned in closer. "I overheard the Patterson's. It's more than what you think. Mrs. Sunshine's got something going on behind that perfectly pinned-up hair that might be to our advantage."

"What did you hear?" I knew Ray said his momma was working on something, but he never got around to telling me.

"Nothing much." His eyes were belying him, and they sparkled like sapphire jewels in a pirate's treasure chest.

I punched him, and he moaned, making the bus driver glance behind him with beady eyes. No one acted up on his bus. Still weird, but true.

"Tell it, Maize."

"Nothing but about Mrs. Sunshine trying to set Daddy up with some woman from the church—some window woman named Macy McCall." He made funny faces at me, and I couldn't help but laugh out loud. The driver glared at me again, but this time it was accompanied by a smile.

"Window woman? Like a window-washer? Or do you mean widow? Like husband-died woman?" He was hilarious.

"Yeah, I guess so. Daddy would have something in common with *her*, not with a window-washer. What would they talk about?"

He was still plain serious, not seeming perturbed by this one bit. Having Mrs. Sunshine thinking of setting Daddy up seemed to cross some sort of line. But then again, if Daddy had a connection to this place, then maybe, just maybe … The brilliance of that woman had no end.

"Okay. I see the potential in this. But still, it ain't going to work." I was still doubtful, but I could see Maize had plans all his own.

"No. That's why we've got our own little secret weapon." He popped his hand like a pistol.

I was too tired to try to figure it out. "What are you talking about?"

He pointed to Bell. "Little, singing, black beauty back there. If we can get her working on that Macy lady, then we've got Daddy shooed in, for sure."

Maize seemed pretty proud of his little, worked-out plan.

I reminded him. "Daddy hasn't tried on any new shoes in so long he wouldn't even know how to start to tie the laces. He'd definitely not find somebody his size that could put up with the specifications of the traveling life ... if you know what I mean."

No home. No security. No steady beat. Who would fall for that? Oh, yeah—Ray. I forgot.

And that brought me back to Ray, a man who didn't deserve this. Me. I didn't deserve him, and I knew this from the beginning. But when I kissed him, I felt all things possible. He kissed me. He loved me. He even told Daddy he was going to marry me one day and take care of me for the rest of my life. I think he would do that for the kids, too. He wouldn't leave them be.

The bus stopped right in front of The Home for wayward families and no-future ramblers. We piled off, one at a time. No one sneered or joked. Some little girl in pigtails told Bell she'd see her at school tomorrow—that was it. The black smoke from the exhaust swirled around us as we made our way through the gate.

The only hope I had was waiting on me four minutes down the road, and I couldn't wait to ease on down there to see my ray of sunshine. He was sitting with Mr. Jackson, playing a game of checkers. It was mighty quiet in the place, and it suited my mood just fine. I went on over to lean across the booth beside them. I smiled at Ray's look of defeat, watching his brow furrow with disappointment.

"I see who must be winning."

Mr. Jackson chuckled with pride. "Of course, honey. Who else?"

He triple-jumped Ray right out of the game.

Ray clapped. "I give up, Mr. Jackson. Pie on me. Come on, Sweet Potato. Give it a shot."

I smiled, tying my apron around my waist. "Do I get free pie, too?"

He laughed. "I'll give you more than just a piece of pie. Whatever you want?"

I smiled shyly at him. "How about a kiss?"

Mr. Jackson hooted. "Come on, now! I think I deserve the kissing. Come on over here, Ray." He puckered up his lips, and we both couldn't help but laugh hysterically as he pulled Ray close, trying to smooch him.

Ray pulled me down into the booth in front of Mr. Jackson. It didn't take me long to finish the old man off, and I hated I had the skill to do it. He seemed to take pride in his perfect record. But game-playing had always been easy for me. With not much to do at shelters but go through the old games, I was mighty good at things like dominoes and checkers.

Mr. Jackson huffed. "I demand a rematch, Sweet Potato."

The bell jingled, and a new group of customers came on in. I stood up to welcome them, apologizing again to Mr. Jackson for beating him. He swatted at me. "Tell me how that kiss is, Ray, when it happens. If it ever happens."

Ray shot him a wicked glance before going through the double-doors. "I don't kiss and tell, Mr. Jackson. Sorry."

I wanted to kiss and tell Ray how I felt shame and love and regret for pulling him into my life. Business picked up, along with the comfortable chaos. The music blasted and so did the energy of the place and then, just like that it was over. Ray took my hand in his and led me on down to our walk. I stopped him at the bench and pulled him to sit beside me. His arm came around my shoulder, and I leaned up against him, needing to steal this moment. Even if it was only a moment.

I would be daring. "You still owe me that kiss."

"I do." He leaned over and kissed me softly on the lips. "What is it? Tell me. I know you've been holding in something weighing heavy on you. Tell me."

I didn't know how to, really. If I told him about my fear around my birthday, then I'd have to tell him about Momma and how it all started, and I'd have to eventually tell him about me. So I sat on the bench, watching the bugs dance around the streetlight, wondering if any of them had ponderings about futures or pasts.

"Go on, Sweet Potato. What is it?"

I looked down at his hands over mine, and I decided I could tell this man anything, and he would try his best to love me through it. He loved me through poverty and homelessness. He could love me through the past right up to my present, too.

I laughed out loud. It just hit me. "When we say, 'for richer or poorer,' we already got that taken care of before we even say, 'I do,' and I know it's true."

He smiled at me quizzically. "What are you talking about, girl?"

So I told him. I told him about the afternoon of my birthday when I'd cried my eyes out for a puppy, even though we really didn't have the money to buy anything that would take constant upkeep. But I felt like I deserved it for being eight. The pet shop was a few blocks down from Daddy's hotel. I told him about Daddy warning us not to leave the house, because if we did, Momma would have a chance of meeting up with one of her suppliers. But I'd been naïve and thought she wouldn't need her fix on a special day like my birthday. But on the trip back, she'd got a bad bag, one that was laced with junk, and it hit her hard. Too hard. I'd seen Momma on the trip to Never Never Land many times before, but this time when that white foam came pouring down the side of her mouth and her eyes rolled back in her pretty head—this time I'd known I was in the middle of a nightmare.

I told him all about the years after, in little bursts with captions and short descriptors, enough for him to understand.

"You changed my life. It might be simple to you, but it matters mightily to me. Ray, you love me."

I looked down at his hands again. It was a statement of fact, but it still came out as if I was asking him a question. Would I ever grow past my insecurities?

"Yes, I do, and I always will."

And I knew that it was true, regardless of what my mind tried to tell me. Just like the way that God was above me and around me all at once. Ray was a gift from God. My very own blessing. Amen.

I told him about the calendar and what my birthday meant. I told him I never saw myself with a future, like colleges or jobs or any idea of what might be going down next week. It was inconceivable to even think about me being an adult, even though I'd lived smack into the adult world since I was eight years old. Could he understand the way that my mind was wired? Could I even begin to explain it?

"And you love me poor? With this dirt over me? This past?"

"You're rich in spirit, Sweet Potato. There's a kindness in you that speaks to me. It's your gentle way, your caring way. You will be my wife, and I'll be your husband. I will take care of you and your family. Don't walk around thinking it's your fault about your momma or your current situation. I promise you that I will ..."

My hand came up to shush him. I had to stop this.

"But see? You don't know, really, because you have a bedroom. A roof. A momma. A place of your own. You have never had to live on the street. What if Daddy decides it's time, and he snatches us all away?" It wasn't an accusation. It was truth.

"It's not what you have. It's what God is. Remember that one?" He smiled at me, and I couldn't help but smile right back. It was a good quote to keep handy, because it worked in so many situations. Even this one.

"Having money isn't the most important thing about life. It's love."

I already knew that. I'd come to that conclusion on my very own. "So, you mean you still want to go out on a date with me?"

"What does that mean? You changin' your mind now?" He laughed at me again. "I'll never get used to the way you speak. You surprise me all day long."

"Well, surprise. I don't feel worthy of your love. Sorry, but I have to be honest with you. I don't doubt you if you don't want to date me." I shrugged.

Ray continued to break me down with his way. "What part of 'husband' didn't you understand? You're going to be eighteen on September 24th. I'm about to ask you to be my wife. I've been saving up for something for a while now, not really knowing what it would be for. Now I know." He took my ring finger in his hand, trying to figure out how to measure it.

Then he stopped in his tracks and frowned. "Oh, I see. I won't ask you that day."

My heart hit the pavement, and I stood up, turning to walk away. "Of course, you won't, Ray. That's what I've been trying to say."

"No, no," he stammered, running up behind me, putting his arms around my waist and pulling me close to him. "I meant, that day holds so many bad memories for you. I couldn't do that to you. Mix the good with the bad like that. I want you to remember the day that I ask you to marry me apart from your Momma passing away. Baby, I love you," he whispered in my ear, and my heart found its way back to beating again, and I was sure he could hear it.

"Just show me."

Could I love him back the way he needed? What did he expect out of me? Out of a wife? I wasn't as good as Mrs. Sunshine, and I never would be. He had his parents and a solid upbringing. How could I ever measure up to that kind of love?

He squeezed me tighter as we walked awkwardly down the sidewalk, and he buried his face in my hair. I froze solid. I wanted to memorize how it felt to be held by him. "If you were going to leave me, I would've barricaded you in somewhere, had petitions signed, stopped the wrecking ball from swinging. I was working on mighty hard prayers to keep you here with me."

Date. Time. "Oh, Ray!"

I looked down at my watch. It was reaching ten thirty. Daddy wasn't here looking out for me. We had forgot all about the time. *Oh, Lordy, no!*

I took off running, Ray right after me, laughing. "We in it now, huh?"

All I could pant was the word, "Pray!"

We made it through the gate and up to number seven, and I creaked open the door. Everybody was up, and the flashlight was on Bean. He was doing one of his standup routines, telling knock-knock jokes that never quite worked out, but we would laugh at him anyway.

Ray whispered behind me, "What are y'all doing with the flashlight?"

Bean turned to me. "Why did the chicken cross the road?"

I shrugged. "Don't know, Bean. Tell me."

"To run from Daddy fox, because he's about to eat you alive." He busted out laughing hysterically.

I rolled my eyes. "Very funny, Bean."

Daddy nodded. "Come on in, baby. Ray. Nice to see you again." What? No "where you been?" No "I'm going to ground you from date night." No nothing. Just "nice to see you." Hello?

"I'm really sorry, Daddy. I had a lot of explaining to do with Ray. We were down at the park bench between here and Soul Food. I promise that's the truth."

Ray stepped up beside me and held out his hand to Daddy, who shook it without twisting him around into a chokehold.

"Sorry, sir. It's my fault. I was caught up in spending time with Sweet Potato, and we were talking about so much that the time truly did pass by without our being aware. I'll try my best, sir, to respect your wishes in every way in the future." The way Ray spoke to Daddy was so commendable. Who could even go against it?

Daddy asked with a smile, "Do you own one of them cellphones?"

"Yes, sir." Ray pulled it out of his pocket. "Just to call in with Momma."

Daddy nodded. "Do that now, son. She's probably worried right about now. Ask her can you stay a little bit longer. That way you can listen to Bean's act. I don't think you should miss it. He's actually on a roll tonight."

"Yes, sir." Ray quickly called his momma to report in and to say he'd be only a little while longer.

I snuggled in beside Maize, resting my head on his shoulder, as Ray squatted cross-legged against the bunk and leaned back. Daddy looked over at us, making sure we were proper, and I mouthed to him, "Thanks."

He tried to give me the evil eye and whispered, "First and last time, young lady."

I saluted him and turned my attention to Bean. The flashlight beamed right off his big eyes and bright, white teeth. "Knock, knock."

I whispered to Ray, "Here it comes. Get ready to laugh."

We all said in unison, "Who's there?"

He flexed his muscles and spun in a fast circle. "Broccoli."

We all used that same voice. "Broccoli who?"

"Count Broccula, baby, and I vant to suck your blood."

We giggled as he came at us with arms raised, trying his best to look wild-eyed, which didn't take much effort. The mystery of it all was that we could continue to laugh—the genuine kind. It was the love of a family that could withstand all storms.

A tear escaped the corner of my eye after Ray had long gone and the room had gone off to sleep. That was what Mrs. Sunshine had seen in my eyes. I didn't know what she meant until this very night. Now, in the quiet of the night, I knew. Jesus was always calming my storms. Jesus was always my boat, my sea, my in-between. My faith, and Bell's prayers brought us to this place. I had faith in what could be, and the word "future" didn't scare me anymore. Even if I didn't have it all figured out, I knew I wasn't navigating this life alone. I could cast the burdens to Jesus, and we could build ourselves a life that mattered. What I always knew deep down could be for us. Faith materialized it into very existence, and we could claim the sky.

The next morning, when I stared at myself in the mirror, I could see a new light there in those pupils. It was the recognizing of a faith that could move mountains, no matter the circumstance. I smiled all the way to school, knowing my secret about myself was all good. And now that Momma's secret had been revealed to me, I would carry it for the world to see. It was about time I let some love in and out.

And it was comforting to know that there could be a tomorrow, and a next day, and a next day after that in a place called Newport News, Virginia.

SIXTEEN

Mrs. Sunshine surprised me at the restaurant door on Thursday, after school. She was dangling her gold keyring in her hand. "It's up to me and you today, child."

I frowned. "What? We are running the place by ourselves?"

She laughed, squeezing my shoulder. "Honey child, no. We are leaving that to the menfolk. We are running to that mall right by ourselves. Let's go. Hang back up that apron."

Ray came up, waving my waitress pad. "Looks like I've got mighty pretty shoes to fill. Hey, Sweet Potato."

"Hey, Ray." *Hey, love of my life. Hey, you handsome somebody.*

Mr. Joe called out, "You better not spend all my money, woman. I'm wanting that Bahamian cruise, I tell you."

Mrs. Sunshine rolled her eyes. "I've been the one wanting that cruise. You are a lying Jack Rabbit. And one day I'm gonna leave you here stirring up them collard greens by your lonesome and soaking me in that Caribbean sunshine all by my grown-up self."

He stuck his head through the diamond shaped-cut-out. "I soak in your sunshine all day long, baby. No need to have some sunburn out across that Atlantic. You got me all fired up just thinking about you in one of them 'kinis."

Mrs. Sunshine grabbed my arm and pulled me away from staring at Ray, who had apparently forgotten all about how to take an order when I smiled at him. "Tell your Ray bye, now. You'll see him in a little while."

"But I just got here."

My time with Ray was very precious, and I didn't want to waste a single day. Seeing him in the afternoons made my life worthwhile.

Mrs. Sunshine led me out through the kitchen before I could even tell Ray bye. We went through her pretty, little attached house and out to the car. "You ever been on a date before?"

Before I could even answer, she did it for me. "No, of course you haven't. So, that's the purpose of this outing. Go with the flow, Sweet Potato."

"You're taking me out on a date?" I was so lost with this woman sometimes!

"I guess you could say that. I'm taking you on a date before the date. Let's call it the pre-date."

She backed the car out, turned a few corners, and hopped back on that scary freeway as I held on to the little door handle for dear life.

"Dear Jesus," I whispered as she swerved onto an on-ramp.

"Jesus is, child. Dear He is."

But I was more about asking dear Jesus to get me safe and sound through the pre-date so I could make it to the *date* date.

She pulled up to the Macy's parking lot. I'd never once been in a mall. We had ventured to the Wal-Mart on very rare, special occasions. Been to a few thrifts when we'd outgrown our hand-me-downs. We did the Saturday-yard-sale-shopping like champs, and if anyone ever asked us where we got our outfits, we said "The YS," like it was the name of an actual store. Who knew? With all the online shopping today, we could get away with it. The bottom line was that we were clothed. We were the walking testament of not holding on to worldly possessions or taking stock in treasures of this Earth. That's how I'd explained it all to Bell, to make her believe that what we lived was for a purpose. Honestly, I believed that down to my core.

I tried to hold in my twinge of pleasure as I looked at all the mannequins dressed up in fancy, frilly shirts and matching six-inch heels. I shifted my feet beside Mrs. Sunshine as she pulled hangers across silver, spinning racks. The scraping noises sounded like a cash register already ringing. She wasn't even looking at the tags hanging off the clothes, holding up one shirt after the next, swishing them to and fro in front of me, hanging them back up again.

She turned to me, putting her hand on her hip. "Don't act like you ain't never went to no mall clothes shopping. Let's look, now."

I stood there, watching her slinging clothes around. Her hand was still on my hip. "No, ma'am."

"No, ma'am, what? You ain't never been to no mall?"

She answered her own question again. "No. I guess you haven't. Okay, let's go. We going to go walking for a little bit."

She took me by the smell-good counters, and I got sprayed without even being asked if I wanted to. I felt like I was in some automated carwash. When we stepped out into the massive, windowed world of pristine tile and columns, I wondered how many trees had to be cut down to make this happen.

Echoes bounced off the walls, rising above the escalators: children's voices, baby buggies with squealing tires. Teenagers walked past in groups. They didn't look like Dream kids; they looked like they went to preppy, private schools.

The fountain in the middle of the atrium seemed like a safe haven. I needed a rest from all this excitement. It wasn't that I was out of shape—heavens, no. It might take me a minute to get it all together. I sure knew Bell would adore this place. I hoped one day she'd have a chance to experience it.

"I thought it might be nice to take you shopping to get you an outfit to wear out on your date with Ray. Would you like that?"

Mrs. Sunshine was rocking back and forth on the concrete fountain edge, and by her body language, I could tell this meant something to her.

"You've already done so much for me. Can't you see that?"

Her arm came around me again. I loved how she wasn't ashamed to reach out for me, and she always seemed to do it right when I needed it. A hug from her was something special, and each time it made my heart seem to grow a little more. But that beating heart also reminded me it could break, and it could hurt mighty hard. *Please, God, let this all be real.*

"I ain't done nothing for you, not yet. You've got your whole life to be with me, child. So, get used to me and my ways. I wanted this. Thought about it since the minute Ray told me about the date plans. I want this to be memorable for you. You don't ever get another first date." She winked at me and nudged my arm.

"So, you remember your first date? Was it with Mr. Joe?"

By the look on her face, I thought she'd fall over into that fountain and make a splash.

"Honey, no! Let's not go that far back in time. But do I remember my first date with Joseph Patterson? Sure do. He took me to the movies and held my hand the whole time. When we were driving back home, he told me he was never getting serious with no woman, and I needed to know that about him right away. You see where that got him, don't you?"

I couldn't help but laugh, imagining Mr. Joe trying to act tough around Mrs. Sunshine. She always seemed to put him right back into his place. I loved that.

"Sure do. Can I ask you one thing?"

"Yes, child. Just don't ask me to start naming out all them boys and dates and stuff from the past. The past is in the—"

I cut her off, not really wanting to go there at all.

"No, ma'am. I want to ask you one thing about today, please. If it's not too much to ask." I bit my lip. I hated to be so greedy.

"What is it? Anything, Sweet Potato. Ask away." She seemed all ears, probably expecting I needed advice or some such.

That wasn't it at all. I didn't need no advice about my Ray. Me and him seemed to be fitting together all right. "Instead of trying to dress me up, can we get something pretty for Bell, like a simple, pink dress? And maybe new shirts for Bean and Maize. I don't need anything, I promise. I think Ray loves me all the same, without me getting anything pretty. Those kids deserve it more than me, and it's gonna be their first date, too."

For some reason, that made Mrs. Sunshine cry. Right there in the mall, right at the fountain, in front of onlookers and passers-by who gave her second and third glances. I felt a rush of regret, but I couldn't take it back. It was already out there, echoing all around.

Mrs. Sunshine reached for a tiny Kleenex pack out of her pocketbook, tore out half the pack trying to get at one, and waved the wad across her eyes.

She apologized through her tears. "Oh, me! I'm so sorry. Sweet Potato, you don't know how big your heart is, even. But you don't know how big my pocketbook is, either. So, I say let's get that pink dress, them shirts, and one outfit for you, too."

I insisted. "No pink dress for me, please. That won't do."

She sighed through sniffles. "You don't like dresses?"

I hadn't ever seen Mrs. Sunshine in a dress, either. She always wore her jeans like me, every single day. Except for Sunday, that is. That was black choir-pants day.

"I really don't need a new pair of jeans. These are just fine. See." I stood up and twisted around.

"Okay. Here." She pulled out a penny. "Throw it in that fountain, and let's go on."

I wouldn't dare. "Why would I go and do that?"

She shook her head. "I don't really know. Everybody does it, I guess. You make a wish, and you throw it in." She pointed to the bottom of the fountain, and I tried to guesstimate how much change was scattered about on the black-and-white patterned tiles of the bottom of the fountain.

I stuck the penny in my pocket. "I don't think I'm everybody, Mrs. Sunshine. Think of all those people that threw in that money. If they would have thrown it in a church plate, they might have helped somebody in need, you know that? We don't need wishes, only prayers. I'm resigned not to be a wisher woman." I tried to shake off the thoughts of Momma that were trying to creep into my perfect day.

She put her arm around me again as we walked into the Belk's department store. We went right to the little girl's department. There on a dress rack hung a precious, straight, pink dress with a matching gingham coat.

"You know what, Sweet Potato? When God answers prayers, He sure does it with style."

"What? You are giving God credit for making this dress, too?" I held it up, trying to measure it to see if it would be a perfect fit for Bell, and I was sure that it would be.

"Yes, honey, and something more. I'm giving Him credit for making you. I'd always prayed for a godly woman for my son to love. Loving a preacher man ain't going to be the easiest to do, or so I've heard. It takes a whole lot of woman and prayer to help lead a congregation. But right when I saw them eyes ..."

I smiled at her. "I see it now, too, Mrs. Sunshine. And there is one thing I can tell you. It is mighty easy to love a preacher man when it's going to be Ray Patterson. After all, it won't be me helping to lead a congregation. It will be the Lord moving through me. So, it'll be all right."

She clapped, never minding the other shoppers and found her way to the boy's department, straight to the fancy polo shirt side. She held up a teal-striped shirt that would look mighty fine on Maize and a darker blue matching one for Bean.

"Well said, Sweet Potato. Now, let's go get what you want for your date."

I stopped her. "Where are we off to tomorrow night?"

Ray hadn't spoken about it since. Every second that I was with him, I was happy to be with him in the moment, and I forgot all about our Friday night Jones Family First Date. But every second of my day without him, I had daydreamed of it, wondered about it.

"You'll find out soon enough. Let's see what would look nice."

She held up a shirt with silver buttons on the cuffs. Way too dressy. One shirt after another—I didn't even have to tell her. She'd snatch it and put it right back up.

"Okay. This is getting us nowhere. You only wear t-shirts, I know that. Don't you want something silky?"

We went from polka-dotted, pleated stuff all the way to tie-dye, and she was laughing through her pain at not being able to match me up with an outfit.

She paid for the kids' stuff and took me out of the fancy store. She led me down to a record store that had all kinds of music shirts and shirts with silly prints on them.

"Oh, look!" I squealed, covering my mouth.

It was perfect. *Lordy!*

I held up the t-shirt, and she gave me a look. "You want a t-shirt over a blouse?"

I smiled wide, nodding. "Every day of the week."

It was a pale-yellow shirt with a Care Bear on the front—Hopeful Heart Bear. Six colors of rainbow light shone from the heart on her chest. It seemed like my heart was bursting with so much love for my God and my world. The words underneath spelled out *Hope Springs Eternal* in purple, bubble letters. A butterfly swirled among the letters.

Mrs. Sunshine shrugged. "I was thinking more along the lines of a dressy-up blouse for a first date. Something to make you feel special."

I said, "Don't you get it? This is what is special. Look at those colors bursting out of her heart. That first blue—this one right here. This is where I feel most special. That is the water, the living water of the Spirit covering over my soul. Bright yellow is the ray of light from Ray, shining in my heart. The orange beside him, it's you—the orange sun warming me with acceptance. The red is for the color of the Assembly Revival pew, and I know that it will be a shelter for me to worship for many years to come. That violet, well, that's Soul Food. And don't get me started on what you and that place did for my family. And that last blue is for my family. Blue sky claiming for us from here on out. So, that is my date shirt, if it's okay with you."

Mrs. Sunshine didn't say anything, just took the hanger from me and paid the nice cashier. We headed on back to the car. She didn't speak on the short ride home neither, turned up the radio and went off into her own little world.

When we made it back to the house, she grabbed the bags and went straight on into the restaurant. I followed, scared I'd made some mistake. Did I hurt her feelings? Should I have let her buy me that black-and-pink polka-dotted shirt? I would have worn it if it would have made her happy. Had I overstepped myself by asking for the kids? What had I done wrong? I knew I would mess this all up.

She went right up to Ray, who was talking to a young customer. Before he could finish his sentence, Mrs. Sunshine grabbed Ray and gave him this big, old hug, lifting him right off the ground, shocking me and him in the process.

He laughed, shaking his head. "Momma, are you all right?"

"Praise Jesus, boy. You hear me, now? You praise Jesus, and you thank the good Lord with every single breath you got for bringing that girl into your life. You hear me?"

I was frozen solid by the counter. Did that mean I didn't do anything wrong?

"I know that, Momma. I do every day. Trust me."

She patted him on the head as she sat him down. "You better, or you'll be answering to me. Not just her daddy, but me first. You got that? Don't you forget it."

Ray's laughter was one of the best sounds I knew, next to Bell's singing, and I smiled at him, reckoning that I was okay.

"What did you say to Momma, Sweet Potato?"

I shrugged. "I don't know. She bought me a t-shirt to wear to our date tomorrow night."

Mrs. Sunshine said, "Just a t-shirt! Just a t-shirt. Don't get me started, because I'm going to be testifying right up in this place." She waved her hands. "Let me go see Joe. Go on and get to work."

I took the pad from Ray, and he leaned over and kissed me quickly on the cheek. "Whatever it was that you said to Momma got her spirit all moved and working. That's a good thing, Sweet Potato. Why do you look like you got in trouble with the principal?"

"Just figured I probably did, that's all. Glad to know that I'm off the hook." I checked the pad and wondered how in the world Mr. Joe could follow Ray's order-taking. I was glad that I was back. Not to help the whole place run more smoothly, but to get that kiss on the cheek. To get that smile.

I whispered, "I love you, Ray."

He whispered back, his voice thick with emotion, "I love you, too."

I wanted to fall into his arms right there, to let him hold me. I was so filled up with love for that man, but it wasn't the proper time. I smiled at him and watched as he went on back to his duties in the kitchen. Mrs. Sunshine would come out to greet customers and cash them out, giving me this look the whole night through. It wasn't a you're-in-trouble kinda look, but a warm toaster-oven kinda look that told me for some strange reason she approved of me for Ray. And for the life of me, I still didn't know why.

SEVENTEEN

When the bell jingled its last, I knew we'd better be out of there. Two nights lingering in a row wasn't going to work. Daddy had whispered to me last night and again this morning that he could let one slide, because he understood my need to talk it out, but no more. I knew not to push him, especially since I had already picked out that pink dress for Bell. I couldn't stand the thought that she wouldn't get to feel all ladylike on our first date.

"Thanks again, Mrs. Sunshine, for everything." I waved the bags at her.

"No, honey. Thank you. Every now and again, I need a little jolt in my spirit. You jump-started me into next week."

She warned Ray not to let it go long tonight. When Ray spoke his "yes, ma'am" and opened the door for me, I felt so much admiration for the way he was with his family. He was always there for them—working, smiling, helping, and never once complaining. He was a grown man now, could have done what he wanted—went on off to college with Denise, or to someplace even farther away. He could have left on that Army train and gone. But he stayed right on here. Stayed on for them, and now for me.

"You know you don't have to do that now." It just hit me. I loved that and hated it all at the same time.

We were swinging hands, walking at a snail's pace despite the clock. "Hold your hand?" He pulled my hand up and kissed it. "I must. You know that. For the rest of my life, I'm grabbing your hand and staying as close as possible to you. As close as I can get."

"No, that's not what I meant, silly. I meant you don't have to go to the Army to take care of me. Can't you go on and follow behind Denise, if that's really what you wanted to do before I fell into town?"

"I want to stay right here, for now. Sorry. You can't get rid of me that easy. The spring will be here before we know it, and then it'll be a hard day when I'll have to go to that base for basic." His arm came around my shoulder as we approached the gate.

"Ray. I love you. And I'll be here or follow you when I graduate, one or the other. Whenever. Wherever. But don't let me stand in your way. Either way, it can work out, but if you want college first, then go for it. We'll make it, Lord willing."

He wasn't stopping. Now, after his first few visits up to number seven, I wasn't ashamed of it anymore. He'd never judged me, even from the beginning. So what? A room was a room. He would have accepted me in a broken-down squatter home.

Daddy welcomed him in.

Ray said, "I can't stay but a minute, sir. Momma is clocking me, too."

Daddy laughed, patting him on the back. "Good woman, your momma is, and you are a good young man. Thank you for walking Sweet Potato every night."

"That's all for my benefit, sir."

He smiled at me, but what he didn't know was that those few moments alone with him in the world were the best benefits I'd received in my whole life.

Bell beamed. "It's your night, Sweet Potato. Bean decided."

The flashlight hit me, dancing across my face as I shielded my eyes.

Not in front of Ray. Oh, Lordy, no! No spotlights for me. "I ... I ..."

Daddy clapped. "I ... I ... nothing. Ray, call Mrs. Sunshine and ask her is it okay for you to stay a little while longer for Sweet Potato's concert."

For that—for more time with Ray, for Daddy requesting it again and accepting Ray into my life—I would sing my heart out. I would sing like there was no tomorrow, even though tomorrow was going to shine, Lord willing.

Ray fumbled for his cellphone in the dark and called Mrs. Sunshine. By the smile on his face, I was sure that the time extension was granted.

He confirmed my suspicions, because he went back to sit down in front of Maize—his spot, it seemed. Bean centered the light in the middle of the room. "Okay, sis. Let us have my favorite."

"No." Daddy's voice was firm. "We have a guest. I think that if anybody is getting special treatment, it would be him." He turned to Ray. "What is your favorite song, son?"

That was mighty important to Daddy. When he asked someone that question, it was like asking what their name was. He always said a song defined a person like no other way. Daddy could read the person to know if they were serious, God-loving, stable, whimsical, or wild. I hadn't had a chance to warn Ray about the possibilities of a jukebox selection, and how his choice could make or break him in Daddy's eyes.

Ray was quick to answer. "I have two, but since I'd already heard your family sing one of mine, 'Amazing Grace,' I'll go to my second favorite. Do you know 'How Great Thou Art?'"

Good selection on the jukebox, sweetheart. "I love that one."

Daddy would approve of that in a mighty way. We seemed to like the traditional gospel music the best—the older hymns. That contemporary stuff was fine and all. Bell, especially, liked those songs the best—when we would choir-sing and clap up a frenzy. But I liked the stuff from long ago, like Daddy did. Those old spirituals got me like no other.

Daddy clapped. "All right, Ray. That's my boy. Go on ahead, Sweet Potato. 'How Great Thou Art.'"

I sighed, finding my way to the center. My voice could probably be heard throughout the whole shelter, but nobody ever seemed to care. Never had any complaints from any of the other temporals. So, we kept it up.

When Ray was leaving, he gave me that smile, and I could see in his eyes that he hated to take off. It seemed harder and harder the more I was with him. I hated that nights had to end. Could love operate like that? Could it grow more *and* hurt more every single day? The next day would be the date night, and I would get to have him all night—no customers to wait on, just me and the youngins. *Amazing grace, how sweet the sound.*

I held up the bags after he left. I'd forgotten about the presents from Mrs. Sunshine.

Daddy frowned. "That woman already done enough for us. She doesn't need to be going and buying you kids no more clothes. I think I need to remind you about handouts."

I stopped him. "Daddy. Can they try on their clothes while me and you go on up and talk a minute?" I would have never imagined that I'd be requesting an upstairs meeting, but there were a few things that needed to be discussed properly.

Daddy eyed me curiously as I paced back and forth on the rooftop, giving me time before I spoke. I looked up to Jesus to make sure I was doing the right thing. No more disrespecting Daddy or outbursts like before.

Okay. I was ready. "Daddy, no matter what outbreak I had, don't think about moving us away from The Dream. Whatever plans you have for living arrangements, those kids have to go there, so we gotta think bus routes now. We never had to think about districts, but now we do. I mean, they have to go there. Trust me, this is the best place on the other side of heaven for them to get their schooling. So, the bottom line is no moving too far away. Deal?"

That wasn't really a negotiable one, but I wanted him to think so.

"Deal. Go ahead. I know you got more. I'm listening."

Daddy crossed his arms and leaned back against the brick wall, smiling at me. He liked this new role, I could tell. My secret was probably about to eat away at him. He didn't know that I had faith now to claim this land. Watch out for the girl with a prayer on her lips and faith in her heart. It could get me somewhere.

"When we get to that place, you get a big enough place for us kids to share equal rooms. Me and Bell, Bean and Maize. We only need the basics. We ain't those kinds of kids, and you don't try to impress us with new things or expensive toys. We never were like that, and we ain't going to go changing our fundamental outlook on life because we might have some money coming in from Soul Food."

I hoped he got that message.

He nodded. "Okay, go ahead. I wouldn't think of that, no way."

"You let me still work at Soul Food and pitch in and help with all of our necessities. You can't be the only one responsible for this family, and now that I can do my duty, it's only right that I work as much as I can. Maize will be soon to follow, and he will learn responsibility early to keep him on track."

Daddy cut in. "Listen to me. You think I'm the kind of man that's going to lie on some sofa and watch some TV while—"

"No TV, Daddy. Promise me. No gaming boxes or TVs or cellphones."

"You are getting a cellphone. If you're going out with that boy, the bottom line is you are getting a way to check in with your daddy. In fact, here it is now." He pulled a little, red box out of his back pocket.

"Mrs. Sunshine put you up on her plan for right now, until we can get things settled. It comes right out your paycheck, but you got some family plan with them that you can call Mrs. Sunshine, Mr. Joe, or Ray for free. But don't go burning up them minutes with friends."

"Daddy. Please. I will call no one but who you say." I swallowed hard. "I can call Ray?" *Anytime I want, for free. Oh, Lordy.*

"You can call Ray. That's what I did say. You got any more words of wisdom for your old Daddy?"

I laughed. "No, I think that about covers it."

He smirked. "I'll try my best to abide by your wishes. Tomorrow, when you go to Soul Food, you pull out that apron from my drawer, and you turn it over and read it. I'm not ready to show it for testifying just yet, but when I am, you will know it."

He put his arms around me and gave me a papa-bear hug. I whispered, "Give us a life, Daddy. Not only breathing air and surviving. Give us a life that matters—where we can make a difference for someone else, too."

He opened the door and led me down the stairs, shaking his head. "Don't you know we already done that? We're still doing that, Sweet Potato. It hasn't hit you yet, that's all. There's more that I can be giving you, but you wouldn't learn anything from it being handed to you. You learn through working out life, and I think I've raised you up right. It is showing well on you."

The kids were in their bunks, ready for the night to end so they could all go out on their first date.

Daddy spoke low. "Don't be calling and talking to Ray until we all go to sleep. Let these youngins get a good night's rest."

I frowned. "I don't know his number." I'd rectify that tomorrow.

"Think of this as an early birthday present. Mrs. Sunshine is number one. Hit number two. He's on speed dial." He chuckled softly. "Goodnight, Sweet Potato. I love you. No matter how old you're getting, you're still my Sweet Potato Pie."

"I love you, too." I held the phone close to my heart. "Thanks for Ray."

He turned over. "I don't think that I had no workings in that. It was all God. Thank Him."

I smiled up at the heavens to Jesus. To Momma. I said, "I thank Him every day, don't worry."

"I don't worry about you at all. Now let me get some sleep. I got the early morning." He was snoring right after he spoke his last word, it seemed.

The room was quiet, but my heart was thundering out of my chest. Could I truly call him? Could it be possible that I could push the number two and hear his voice? I hit the button, and it startled me because it beeped so loudly.

"Sweet Potato, is that really you?" He seemed as amazed as me.

I whispered, "Yes."

He laughed. "I guess you're trying not to wake anybody up, huh?" He knew my living arrangement. He added, "I'll do most of the talking tonight, then, if that's okay with you?"

I whispered back that it would suit me just fine, still in wonder that I could have this time with him. Second best to being in the same room with him. I could close my eyes and see his smile right now. It helped ease my panic about holding a phone up to my ear.

"Please. Let me hear you."

We talked well into the night—well, mostly him. I made him tell me all about him growing up, school, football, church, and what he loved most about his life. As I listened to his soft voice weaving me closer into his spell, I saw myself with him in all of his stories. Watching his life as I sat on the sidelines. Now, we walked down a cracked, concrete path, but I knew that one day I would see him waiting for me at the end of the aisle.

Even though I knew I was too young to be thinking of such grown-up things, I could see us having children of our own. I'd name them all after flowers—at least the girls, that is. Ray said if we had boys, they would get Bible names, like Solomon and Samuel. And he wanted at least five kids, he said. That was fine by me. My girls would be called Lavender, Lily, and Daisy. With my three, that would make eight, and that was enough.

He told me how he'd saved up all of his money from working at Soul Food since he was fifteen, and he was leaving it all with his momma for things I might need when he went to basic training in the spring. He told me more about his plans for the future and how being a chaplain assistant in the Army was the place where he was supposed to follow God's calling.

I said, "But I told you, you don't have to worry about me now. Daddy is going to take care of us. I told him that he ain't carrying us away from this place, so he knows he better start getting his act together. I didn't want to tell him the truth, and I guess you need to hear it right now before you truly accept me."

I had always known this but had never told another soul. Maize figured it out for himself and told me once that he secretly wished it would happen. Poor child.

"Tell me, Sweet Potato. You can tell me anything," Ray spoke softly, and I hugged the phone against my ear.

"If Daddy tries to move us again, I'm taking those kids as my legals. I can do it when I turn eighteen. I can make it happen, if your family could help me. I've meant to talk to Mrs. Sunshine about it sometime or another, but first I want to put my trust in Daddy to do the right thing."

"You will be my wife, and soon I will take care of you and those youngins, too. Don't you worry about a thing, because together we'll always be able to do right by them." He brought me back down with an over-and-out. "You need to get some rest. I don't want you falling over on our first date."

"Date ... Mmm ..."

Just saying the words was like a triple scoop of rocky road ice cream. We said our goodnights, and even though I couldn't believe the time had gone by so fast, I was far from sleepy. My mind replayed our conversation, hitting the parts where his life had changed since he met me—how he felt complete and not alone. How God was working us all out together, soothing our fears. His words washed over me, and once again I had to remind myself that this man was *mine*.

When girls would talk about boyfriends at school, I rarely listened to them. Since I was never truly included in those kinds of talks anyway, I always was on the fringe of the goings-on. I stuck my head in a schoolbook and went on about my day. It had never been on my priority list to even once contemplate what it would be like to have a boyfriend.

As the sunshine brushed against my face, making me feel right pretty for the new day, I knew what mattered most was in this place. How appropriate for us to start us a new life here. God sure knew what he was doing. Funny how I'd always loved a good, romanticized story about how a name could come to be—from restaurant names to people.

I could not go back. My family had always been enough. Now, with Ray and Soul Food and that school for the youngins—I could rejoice enough to jolt my spirit just thinking about it.

EIGHTEEN

As soon as I tied my apron, Mrs. Sunshine was loosening it. "What do you think you are doing, child?"

I shrugged. "Getting ready for work, looks like to me."

"Getting ready for your date—I think so. Did you think you were working today?"

She waved that famous finger at me. I hadn't seen Ray or heard his welcome call, so I figured she had sent him scurrying away, too. What did people do to get ready for such things? Wash? I'd already done that.

"I need to work extra for that special gift you gave me yesterday. Thank you so much for that."

I patted my pocket. The cellphone had one message on it—sweet words from Ray telling me he couldn't wait to spend the evening with me. That reminded me. I needed the instruction manual on the thing, because I didn't know how to send a message back, and I was too embarrassed to call and ask.

"That was your daddy's idea, and a fine one. Kids today don't need to go off alone without having some way to contact us—not with all that evil out there in the world, I tell you. And speaking of your daddy, here he is now, right on time."

Daddy jingled the bell with his finger. "Hey there, girl. Didn't I just see you running down here before I could stop you?"

He had all the kids with him. Bell had on her pink dress, and the boys were practically prancing in their new polo shirts. And they were a right handsome family, if I did say so myself. Right proud of them, I was.

"Daddy, what is this?"

I watched as he went to the drawer and pulled on his apron backward. There went my chance to look. He sure wasn't going to let me do it in front of the youngins, I had a feeling.

"It's me working your shift. You are doing double tomorrow. I can do you a favor by letting you have the day off. Ray is picking you up soon, anyway."

Ray was picking me up? Like coming to a house with a porch swing, shaking hands with the parents as they take pictures? No way was he going to come get me from number seven.

"He ain't got to pick me up. I'll be here. I'll save him the time."

This was as good as it was going to get. My Care Bear shirt on, my hair miraculously perfect in place. What else was there to do, people?

"Well, go on back and get ready. I got the kids with me. They already used up the bathroom. I had to make them hurry up. It's all you, child."

He pushed me out the door, and I stood there staring at them through the glass. Bell was twirling now, with Mrs. Sunshine holding her finger, letting her spin that beautiful dress of hers and praising her up and down. Her voice carried right on out to the outside, and I smiled. Maize was already opening one of the glass pie dishes lining the counter, and Bean was right behind him, pushing for position.

I decided to go on back to The Home, maybe this time to myself would be exactly what I needed to pray myself up some courage. Maybe I'd try to memorize a little bit more of that poem and surprise Ray by reciting it to him tonight when I would find myself at a loss for words. I needed something to calm my nerves.

The room was wrong without the kids in it. I had never noticed how dingy the place looked until I was here by myself. The tiny bathroom was barely lit enough for me to see my eyes in the mirror—Momma's eyes.

I tried to put on a smile, but it was a little forced. "Hey, faith. Nice to see you."

I imagined Momma speaking to me. Even though I could not remember the exact tone of her voice, I made up one in my mind.

You did good for the kids. Now do some good for you.

"Don't worry, Momma." I started to sing one of our prayer songs. "Do good unto others ..."

I heard a thump. But something sent me straight from feeling high on life to not right. The tiny, little hairs on the back of my neck stood straight up. *Thump*. Ray wouldn't knock like that.

Oh, Lordy! That was our door—number seven. It was daylight and after four. Was Ray ready for our date? Thump. It was more of a body ramming the door than a rap of the knuckles.

I ran to the door and swung it open, but it wasn't Ray or Daddy or one of the kids. It was a stranger, with long, stringy hair and a look that let me know he was up to no good. He had the Devil in his eyes and some foul odor seeping off him. I couldn't find my voice, but I could find my strength. I pushed the door to as best as I could, but his black boot was stuck in the doorframe, and his slurry talk weaved through the crack and found me.

"I've been watching you, girl. Now, let me in."

I wasn't a little girl. My six-foot frame came with some power. I'd wrestled down Maize and Bean both while we were playing. I could hold this drunk man out this door. *Praise God. Jesus, help me.*

"Mrs. Betty Atkins!" I screamed as I fumbled for my pocket,

found the cellphone, and hit two. *Lordy, no!* It went straight to his message center. *Ray! Ray!*

I hung up the phone and tried again. When I hit the number one, it showed Mrs. Sunshine's name. *Thank heavens.* It was ringing. *Lordy!* The man was bearing down on me, and as hard as I tried, I couldn't hold him off much longer. I screamed again for Mrs. Betty Atkins as loud as I could. *Lordy!* Where were the people in this place? It was daylight, even!

He crashed into the door with a force too mighty for me to hold back, knocking me onto the floor. The cellphone flew clear out of my hands. It slid across the black, mosaic tiles, but I could faintly hear gospel music in the background, and Mrs. Sunshine's confused voice repeatedly saying, "Hello?"

His hands slid around my neck as I wailed and kicked. My voice was a squeal, and I prayed they heard me. "Mrs. Sunshine! Daddy! Ray! Help me!"

The man slurred, "I gonna help you right fine. Come here, girl. I've been watching you. Waiting. Now, it's time to get this over with for good."

He was on top of me now, white foam at the corners of his mouth, spit falling onto my cheeks. I pushed and knocked, flailing at him with all that I had. His hand closed over my mouth, but I bit down hard, feeling the dirt of his fingers in my mouth. I felt like I would choke from the pressure. His other hand was on my throat, closing in tighter and tighter, and I knew he was going to kill me. This couldn't be it. God, I'd just started. *Oh, Lordy, no!*

I saw hands. Strong hands were on the man's shoulders, lifting him clear off the ground. Daddy slung the man up against the wall with a *bump* that left a crack in the plaster. A knock or two later, and the man was against the dingy floor, crumbled up in a heap. Daddy's strong arms lifted me and carried me out through the hallway, down the stairs, out the door, up the sidewalk, and through the gate to a place where I knew I was safe.

Ray was running, his shirt unbuttoned, holding onto his pants with one hand. "Sweet Potato!"

His voice was panicked. Daddy kept on walking, and I buried my face back into his neck until we'd made it safely inside Soul Food.

Mrs. Sunshine was crying. "What happened? What happened, child?"

Daddy pushed on through to the back room.

Mr. Joe hollered, "What's this all about? Let me find out!"

But it didn't take but a second for him to hush up his complaining. My youngins and Ray were all right behind Mrs. Sunshine, crowded up in the small kitchen. She slung open the door and led us into her home. Daddy sat down on the couch with me still in his lap.

He shushed me about a thousand times, pulling me back. "Oh, God! Sweet Potato, I'm so sorry, honey. I'm so sorry."

I cried a little before I could get the courage to speak. My voice was broken. "I ... I'm o ... kay."

Mrs. Sunshine had not stopped crying, and Ray was at Daddy's knees, holding on to my arm. "Sweet Potato, what happened?"

I didn't know, really. Daddy explained to them what he had walked in on, and Mrs. Sunshine fell back into her recliner, rocking it as she went.

Ray reached out and touched my hair, then my cheek. "Baby, are you okay? Did he ... did he hurt you?"

Mrs. Sunshine hollered, "I'm calling the police! You hear me? I'm going to go get the shotgun."

I shot up. "No! No! You can't!"

She had the phone in her hand, and I jumped up from Daddy and knocked it out of her hands. "You can't do that none. You can't go reporting anything, or they could take us away—all of us. No!"

My tears fell between my words, but I was sure they could understand what I was trying to say. Daddy knew what could happen, all too well.

Ray's hand came to rest on my shoulder. "It's okay, Sweet Potato. Nobody is going to take you away, but we have to report this man."

Daddy shook his head. "She's right. If you say something, they'll come investigate. We can't have that. He won't bother you no more, Sweet Potato, let's go."

"No," I protested. Ray's hand was still on my shoulder. "He told me ... he said ..."

"What? What did he say?" Ray's voice was threateningly low. I'd never heard him at the brink of anger until this very second. "Tell me."

"He'd been watching me. He had to get it over with. What did that mean?" Short. Simple. Enough.

Mrs. Sunshine threw her hands up in the air. "That does it! That's it!" She stood up, waving her hands in front of Daddy's face. "That's it!"

Mr. Joe busted inside, swinging the door back. "What is it, woman? What's going on in here?"

"Joe! You hear me, Joe? These kids aren't going anywhere. They are staying right here with us. Enough is enough." She pointed at Daddy, talking more to him than to Mr. Joe.

Daddy switched his mouth back and forth, twitching his mustache. He always did that when it was decision time. I could see his eyes working and his heart breaking like a big, old duck egg cracked on a sidewalk.

He looked at all of us, starting with Bell in her pretty, pink dress. Her face was stained straight down with tears. Maize's face was pensive, pulled tight as a clothesline cord. It was obvious that he wanted to go and hurt somebody, but it was like he was channeling it right toward Daddy. Bean was dancing from one foot to the next, confused and angry. His eyes fell on me, and it took all I could muster to keep a steady gaze directed toward him. Nothing else could be said. What was left? We'd had all of our conversations, all our talks. We were finished with that. Mrs. Sunshine was right. It was time.

Daddy finally said, "We ain't going back."

That was straightforward enough.

But Mrs. Sunshine misinterpreted. "You aren't leaving here, Eli Jones. These kids are a part of us now. There is no snatching them up and running, and as long as I have a breath in my body, I'll fight you if you drag them down a road again."

Bell's sobs rose over Mrs. Sunshine's words, and I reached out to her. She pushed me away, almost knocking me over.

"But I got a solo on Sunday, Sweet Potato. I can't leave here. Bean got a hundred on his spelling test today! Did he tell you that?"

Daddy put his hand on top of her head. "Come here, baby." He picked her up and held her. "We are not going anywhere far. I was trying to say we are not going back to The Home."

Maize seethed. The anger was twisting his face. "What do you mean? I thought you were finally committed to leaving the map behind, Daddy? Just go on. Leave me behind. I'll call the police myself."

I knew this place had his heart now, too. It might have had something to do with pie and that ponytailed girl who was waving at him when he got on the bus this morning.

Daddy's voice was stern. "Nobody is calling the police, and nobody is going anywhere unless I say. I knew who that man was, and he won't find us again. He's long gone." He motioned for Ray. "Son, come on with me. You youngins, you stay here with Mrs. Sunshine."

Mr. Joe frowned, confused as ever. "Well, I'm getting back to work. Sunshine, you need me, you holler, now."

She rolled her eyes. "Go on, Joe. Get on."

Mrs. Sunshine put Bell on her lap, trying to console her fears, humming all the while as she rocked her.

I crawled over to Maize, and he put his hand on my back. He growled low as I nestled into his arms. "Where are you two going?"

Daddy sighed. "To get our stuff. You stay here."

Maize stood, dragging me up. "I'm going, too." He balled his fist up, pounding on his hand.

Daddy held out his hand in the stop-in-the-name-of-love sign. "No. You are staying here with Sweet Potato. You don't let her out your sight, you hear me? You protect her."

Maize laughed. "Like you did? Like you protected her? Us?"

I whispered against Maize, trying to convince myself. "This wasn't Daddy's fault."

He put his arms around me, and we slid back down onto the thick carpet. "All this is Daddy's fault. All of this."

I hid in the crook of Maize's arm, too afraid to agree with him in front of Daddy. It wasn't the appropriate time for *I told you so*.

Ray and Daddy left us, and as soon as I knew it was just the two of us, the tears came thick and fast. I couldn't stop shaking, and Maize held on to me tighter. When I closed my eyes, I could see that devil's face. I trembled from the inside out, tiny ripples of fear coursing through my veins.

It didn't seem as if Ray and Daddy were gone five minutes. This time, they came in from the back door. Was the man still there? Had they finished him off?

Daddy must have sensed it. "He was gone, Sweet Potato. He won't be back. I promise."

But that was something I knew Daddy couldn't promise. He couldn't see inside the workings of an evil mind. Only God could do that. I prayed that God would make that man never come back. *Lord, help that man mosey on down the road and fall into a deep, dark pothole, never to hurt anyone or see the light of day again.*

Ray set the five drawstring bags down on the floor beside me. Daddy slung the four bookbags down, along with the purple-top tote. Mrs. Sunshine was shocked. "Is that all your things?"

Daddy nodded.

She exclaimed, "Oh, me."

Maize was still holding on to me. I whispered to him, "Don't be mad, Maize."

He spoke through clenched teeth, "Mad? Mad? I'm ... I'm ... out of control right now. I can't even begin to think what could've happened to you."

He pushed me off him and stood up to Daddy. He seemed like such a man in that moment, not a fourteen-year-old boy. The way he was standing, shoulders wide, reminded me he was growing up right in front of my eyes.

"Daddy, what if that would've been Bell? What if she couldn't have got to that phone? What if Mrs. Sunshine hadn't given her a phone to call out in the first place? She would be lying there bleeding to death on that floor."

I stood up beside him, my legs feeling like spaghetti noodles. I tried to put my hand on him to calm him down, but he shrugged me off.

"But it wasn't Bell. And I did get to that phone. So, don't you play the what-if game. What-ifs hurt too much, and you know it as much as me."

Maize turned on me, eyes flashing hot. "Don't take up for him anymore, Sweet Potato." He turned back to Daddy. "You are the sorriest excuse of a man that I've ever seen. You ain't got no stable place for us, no place for this family, so you haul us all over creation— to do what? To satisfy your need to hide from your hurt? Like we don't hurt? Like we don't have that same pain? Like we didn't see her foaming on the street ourselves? Momma is dead, Daddy! She died long ago, and so did you, that very day. And today, this family is dead. Dead to me, do you hear me?"

His hands were clenched, but I held them anyway. "You don't mean what you are saying, Maize. You don't know everything."

"I know everything! I know that Mr. and Mrs. Foster is going to be better than this. I know the street is better than this. I can't stand it to know that Bell could have—or ... or ... Sweet Potato ..."

Daddy put his hands atop Maize's shoulders and shook him a

little. "Listen to me, son. We ain't going back to that kind of life. We might be going to a hotel right now, but it will be a temporal thing, until I can get us settled into a little place."

"Temporal. That's all it's ever been—a temporal thing. A hotel. Whatever."

He hung his head in defeat, and the anger whooshed right out of him like a deflated balloon. He was done.

Mrs. Sunshine shouted, "You ain't taking these kids to no hotel. You might as well sign them over to me. All of them. You can forget breaking these children's hearts anymore."

Ray interrupted her. "No, Momma. Me and Sweet Potato are going to take the kids. When she turns eighteen, we'll get married then. We won't wait. We'll go down and fight for them ourselves."

Bell perked right up and said, "Sweet Potato? You want us with you like that? I want you, Sweet Potato. I want you and Ray."

For once, Daddy was outnumbered. He pushed Maize down beside me on the floor and sat down on the couch beside Bean, putting his arm around Bean's bony shoulders. And he started talking. He started where he should have—at the very beginning, right after Momma had gone up to heaven or down to hell, whichever was her choosing—and he ended up at the plans for our future. Through it all, Maize looked like he didn't believe a single word. Bean and Bell kept looking to me for confirmation, and all I could do was nod like I believed him. To be honest, I was doubting him on this one. I would have to see this to believe it. An actual drawn-out plan, including minute details, was a rarity from Daddy.

Bell said, "Does that mean we get our own room, with a fenced yard and a swing set? Or maybe one of them fancy, white porch swings? Does that mean we can have a kitchen and you can cook us some food again? I can have a plug to charge my music?"

It broke my heart, and I was sure it did Daddy's, too.

"Yes, girl. No more life like that. We're starting fresh. This is it, children. I mean it. I'm so sorry. I'm moving forward, this time.

You don't need to jump in and try to save my children, Ray. Mrs. Sunshine, I know your intentions are in the right place, but I can take care of them myself."

Maize's eyes filled with disbelief. He knew it would be a stretch for Daddy to settle down in one place. Bell was already throwing herself at Daddy, her arms squeezing him tight around the neck. Bean was sitting there, still not quite grasping our new reality. I understood the feeling wholeheartedly. I was still grappling with it myself.

I continued to hold on to Maize. "It's going to be okay, Maize. Daddy is right. He's going to do this the right way, so go ahead and tell him so."

He sighed heavy, like the weight of the universe was on his shoulders. "Tell him what? That he's done you right? Done me right?"

I said, "Daddy loves us. He has always been a good daddy to us. Daddy has given us a whole forest of love. So, we walk down the crooked path that now has been laid straight by the Lord and move with what He has made for us, and we find our way together side by side. God's been our North Star this whole trip. Let Him lead us out of here, too."

Maize nodded but couldn't find his voice. Daddy stood up, straightening Bell.

"Can I borrow your phone and a phone book, Mrs. Sunshine?"

Mrs. Sunshine eyed Daddy suspiciously. I was sure that she was still as confused as could be, but I got him, even if nobody else did. He flipped to the yellow pages, looking up hotels.

He asked, "Do you think the Holiday Hotel is a safe enough place?"

Mrs. Sunshine nodded. "Guess so, but what about school?"

Daddy sighed, frustrated. "I know, Mrs. Sunshine, but what do I do?"

She grabbed the phone out of his hand. "Give me a minute, will you? Kids, excuse me." She pointed to the little kitchen. "Ray, get them something to drink, will you?"

He grabbed some sodas out of the fridge and passed them around.

When he got to Maize and me, he held out his hand.

"Maize, can I?"

Maize hung his head, not answering. Ray slid down on the other side of me and put his arm around my shoulders. I could smell his clean, just-took-a-bath smell. I buried my face in his neck, and I felt the warmth about him.

I whispered, "Why didn't you pick up when I called?"

He squeezed me tighter. "My battery went dead after our talking last night, and I forgot to charge up the phone. I promise I won't ever do that again. I'm so sorry. If I wouldn't have pushed you for a date, then none of this—"

Mrs. Sunshine busted in, clapping. "Okay. Got it done. Eli, how much you got?"

He grimaced. I knew how much he hated to tell his business. "Probably enough for about a week."

She waved the phone and put her hand on the Bible on the countertop. "Preacher and First Lady Anderson are about to go to a conference in Georgia for a week after church on Sunday. You all can stay at the parsonage for that week, keeping watch over the house. We always have somebody do it when they go on trips, anyway. That worked out perfect. After they return, Ray can sleep on the floor here in the den, and you and Maize and Bean can take the pull-out sofa. Bell and Sweet Potato can take up in Ray's room. That's settled."

Daddy looked at all the kids. "You up for that? Just until?"

We fell silent. What was there to discuss? I prayed with all I had that what Maize had said about Mr. and Mrs. Foster was trash talk. We had to be the family that I knew we could be. I knew in my heart that we could withstand this hiccup. We'd sure been through our share of messes before.

Anyway, this was nothing, because it had happened to me. Now, if it would've happened to Bell, or Maize, or even Bean … that would've been something major. But since it was only me, I could store it away and make like it never happened. I could put on the front like always, and we could get out of this one fine. I prayed for it to be so, anyway.

Ray said, "Stay here until Sunday night."

Daddy stopped those plans from taking root quick. "No. I think we'll go on down to the Holiday for the weekend. The kids can play around in the pool, and then we'll go to the parsonage on Sunday, if you are sure it's settled with the preacher. Can I speak with you privately, Mrs. Sunshine?"

The house was too small for private conversations, so they went out to the yard, out of earshot.

Daddy came back into the quiet house and said, "What is all this sadness about? Don't you guys have a date to go on?"

I shook my head against Ray's neck. He answered for me. "I don't think tonight would be the best night to have our first date, sir."

He coughed. "Nonsense. Sweet Potato, look at me."

I lifted my head, wondering what my eyes showed now. He turned his head sideways at me, his mustache twitching back and forth. He ran his finger down my throat, where a bruise was starting to form. His voice caught.

"Life moves on regardless of what happens to us. We can't sit still. We have to keep moving. Go on out, Sweet Potato."

"I don't think I can do that tonight, Daddy." I turned to Ray. "I'm sorry."

He sighed, circling me with his arm again. "I'm the one that's sorry."

Bell stood up. "Well, I got all pretty for nothing, then. Guess I can save this dress for my singing Sunday. Can we go on down to that pool, Daddy?"

Bean frowned. "We ain't got no swim trunks, and I don't think they'd let me go in my boxers."

Mrs. Sunshine hollered to Joe to close shop and take no more orders, but he popped his head in to announce that Denise had come home for the weekend because she was so homesick and had stopped by for a visit. It was the perfect time to throw her to work, since Mrs.

Sunshine was dead set on escorting us to the hotel. I looked at Ray, trying to figure out a way to convince him to tag along.

Daddy put his hand on my shoulder. "I think it's best if Ray comes with us. Let's go, then."

Ray helped me up, and I felt faint right there, and he might have to catch me. He must have known it, because with a sweep of his hand he was carrying me out to the car. He crawled into the backseat beside me, holding my hand.

During the drive, Daddy told Mrs. Sunshine he still hoped that we could work at Soul Food, even though we were 'bout to move out of The Home, which was the perfect walking location for Daddy. Mrs. Sunshine said that without us she'd have to go on and close the place up, because it wouldn't be the same. She eyed me through the rear-view mirror, and I tried to smile at her reassuringly, but my face wasn't working right.

At the hotel, Mrs. Sunshine and Ray went with us to check in. Ray was still holding my hand. Bell pointed to the sign for the presidential suites and asked Daddy if we could check in there, like she was a princess.

He picked her up. "You are a princess, Baby. Look at you in that fine dress. It doesn't matter about no name of a room for us, as long as we are together."

Mrs. Sunshine took Bell by the arm. "Honey. You tell that man which room you want. I don't care about it. You tell him it's for the weekend and I'm paying."

Daddy stepped in between them and said, "No, ma'am. I ain't taking nothing more from you. That's way too much for generosity. I got my pride, and I've got this covered, or I wouldn't be here right now."

Some of the guests turned and looked at us. One couple pulled their children behind their backs, like we were there to rob them or something. If the people of the world knew just what we were made of, they'd come trying to shake our hands solid, so our good could rub off on them.

Mrs. Sunshine bumped Daddy right out of the way and got the clerk's attention. "You listen to this pretty, little princess. She wants that president suite. Give her a nice room for the weekend."

She passed over a little, plastic card, but Daddy pushed it back toward her with his left hand and handed the man behind the counter the bills. The man looked one button shy of calling security, but he decided to go with the safest bet, and that was Daddy's cash. What was it about us that made the world suspicious? We were all cleaned up and smelling good, especially my Ray and that little princess of mine, still twirling around the lobby of this fancy place like she hadn't a care in the world.

When the bill was settled, Mrs. Sunshine motioned for Daddy to leave a tip for the man who wheeled our bags on a golden cart. Bean had climbed up there with the bags, and the man didn't even seem to mind. Daddy pulled out his tattered, black-leather wallet once more and come to find out there was still money tucked inside there. If they made magical reappearing-money wallets, I'd believe Daddy lucked up and found him one.

That suite was seriously fit for a president, not for some Jones family who resided in The Home that very morning. The luggage man showed us the kitchen with the fully stocked refrigerator. There were even little packets of popcorn by the microwave. We had two gigantic bathrooms. One was as big as the entire room number seven. Daddy couldn't even find the words to begin to express himself, but Bean did the honors for all of us. He let out the biggest yelp as he fell onto the big, white bed, as if he'd been caught in a bear trap.

"Hallelujah, heaven on Earth. Called it! Dibs!"

The man showed us the extra pull-outs from the sofa and the rollaway cot. He told us if we needed anything, we could use the button on the phone to call room service. We'd stayed at hotels before, but always the ones with leaks in the bathtubs and roaches for tour guides. Nothing in the world would have ever prepared us for this.

Mrs. Sunshine patted my arm. "Good times, Sweet Potato. Now, go on down with them, Eli, and get them some sweets from the gift shop. I'm going to stay up here with Ray and Sweet Potato."

There was an actual store inside the lobby? This place was unreal. Mrs. Sunshine fell into the oversized, blue chair as they closed the door behind them.

"Okay, girl. You got some decisions to make."

I frowned. "Sorry?"

Ray was sitting beside me on the couch. "Do you want to come live with us starting tonight? That's what Momma is offering."

Yes! No! "I can't do that, Ray. Not while Daddy is trying to make a step forward. That could put him two steps back."

"You can stay in my room. I'll sleep out on the couch. Just until you turn eighteen and we can get married. You'll come to me after my training is done and I'm assigned. We're going to stay at the family housing on base, and it will be big enough for all of us—with the kids, too. I can have a request in for family housing as soon as everything is legal."

I said, "No. I love you, Ray. Don't get me wrong. And Mrs. Sunshine, I love you, too. For that week we'll soon spend with your family, we'll be much obliged, but I can't leave them. Not now. Daddy says that he is going to try this, and I need to give him my full support."

I had to see this through. No matter how easy it would be to hide in the Patterson's' place forever. It would do my family no good if I ditched them now.

"I knew before I asked exactly what you would say. But I wanted you to know I'd take you and all the kids, if it meant you'd be safe and happy." Mrs. Sunshine had tears welling up again. "I love you and those little ones. That Bell, she is a precious sight. And Maize, and Bean ... Lord bless you all."

"What happened today wasn't Daddy's fault. That was just something evil that happened to land on me, but we shooed it away, and it's over." I shook again at the thought of it. *Lord, help me.* I was so good at faking. I could fake that it hadn't phased me at all, even though my core was still shaking.

Ray's hand was in mine. "I can't stand the thought of you not being able to work."

Mrs. Sunshine laughed. "Boy, tell her the truth."

"I can't stand the thought of not spending every single day with you, Sweet Potato. If you stay here at the hotel, I'm happy for you … but it will be so far away." He whispered, "So, stay with me."

I had to erase his soft voice from my mind to focus on what I knew I had to do. "I'll get the bus to drop me off at Soul Food, if that's okay with you, Mrs. Sunshine? Could you drive me home each night? Daddy could probably get the local transport to take him in the mornings and afternoons. We've used them transits before. He promised me that I could work, regardless of our location.

We could do this. It could all come together. I still had faith. That one devil couldn't squash the Lord out of me. A whole legion of demons couldn't touch the hand of the Lord over me and mine. *Amen.*

Ray leaned in closer. "I know what I could do, Momma. With my savings, I could buy a car, couldn't I? What do you think of that?"

His eyes registered a new hope. This man with all his plans. *Lord, I thank you for him.*

Mrs. Sunshine beamed with pride. "That could work. When you get out of basic and start base living, you'll be able to drive back and forth to see your old man and your dear, old momma and this here girl. So, car shopping we'll be going, it looks like."

She winked at me when the door opened. "Keep that discussion to ourselves, girl."

So, she hadn't approved that one with Daddy. If I had told her that I'd stay with her, I would have been stepping over the imaginary line of trust I had established with Daddy. A war wasn't to be waged today. We could figure this all out with peaceful negotiations.

"Look, Sweet Potato. Look what I picked out for you."

Bell held up a bathing suit with matching shorts. As if I was going in the pool. "You, too, Ray."

She threw a pair of red swimming trunks at him, hitting him in the face. She giggled. "Sorry."

He warned, "It's okay. I'll pay you back when we get in the pool."

I frowned. "Wait. I ain't getting in no pool, and I'm not wearing that in front of you." Wearing bathing pieces in front of Ray didn't seem right proper.

Daddy pulled me up. "Go get changed. You ain't turning down them kids for a swim. I tell you that would be a good time missed. Get over this shyness and let your guard down, Sweet Potato."

He held up his swimsuit. "See, they even had one for your daddy. So, go on, kids, let's go."

Mrs. Sunshine smiled. "I'll be back to pick Ray up by ten." She kissed Ray on the cheek and chuckled. "Funny how your first date turned out to be checking in to a hotel. Don't get no ideas, now."

We all laughed. As wonderful as my day had begun, it had gone straight down to a bottomless pit of fire, only to bounce back up to heaven by six. We all seemed to be back at what we could do best—laugh despite our circumstances, love with all we had. I loved these people, all dressed in swim trunks. Bell—excuse me, *Princess* Bell, as we must call her at the president's suite—had color-coordinated us like we were on some Olympic swim team.

I loved the way Daddy watched Ray like a hawk around me, still protective as ever over his baby girl. I loved the way Ray played with the kids, dunking them and spinning them in the air to the middle of that gigantic, indoor swimming pool. The fancy, soothing jets helped my aching muscles that were starting to knot up from my knock down to the floor. I ducked under the water to hide the tears forming.

When I came up for air, Ray was right there. I pushed my hair back, embarrassed to be with him in front of the entire family. He found my hand under the water.

"Having fun?"

I bit my lip. "Trying."

He moved along with me to the side of the pool and leaned back. "Look at them. I admire them so much."

I followed his gaze to my kids. They were squealing. Maize had Bell's ankles, swishing her around, playing a new game called "washing machine." "Admire them? Why?"

"I've never met anyone like your family before … like you."

"I'm sure of that."

He whispered, "You don't let things touch you. I see how you push it all away. I don't know how you compartmentalize like that and handle your business, but you don't have to run anymore."

I looked to Daddy. "I was never the one running."

He was sitting poolside, looking through some magazine, lounging back like this was the most natural setting in the world for him.

"I think so, Sweet Potato. Running from your name, your past hurt. Look at today. Hurt hit, you ran. You're in this pool like nothing happened. How do you do that? Just close yourself up like that and make like nothing bad is happening around you?" He leaned back. "See? You're doing it now."

"What?" I was confused. What was I doing? Coping? Surviving? Breathing?

"Closing up. I am trying to talk to you, and you are—I don't know where you are." He didn't sound angry, just frustrated.

"I was thinking about how nice you look, that's all." Did I just say that? Was I saying I liked the way he looked half-naked? I didn't mean it that way at all.

He laughed, realizing my stumble. "What am I going to do with you?"

I put my arms around his neck and let him spin me around. Bell wouldn't get all the fun. "Love me, thank you very much."

He kissed me on the cheek quickly while Daddy turned a page. "Easiest thing to do in my life, and you are very welcome." He dunked me under the water with both hands on top of my head. "And thank you for loving me!"

NINETEEN

I loved the way God could turn a day around for good. I would also appreciate it if God could cut the images right out of my brain with some extracting surgery, but only the part that happened after four and before four fifteen. Just fifteen minutes—that wasn't too much to pray for, right? Ray thought I could close things away, but he was so wrong. I was trying to make it through till the lights turned off. In the daytime, I had all their eyes on me.

Daddy ordered us all filet steaks, and we ate at our very own table in the presidential suite. I wanted to gather the courage to ask him where he got that room-service money from, but I decided to keep quiet a spell. Ray kept the conversation going with all the kids. I couldn't find words to say, and neither could Daddy. He kept exchanging glances with me, and I was sure he wanted to share the conversation he was having with his conscience right now—about how sorry he was, and how he hoped that one day I would be able to forgive him for what had happened. I loved him unconditionally; being merciful with him had become second nature to me.

Daddy was trying to clean up after everybody, and Ray stopped him. "Sir, that's what you pay them for here. Just wheel this cart on out the door."

Bean was already opening the big TV cabinet and flipping through the channels. Some movie was on about talking cars, and we all settled in with a bag of popcorn each, even though we'd stuffed ourselves with steaks. Ray sat beside me on the couch. He was mostly watching me, not the movie. So was Daddy.

I stood up and stretched. "Daddy, can me and Ray go out to the balcony?"

He nodded, intent on the movie now that he knew I was watching him. But before Ray could slide the door shut, he hollered, "Leave it open! That breeze feels nice."

I rolled my eyes. *Whatever!*

Ray smiled at me, leaning against the railing. "So."

"So."

"Are you okay?"

I avoided his question. "What kind of car do you want?"

"Don't know. Thought you should be the one to pick it out."

His hand came against my cheek again.

"Why me? I never took the driver's class."

Sixteen meant driver's ed for everybody in the universe but Sweet Potato Jones.

"You'll need to, because it will be *our* car, soon enough."

He took a step closer, but I heard Daddy laugh out loud—a little too loud.

"Ray, why do you do this?"

His finger was rubbing across my hand. I thought about how it felt when we kissed and how tonight would have been our first date. We stood on a balcony with a perfect view of the James River, watching the boats with the tiny, blinking lights make their lazy way to the harbor. What would we've been doing, if he could have planned it?

"What? Do what?"

He looked at the scene behind us—my family gawking at us until we looked, then snapping their heads right back and pretending to laugh at the TV screen. What did they think they were doing? Who were they kidding?

"Why do you put up with this? Come on." I pulled him along back into the living room and cut off the TV.

Maize yelled, "Hey, we were right in the middle—"

"Of minding my business. You guys weren't even watching that movie. What was the name of that car?"

"Mmm ... Mmm ..." they all said in unison.

"Exactly my point. Now, what was I saying?"

Bell clapped. "Oh, I know this one! What color car do you want? Ray, get her a red one. She loves red the best."

I pointed my finger at her. "See there. Ray, why do you put up with this? Don't you think you deserve some normal girl with a normal life and a normal family? Not this. Look at what our date night has become."

"What? One of the best nights of my life, because I am right here with you?"

Daddy stood up, pointing at the clock. "See the time. See how it's flown. Okay, Ray. Time for your momma to come on. I'll walk you down."

I tried. "Daddy, can I walk him down?"

Just the thought of not getting to walk down to the lobby with him—devastating.

"Bean, you up to getting some exercise?"

Bean jumping-jacked at Daddy's suggestion. *Oh, Lordy!*

Maize spoke quietly, but his jaw muscles tensed. "I'm going down with them, and Bean is staying here. After what she went through today, I think ..."

Daddy stopped him. "I get what you're saying. At least let me walk you to the door."

He looked at Ray when we were away from the kids. Bean had opened the big cabinet and was trying to climb right into the part where the DVD player was. Knew it.

"You don't need to worry about Sweet Potato and no transport systems or the back-and-forth from here."

Ray shrugged. "It's a part of me now to think of her. If my family can help in any way, we will. You know that, sir."

Daddy leaned against the doorframe. "Call me Eli. I think you deserve it. You have shown yourself to be a proper, young man, and I've decided something on my very own."

Oh, Lordy, no! Daddy couldn't go making decisions about Ray and me. "You also deserve to take my little girl out on a right date without them youngins."

I was shocked to the core. "You decided? When was that?"

"When I saw the look in his eyes today. That was enough for me."

Ray held out his hand to me, and I took it. He always knew when I needed him. "You know that I would never hurt her, sir. Mr. Eli, I will do what I can to treat her with respect and with God at the center in all that we do."

"Right you are. Keep God in the center. I've found an inspiration well from you and your family. A strength I've needed for a very long time. You people set a mighty fine example for the world to follow. I've got big steps to take on how to be a right man for this family."

Ray nodded to Daddy. "Pray through all things, Mr. Eli. Pray through all things—that's what I can say to you."

"Well, I pray your momma don't get ahold of us, because we've lingered talking, and this time it's my fault." He laughed as he pushed us out the door. "Don't worry about the early morning pickup for Sweet Potato. I'll get her there by six o'clock. We are doing the pancake breakfast at the church, anyhow."

"Yes, sir. Thank you for this evening. It was nice to spend time with your family."

Ray shook Daddy's hand again, but Daddy grabbed him and

gave him a gigantic bear-hug. Ray laughed with surprise. I turned away, because I didn't want them to see the tears. I'd been holding them in so long that one false move and *wowza*—out.

"You are family now. I would never have thought Sweet Potato would have her a strong, young man like you courtin' and calling. If it had to be some boy, Ray, I'm glad it is you."

Ray was mine. My first and last boyfriend, I was sure of that. It would be nice to tell our kids that we fell in love with each other on a summer morning, and God had brought us all here, not a tiny finger falling on a map by chance. That would be our love-story testimony, passed on for generations to come.

Ray swung my hand, then roped his arm around my waist. Maize walked a few steps behind us, giving us space, but I could feel his eyes on me.

Ray said, "I'm glad it's you, too. Sweet Potato, you think I'm joking, but that was the date to top all dates. Spending time with you and the kids in the pool, the balcony—anything with you makes perfect sense."

I sighed, leaning up against the wood railing in the elevator. "Dates end with a kiss, right? Good ones, anyway. And since you did say that it was one perfect night …"

We made it to the double elevator doors. Maize told us he would meet us in the lobby and took the one beside us. As soon as the elevator doors closed, giving us a moment of privacy, Ray put his arms around me, and his lips found mine in the sweetest of kisses, soft and safe. I wrapped my arms around his neck and let him hold me. I dared those tears to come in my moment alone with Ray. I wouldn't let that evil steal no more of my precious moments.

Get behind me, Satan. My shoulders relaxed at the release of the power of the Spirit.

"What was that about?"

"Just letting it go. That was easier than I thought."

He pulled back. "You don't have to hold it alone anymore. I'm gonna prove to you that I will do right by you."

I leaned against him, praying that it could be so. "We will wait and see."

We went out to meet his momma at the entrance. The lobby doors opened, and he stopped me. Maize was already waiting, standing with his arms crossed, with legs parted wide like a bodyguard.

"This is as far as you should go. I'll watch you get back on the elevator. Go ahead."

We waved at his momma, and she waved back at us.

"I love you."

He quickly kissed me on the cheek again and stayed put until the elevator doors closed. As we rode back up, I looked into the eyes staring back at me from the glass doors and whispered, "Hello, faith. Thanks for showing back up. It's nice to see you again."

And I imagined the voice of the Lord whispering in my ear, "Nice to see you, too, child."

TWENTY

Denise was working the weekend with us to help cover my absence. They must have had that one all planned out, because as soon as I entered, Mrs. Sunshine ushered me through the back and onto the couch. I looked up to the peaceful look of Jesus and wondered what plans he had in store for me. No matter what came at me, I was the better for it here than anywhere else in the world.

She handed me a soda from the fridge and stirred her coffee. "I'm fixing to ask you something, and I want the truth. You hear me?"

Her voice wasn't harsh, but it had that matter-of-fact tone that let me know she didn't play.

I crossed my legs, nervous. "Yes, ma'am. I don't lie, Mrs. Sunshine."

She nodded. "Of course you don't. Now tell me. Has this ever happened to you before?"

I frowned. "What?"

"About yesterday. Sweet Potato, Ray was right. You go blocking punches. One day life is going to knock you down for the count if you don't stand up from your corner and fight. Child, you tell me the truth, now. Has yesterday ever happened to you or one of them kids?"

But I did fight. I did fight back, the best I knew how.

"No. I knew that it could happen, though. That's why we never stay alone. We slipped up, that's all."

Mrs. Sunshine buried her face in her hands. "It's all my fault. I was pressuring you to go and get ready for the date, and you were trying to tell me that you were already ready. And Sweet Potato, you looked beautiful. The day could have gone about its business, and you could have gone on with Ray to the music festival and that big fair. And Bell could have ..."

I put my hand on her shoulder. "Mrs. Sunshine, I'm fine. I'm telling you the truth. I'm right at fellowship with the Almighty right now, because the last time I checked we are better off now than we were yesterday. Don't you see that? Those kids got to swim in a pool, eat steaks, and sleep in these pillow-top beds. I didn't even know they made those things."

"Blocking, Sweet Potato. You're blocking again. What happened to you? Were you hurt?"

Tears coursed down her face, and I hated I'd made her cry. She was such a strong tower of a woman. To see her crumbling down was hard.

"No. I told you I was fine. I'm sore as all get out, but that too shall pass."

I rubbed my back and neck at the thought of it. If I'd had a scarf, I would have wrapped it around my neck, because the skin looked so bruised. I prayed nobody would ask me questions.

"Physically, that is all. Mentally taken care of, too. I told Satan to get out my way, and I didn't think another thought about it. That is the truth. As soon as my head hit the pillow last night, I was gone, with all my fears prayed away. Ray told Daddy to pray through all things. I'm really good at taking other people's advice when it matters, and that was an ordeal that needed praying through."

Definitely so.

"If something like that would've happened to me at your age—shoot, at my age—I don't know how I'd handle it, Sweet Potato."

She held her arms out, shaking me lightly. "And you see something positive out of it?"

"Yes, ma'am. I do. I wasn't hurt. God showed me how He could get me through the next fire trial. My feet weren't even singed. I'm blessed, Mrs. Sunshine."

She patted the chair corner. Somehow, I managed to squeeze next to her. She put her arms around me and gave me a big, old hug. She could've been my very own chiropractor, because she cracked me right.

"I misjudged you, child. I thought I knew you, but you surprise me at every bend in the road. What I do get is that you're a fine girl that deserves the best this world has to offer. You sure you don't want to stay here with us to finish out your school year? If I have to call that contractor, I'll be adding an extra room on here for the kids, too."

I hugged her back. "Daddy has us covered. The youngins are beside themselves with joy. Daddy said that Ray deserved to take me out by myself. Them youngins deserved the night they had, and today, and the next day after that. It's all working for good. We know how to take care of each other."

She clapped. "A date tonight, then?"

I nodded, biting my lip. Tonight. Another night with Ray? *Thank you, Almighty.* I wished that I had a way to call Ray to see if he had made any plans.

"Oh, Mrs. Sunshine. I hadn't even thought of that phone up to now. I'm going to pay you back somehow. I'm sorry I left it behind."

"Hush up now. You got more important things to think about than a blessed phone."

"About Ray. Where is he, anyway?"

"He's out with his Uncle Clarence, Denise's daddy. They went off to get him a car, and Clarence knows an honest dealer in the city that went to school with him. So, I let them handle that today."

When the Pattersons set their minds to something, they didn't waste any time. "I told him not to worry about the car thing. He doesn't need to go and spend his money now because of me. Daddy is going to taxi us back and forth until he decides his next move."

Mrs. Sunshine laughed. "Honey, Ray didn't need no reason for the car thing. He's been wanting one for a while now. He's a man, after all. And poor ol' Clarence loves to help and needs any distraction of good he can get. It makes him feel worthwhile."

"It must run in your family."

"Helping is all we've ever known, I guess. It's our godly purpose."

Denise was lounging at the counter, drinking a chocolate shake. She was rolling her eyes like she was getting a pure taste of heaven through a straw. She giggled when she saw that we'd caught her. "Okay. Don't even joke me. I've had cafeteria food only, people. I've missed this goodness, and I've sure missed this place."

Mrs. Sunshine swished her hips. "Well, you'll get a set of these in no time, if you keep drinking chocolate shakes all day long."

"That's all right with me!" Denise swung her hips right back.

We worked together all morning. She was truly a nice girl, easy to be around. Her talk about college with all the customers had them all 'bout asking me at least fifteen times what I wanted to pursue after graduation, or where I wanted to go. They all knew I was a senior, so they were laying the pressure on thick. They were taking bets on which alma mater I would choose, trying to sway me to their school. The Virginia Tech faithful rambled on about Hokie sports. It was a lot of hokey-pokey to me, 'cause I hadn't once thought about my future. I had more pressing concerns than college dreams, and I was reminded of that when Ray pulled up in a big, red SUV.

His momma hollered through the window, "You gonna be real safe with all that metal around you, boy!"

Ray was as ecstatic as a farmer with a higher-than-expected yield. Clarence was showing off the SUV to Mr. Joe, giving the whole salesman pitch, as if it was his duty to recreate the whole scene for us—right down to where he ended up with a dealer discount. I stood watching how Ray's face shone in the light. Could anyone else see the simple beauty of that man? There was a touch of God in everything he did. I studied how he danced around his Momma and had a private handshake hello with Denise. He came up to me last, and the way that he dropped his head shyly sent shiver-boats sailing down my spine.

"Do you like it?" He waved the keys in front of me.

"Well, I absolutely think it's fine. Not as fine as you, I tell you that, but fine just the same. Let's call it Big Red."

His momma came up behind him as he took my hand. "Ray, what you need all that room for?"

"Think about it, Momma. We got each other and all the kids."

Her hands were on her hips, sizing him up. "That was a man's choice you made at that lot. If I do say so myself, I'm proud of you. To think of them all, and not just yourself—I shouldn't have even thought any different."

Ray turned to me. "I can't wait to take you on our date tonight."

I bit my lip, wondering how I could say this to him. It wasn't that I didn't want to be alone with him, but I couldn't help but think of Bell and her pink dress.

"Ray, um ... I ..."

His smile let me know that he understood me. "You want them to go with us tonight, don't you?"

I shrugged. "Well, I know they were looking forward to it, and Bell needs to wear her pink dress."

He put his arms around me. "Whatever to make you happy. I wouldn't have it any other way. The festival is through the weekend. I was taking you to the Blues and Gospel Festival at King-Lincoln Park. Would that be okay for a date? I wasn't sure."

I snuggled up close to his neck, not caring in the least that we were in broad daylight right beside a busy intersection. "I'd feel like a queen in that place. Sounds perfect."

"You know the kids will love it." He pulled away. "Speaking of kids ... um ... there's your daddy now."

I blushed. I hadn't quite figured out how to hug up to Ray in front of Daddy without feeling uncomfortable. I put some distance between us.

"Hey, Daddy. Hey, guys."

Bell was skipping and singing. Maize and Bean were passing a basketball back and forth.

I asked, "Where did you get that ball?"

Maize spun it on the tip of his finger. "When we were down at the church, we were playing with a group of the other guys there for the pancake breakfast, and this guy said that we could have it, since we liked to play so much. He came up from out of nowhere and was really cool."

Bell chimed in, "And because I sang so good, I get that stand-up solo in church tomorrow morning, after all."

Daddy nodded. "And because I am such a good Daddy, I ain't going to say nothing about you making a spectacle of yourself in the middle of the street."

He pointed at the SUV. "This is it, huh? Ain't it a little flashy?"

But it wasn't, really. It had regular tires and rims. It was fire-engine red. My color, because Bell had told him so. "Daddy, can the kids go with us tonight on our date? Please?"

He laughed heartily as he pulled open the restaurant door for everybody and did his signature ringing of the bell. He had promised the kids anything they wanted from the menu. I was sure that meant pie and more pie. I questioned this endless money he kept throwing around. Something was unsettling about this whole thing, for sure.

"It *would* be you to ask to bring them along, after I broke down and got up enough nerve to say you could go out by yourself."

I shrugged, smiling at him. "I thought they'd have a good time when I found out that Ray was taking me to a music festival."

Bell clapped. "A festival. A music festival. Please, Daddy, please, please, please."

Daddy rolled his eyes. "Of course you all can go, and I like it right fine like that myself, anyway. Not that I don't trust you, Ray, but …"

Ray pulled his apron on. "Don't worry, sir. I know what you mean. I'll take good care of them."

Daddy nodded. "I'm sure you will. Now, Sweet Potato, are you going to take our order or what?"

It was my turn to shake my head, laughing. "For what? Pie? Please. I already know."

Daddy shrugged. "How did you get so smart, child?"

I said, "It runs in the family, it seems." And it did. Daddy was a smart man for bringing us here, for accepting the past, and for moving us forward. It was right brilliant of him, if I did say so myself. Smartest move yet.

TWENTY-ONE

Denise took up with the kids right away, and Maize took up with her, trying to hit on her even though she was four years older than him. She started giving him girl advice after she got it out of him that his first time getting looked at was here at The Dream. For Maize, the Dream afforded him way more than the educational experience. He'd always missed out on the social aspect, except being the brunt of jokes or hazing. Now, he was right there in the thick of all of the action. He found himself a little crew, and they were always walking the halls together, sitting at lunch at the same table, and were covering each other's' back. Maize always wanted that life, and now at The Dream, it was possible for him.

Denise kept throwing me strange glances as the day went by. Finally, I mustered my courage and asked her, "What you keep wearing that look for? I see the way your eyes are all quizzing me."

"You passed up on a *date* date for a *family* date? Why?"

She didn't quite get me yet. But I was sure she would, by the end of it. Even if it took her through her whole undergraduate degree to get smart on me.

"We kinda come together perfect, all of us. I'm more me when I'm with them, not worrying about them or wondering."

How to explain to someone who didn't have to share an existence with her family the way I did? She was an only child. And she had her own dorm room now—totally different planet than I would ever land on. And even though I might have a semblance of a future now, it was still up for grabs what God would reveal for me.

"What do you think would happen to them? If that's what it's all about, then I'll baby-sit Bell here at Soul Food for my night shift. She won't get in the way like she would on a date."

Her tone was light, and I knew that she wasn't knocking on Bell or me. So, I didn't take offense.

"They won't get in the way with me and Ray. Ray gets it."

He came up behind me. I could sense it by the way Denise seemed to shut down, as if we were talking about something secretive.

"I do get it—and Denise, don't start trying to change my woman now. I love her just the way she is."

He squeezed my hand before passing by to the next table.

She shrugged. "Love, huh?" Her face had fallen, right down to the tile.

Ray heard her sour tone. "It's going to be fine with you, Denise. You'll meet a nice man. Maybe even in the seminary school. Be patient. Don't look so hard. Just let the Lord work for you. I'm proof that if you trust and wait, the perfect one will appear at your door."

That reminded me of Ray's apron, and then of what Daddy had been hiding, not ready to testify. I whispered to him while the kids were busy filling up the salt and pepper shakers for Mrs. Sunshine.

"Can I peek at your apron now?"

He nodded. My hand was shaking as I opened the drawer behind the counter. He had it folded inside out, and I had to twist it to read those Bible words. *But one thing I do, forgetting those things which are behind and reaching forward to those things which are ahead. I press toward the goal for the prize of the upward call of God in Christ Jesus.*

I folded it back up neatly, rubbing it gently in my hands. Was it when Mrs. Sunshine gave him the apron that he wised on up? Or was it my words, or the pressure of the universe, or seeing me lying on my back on the floor of number seven? I sighed, looking at Daddy—maybe for the first time. He was watching me with that same look of intent. When he was ready, I was sure he was going to let me in on what had been plaguing him. Maybe it was about Ray and me, or about that wallet of his that somehow had more money in it than Mrs. Sunshine had divvied out. Maybe it was the responsibility of trying to own his life, not borrow it.

He came up to me behind the counter. I still hadn't moved, thinking of how the Lord had worked us up and down and all around to this very spot. He stood beside me, looking out at the youngins. "Well, what are you thinking about, Sweet Potato Pie?"

How to say it all? "God knows it all, and it's all good. No point in hashing out pasts or what-ifs."

He nodded again. "Good sum-up. Now about this night out. What are you expecting from it?"

"You to go to that hotel and get that pink dress and her sandals and her little, pink bows. Maybe me and Denise can make her over."

I blinked back tears, watching Denise and Mrs. Sunshine doing the bump. When Bell jumped into the mix, Mrs. Sunshine's big hips about knocked her clear into the next booth.

"What you expecting for you, Sweet Potato? I'm talking about you and you alone, for once."

"Me? I don't know what you mean, Daddy."

His mustache was twitching like he was making up his mind about something.

"You really want to marry this boy? I've only heard Ray doing the talking. I ain't heard nothing from you."

His voice was low, and I was sure that he didn't want to have this conversation here and now. Probably never, honestly.

"Daddy. We're talking about a first date. But yes, I want to marry this boy. No matter how strange it might sound to the world. I'm not of this world, I guess, I go by my own way."

He put his hand on my arm. "You don't run away on me. You stay put. You hear me?"

I frowned. "What are you talking about, Daddy? I ain't never the one running. Why do I keep hearing about this? I think you've covered that one for the both of us."

"You're always running away, Sweet Potato, even though you're right here. You're like one of those big projection screens at a picture show. You take in. You only release the colors that have been given to you. You play the part and say what has to be said, then close the curtain. Nobody can grab hold of you, because you are up in that little room, away from it all. You can't do that with this boy. You just got to be you. The you I know you can be."

He wasn't making a bit of sense. "I'm like a movie? What? Daddy, what are you saying?"

"You ain't taking the kids with you tonight. I decided I'm not letting you."

He crossed his arms and braced himself for a showdown.

"You decided, huh? But what if I've decided I need them there with me?"

"I think it's downright hilarious that we keep going 'round and 'round the mulberry on this one, Sweet Potato. I'm pulling rank on this. You can't hide behind them youngins forever. You need to stand on your own two feet, not octopus legs. So there."

Ray came out of the swinging doors, holding his cleanup bucket. Daddy motioned for him to follow him outside. *Great. Go on and tell Ray that I'm some movie, or whatever you were trying to get at.* Was he going to warn Ray I acted my way through life? Did he think I was that shallow? I was deep in it with this family, and he better never forget it.

"Oh, Lordy, no!" I spoke out loud without meaning to.

Mrs. Sunshine rushed over. "What's the matter? What happened?"

"I done happened to get myself in a load of mess." The tears started to form. I double-dog-dared them to show up now.

She followed my gaze out the window to where Ray and Daddy were apparently discussing how to buy tickets to my movie.

Mrs. Sunshine positioned up. "What now? You need me to go storming out there talking to your daddy?" She rolled her quarter sleeves up to her biceps.

"Just find out if I'm off to the Ray date alone, that's all."

I knew I sounded ridiculous. That should be what I wanted, right?

"You sound like that's a dreadful thing, baby girl."

I bit my lip. Ray was laughing through the window. The joke was now on me. *Oh, Lordy!*

Denise leaned over the counter. "You'll be alright, Sweet Potato. It's just Ray."

Could she not see that was the problem? *Just Ray* was the best thing in the world. What if he got me alone and figured me out to be nothing? As empty as I felt?

What about Bell having a wonderful night? But it wasn't about Bell in a pink dress. She could save that for Sunday singing. I knew that. She didn't look too disappointed when Daddy sauntered on over to give them the news. She actually looked at me and winked, letting me know that she probably had something to do with this. What was I ever going to do with these youngins?

I rushed to the bathroom to check my face in the mirror, to see if it looked like something from one of those low-budget horror films from the forties we had to watch in English class for comparative analysis—that fake, plastered-on look, all pouty-mouthed and wide-eyed. But it was plain ol' me, with those eyes full of quiet serenity.

I leaned over the sink. "What you trying to say to me, Momma? What is it, doggone it?"

Momma didn't answer. Her voice wouldn't come to me. I looked down at my watch. It was getting to be about that time.

There was a knock on the door.

My voice echoed. "Huh? Hello?"

Maize coughed. "Come on out, Sweet Potato."

I slid through the door, even though I could have opened it all the way. "What? You got to use the girls' room?"

He took my hand. "No. Come on out." He led me outside. What was this? A meeting out on the street?

"Why you trippin'; going to hide in the bathroom? Daddy told me you didn't want to go out with Ray. I thought you wanted to be that boy's girlfriend. Has he been pressuring you? You in trouble? Let me find out." He wiped his brow. The Lord was turning up the heat, and I was about to boil over.

"No! You know I love Ray, Maize. But … alone? I don't do well without y'all to help carry me. You know that about me more than anyone." I inched closer to him.

He shielded his eyes from the sun. "Listen to me, big sis. You need Ray like the crops need rain. Like the farmers pray for it."

"I know about Ray. I don't know about me."

"I know about you, and you are hands-down the model of what a woman should be. You got this, sis. You know that no one deserves you. You shine that golden. But if it has to be anyone, I guess we gotta stick with Ray."

Maize knew all about my insecurities. I hid them from everybody else, but Maize and I were closer in age and experience, and I knew he struggled with them on his own level. I protected Bell from all my secret misgivings and doubts about myself. Bean was in his own, little zoo yard. Me and Maize, we played the survivor game. He was always trying in his way to build me up, and I loved him for that.

"So, your sayin' you approve of Ray?"

"Yep. Something like that. Go out and have fun, Sweet Potato. Tell me all about it, so when I start asking them lucky ladies out, I'll have a database of moves."

"Whatever. I ain't telling you nothing, but I'm going to ask you for one thing. Pray for me, Maize." I was afraid to speak it too loud, in case the Devil caught wind of my next insecurity. "Pray that he'll love me once he gets me alone."

Maize gave me a big, sweaty hug. "I don't have to pray for that. I know that to be the truth. I don't know about the praying stuff, but I do hope you'll figure out how much you are worth."

"For a little brother, you're awfully sweet."

He swung open the door for me like a gentleman, already practicing his lady-killing skills. "I heard that it's running in the family today. Might as well jump on that train."

Bean came bouncing up, jumping on Maize's back. "Hey, did you hear about the time when the train came to town?" Bean and another homegrown joke.

We all said in unison, "No. What happened when the train came to town?"

He laughed before he could even get it out. "It went *kissy-kissy-choo-choo* ... All aboard the love train. Next stop, Rayville."

I hid my face in my hands. Maybe it was a blessing in disguise that I'd got the chance to have a date alone with Ray. He might not love me at the end of the night, but it sure wouldn't be because my fanatical, little brother scared him off. I'd have to do that all by myself.

TWENTY-TWO

Mrs. Sunshine allowed me time to use the bathroom connected to her bedroom. Angels of all different shapes and sizes lined the countertops. She told me that customers always gave her angels, and she kept every one of them. I couldn't help but raise my eyebrows when she held out a bag from a department store. Inside was a new blouse and a pair of sleek blue jeans that were more for dressing up than my relaxed ones. No cartoon-character t-shirt for me tonight. She gifted me a simple, burgundy, button-up top with a waist belt, looped tie, and little, pearl cuff buttons. The pants were my exact size, which was hard to find. When I tried the outfit on, I had to admit that it suited me. She'd done good.

Mrs. Sunshine clapped. "Perfect. I knew that it would fit you. I slipped it up to the lady when you were picking out Bell's clothes. I was going to save it for your birthday, but I decided differently."

She seemed mighty pleased with herself, and I couldn't fault her. This was a lot more appropriate for a date night than what I had on. Especially *this* date night, the most important one. This was either going to make or break me. If we made it, this one would be the one we'd tell our kids about.

"Thank you so much for everything, Mrs. Sunshine. I guess this is it."

She'd done all that she could do for me. God himself couldn't change me up in the next ten minutes. I'd have to do with what I had been given.

"Why are you talking like this is the end of the world, child? I thought you would've been excited to go out with my boy. If he sees you all glum, he'll think that you don't want to be with him, and that won't do. That won't do at all."

She pulled out her makeup bag and brushed a little bit of pink onto my cheeks, even though I told her it wasn't necessary. You couldn't stop Mrs. Sunshine from doing what she wanted. She clipped a silver, angel barrette in my hair, and after she was finished with me, I had to admit I looked right decent.

"It's not that. I want to be with him. More than anything in the world. I just … it's just that …"

He'll see me, the truth of things, and then he won't want me anymore, and my first date will end in one dirty mess, and he'll sweep me right out the front door. And my youngins would hear of how my first date was a failure, and the wedding bells would never ring with Ray, and …

She turned me to her. "Clear up that mind, Sweet Potato. I see you burying yourself right in the ground. Let me pull you on up, Sweet Potato."

She pulled on my hair a little like she could yank me up, root and all. "Come let that sunshine glow on you. I wish you'd look at you the way that we do."

She forced me back to the mirror, and she got right up to my ear and whispered, "You're a beautiful soul. I can see your heart wide and vast like the ocean. Believe it, 'cause I don't lie, thank you very much."

"I believe I'm gonna be sick." I gave her a look, and she stepped out—just in time, because I let it go right there in her toilet.

She laughed through the door. "Honey. It's just Ray!"

I cleaned myself up and came on out, shaking. "Exactly."

Ray was down the hall. I could hear him moving around in his little bedroom. Did that mean he could hear me? *Oh, Lordy, no!*

"Momma, is she ready?"

Mrs. Sunshine twisted her mouth like she was still deciding, shook her head, and replied, "Ready as she'll ever be."

I took a step out into the hallway. I watched him turn the corner out of his room, and I caught my breath. He had on a black-and-blue dress shirt tucked into a pair of those well-fitting jeans I loved so much, the faded ones with the fringes on the bottom. He looked so handsome that I couldn't breathe.

He whispered, "You look so beautiful, baby."

Baby. Beautiful. Broom, go away. I couldn't answer him and stood there letting the wall hold me up. His hand found mine, and I felt the weight of all my insecurities and fears fly away out the opened bedroom window. *Oh, Ray.*

He never let go of my hand as I followed him down the hallway and through the kitchen, past Daddy and the youngins. He promised Daddy we would be at the hotel by ten. Daddy called a taxi to take him and the kids on back, since they had all finished their pie. Bean was begging to go swimming again. Maize held up his hand to me, and I tried to smile at him, but I couldn't move my face muscles. With all of this emotion building up inside of me, I was scared if I started crying, I'd never stop.

When we made it to his car, I let him help me inside. He leaned in close to me, and I could smell that he'd put on some nice cologne. Lovely. I closed my eyes, letting out a heavy sigh.

He chuckled softly. "I'm nervous, too, Sweet Potato."

Nervous? Ray? He got in and started the car, being extra careful with his new equipment. The air conditioning vents right on me, the music was already set to our Soul Food station. It all seemed lovely, especially when his hand came over to mine after he'd pulled out safely onto the interstate. I wished I could've looked out the window, taking in the road signs and all the details, but all I could do was look at him. He kept glancing over at me. "What is it, Sweet Potato?"

I shrugged. "You? Nervous? I doubt that."

He'd had a girlfriend before. I remembered Denise saying that when I'd first met him. He'd probably had a handful of them.

"I want to make you happy. This is important, so it's pressure like I've never felt before. Like what if I can't measure up and make you happy?" He turned off the main road, and I could start to see the festival parking signs.

"I'm with you, aren't I? That is *happy*."

Just right here was already the best date I could ever have—sitting in the car, doing nothing at all but holding hands. I had my own little festival inside Big Red. Who needed face-painting and cotton candy?

Ray pointed to the entrance. "We're here."

He pulled into a parking space and led me to the gate. Vendor tents lined the community center, filled with crafts and food. Kids yelled and squealed on the inflatable castles and slides.

Ray said, "I thought Bean would've liked that."

Bell would have loved to see the brick stage, all lined up with brass instruments on stands with musicians ready to play. The Blues and Gospel Festival was perfect for us. I could do this date business, but most importantly I could be me.

Ray took me down a long pier that was empty of onlookers. No one else came down from the fancy, white-tent areas, but we could still hear the music finding us as we walked the planks over Hampton Harbor. As we reached the end of the pier, Ray pulled me close, holding me against his chest as we looked out across the endless water. I'd never seen the beach before, and it was downright spectacular—out of the realm of words and knowledge, space and time. It was what I would've wanted the youngins to experience. Riding in a car with someone I loved to a beach with bouncy houses and glory singing. We would have to bring them back someday.

The strong voice of the singer echoed around me. "Hallelujah" was playing as the waves lapped against the beams of the pier. Ray began whispering those beautiful lyrics, his arms circling me tighter, and I knew that all was right with the world.

I turned into him and buried my face against his neck, my lips brushing against his skin as I boldly put my arms around his back. I whispered to him, "Maize was right. You are my rain and my sun, like farmers' lips to God's ears. I hope you know it."

He was holding me so close to him I was dizzy, the world rushing around me and inside of me all at once. His voice was husky and strong. "Why are you so scared to let love in?"

"Love is hard."

He pulled away from me, kissing me softly on the lips. "Love is patient. Love is kind. It does not envy. It does not boast. It is not rude. It is not self-seeking. It is not easily angered; it keeps no record of wrongs. Love does not delight in evil but rejoices in truth. It always protects, always trusts, always hopes, always perseveres. That is love, and that is me and you."

"Don't you know I'm just some homeless girl seeking shelter?"

Love wanted to rise up in my chest, but I was too afraid to let it. Too fearful of what it would do to me if I gave it the control it was seeking.

"The Lord is sheltering you, Sweet Potato. Don't fear anymore. Let your past be and know there's so much love waiting for you. Let me love you."

He held my face in his hands and kissed me, lingering against my lips as we swayed to a song we were conducting. I wanted so badly to believe it all to be true, to let him love me as easy and laid-back as summer. But to do that meant I'd have to trust in the future, another day.

"I say love is too hard, but I guess I do it anyway." I loved him despite me, anyway. "I do love you, Ray. I don't know how you love me, that's all."

"You love everyone around you. Look at you with Bell and Maize and even Bean. Look at you with your daddy and my parents, the customers at the Soul Food. Everybody, Sweet Potato. You say loving is too hard for you. You have more love in you than there are species of birds in the whole world."

But he wouldn't understand what the kind of love I felt cost me. It was a pretty penny.

I pointed to each of my shoulders. "On one side, that's Maize. On the other side, Bean."

My heart was next. "That's Bell. Loving them takes away a part of myself or weights me clear down to the bottom of the sea. That is how it has been since I was little, still playing with dolls. Then they became my real-life dolls. I couldn't put them on a shelf, so I had to shoulder them and heart them. Loving like that is too hard, because it doesn't leave much room for me to figure out how to proper love other people—like myself."

He pointed to my imaginary boys on my shoulders. "See, Maize and Bean. Watch this."

He picked them up and slung them into the river, like he was skipping pebbles. He touched my heart. "They'll still always be a part of you but trust me on this one." He made like he was pulling Bell slowly from my heart. Then he blew a kiss out over the shimmering waves, like broken glass catching light. "Let God take them, Sweet Potato. They're God's creations, after all. You didn't breathe life into them. They are loved and will always be loved by you. Now, love *you*. Love me. Love us all with the freedom of letting go and letting in all at the same time."

He touched my heart again. "Love them like brothers and sister. Love them forever. We'll always take care of them, Sweet Potato. It won't be hard like you think."

He laughed as he drew me back closer to him. "Well, maybe with Bean, sometimes, but it will be our life. One that we will accept with happiness. Not fear or frustration or that devastating kind of love that doesn't know where it will lay its head. Just simply love—the fulfilling kind that makes you whole."

"Ray, you say you know me, and you know how they are to me. Are you truly ready to take on that kind of life? To take care of them with me? You're a man starting out with a whole future ahead of you. We could take you under. The weight of them and me could pull you down."

And I couldn't allow that. I couldn't watch him drown. Even if that meant losing him. I'd have to let him go, because I loved Ray more than me, too.

He smiled. "You still don't know what happened to me that morning you walked through the door at Soul Food. You spoke, you smiled, and I've been soaring on wings of eagles ever since. There is nothing that could bring me down from the clouds, as long as I have the love of God and you. And now, because of you, I'm more than a man starting out. I am a man with a clear focus on my purpose for this life. Don't ever doubt my feelings for you. I love you like this."

His lips came to me, and I knew his love for me was true. I could feel it in the way his eyes searched me out. He somehow could love me as I was. He had a persevering kind of love that was too overwhelming to comprehend. It was humbling to be loved like that.

I whispered against him, "I do love you, Ray. I want you to know that I'm trying really hard."

"I don't want you to try. Just be."

"Now you sound like Yoda."

He laughed. "See? Now you're back."

We swayed softly to a slow song, his lips against my neck, whispering how much he would love me forever. Some jazz-sounding music with a saxophone was now taking over as the darkness began to surround us. He spun me around on the pier under a starless sky. The moon was even hidden behind the clouds, making it an engulfing dark, but one that I felt completely safe in.

We didn't have much to say to each other, and I knew why.

Sometimes, when a farmer is working, he's content to hear the sounds the earth makes under the tiller—the way the seeds seem to crackle against the ground, the way birds fill the air above. That was us. Just listening to the world, we were creating together. The crashing waves, the creak of the worn planks beneath our feet, the wind against my hair.

An urgency of sadness hit me when the music stopped and we sat down on the pier, face to face. It was almost over, and I knew what that meant. The tips of our shoes were touching, my worn, black Converse against his white Nikes.

I whispered, afraid to break the silence but needing to tell him somehow how I felt about us. "Look at us. We are like our shoes, you know?"

He pulled on my laces, untying one of them. "Me? A shoe? What are you talking about, Sweet Potato?"

My voice came out in a rush. "We both got a covering. A different kinda name, our own unique stamp about us. But if you really took a good look at us, the inner workings, we're filled up with the Spirit of the Lord, right down to our toes. You're stronger than me 'cause you walked tighter to the Lord longer than me, but I will get there. God made us both for the same purpose. He breathed life into the both of us, and we became. And now we are becoming together, and I get that now."

"You get what?" He grabbed my hands and entwined his fingers with mine.

"That you and I can be. I know our night is almost to ending, and I thought if you had me alone you wouldn't love me when it was over. That you would somehow see how different I was from you and how you could never love someone like me. But I feel the way you are holding my hands and being here in your strong way. The way you are looking at me right now. I know you love me. I don't need another word from you about it. No more convincing or speeches. I feel you inside of me, like you are a part of my very stitching."

As soon as I finished getting it all out, I jumped clear out of my skin. The noise of a thousand rockets took off from the sand right behind me, and the world exploded above us in a light show—a colorful rainbow of stars and flashes of amazing light.

Ray stood up, pulling me with him, bringing me right against his chest as we looked up at the fireworks signaling the end of the festival and the beginning of my new life. Colors. A living rainbow—a promise never to flood over me again and wipe me out. The world was speaking colors to me even here.

We walked slowly down the pier, hand in hand, him wrapping his arm around me while we still held hands. I loved that. I would have a future. And even if I didn't quite know what that all meant yet, or how it would feel, or what it was supposed to amount to, I knew I had all I needed to survive. No, not to survive—to live. I had it all here. In the godly man right beside me, in a daddy who had come to terms with the life that God now wanted him to lead, in my brothers and sister who would always be my heart, an extension of me. There couldn't be a rainbow without the rain and the sun. The promise of a new day, a new song to hear Bell sing, a new life to grow into, whatever we were meant to be.

Loving wasn't meant to be hard, and nobody ever said that it was going to be easy, either. But it was gonna be worth every single emotion that came with it, I was certain of that.

Back in the SUV when the fireworks were over, I pulled down the leather flap and looked at myself in the little, light-up mirror. I saw Momma's eyes looking back at me, telling me it was okay to love and to risk it all. Loving might mean some hurt, but that meant living. That meant breathing.

I whispered, "I love you."

To myself, and maybe even to Momma, too.

Ray whispered back, lacing my hand in his again. "I love you, too, Sweet Potato."

And that was enough for me.

TWENTY-THREE

"Your birthday's right around the corner, Sweet Potato. I've asked you time and again what you would like. Just one little hint," Ray whispered to me while the kids were lounging on the huge sectional in Preacher Anderson's living room.

"We don't do presents. Didn't I tell you that already? That's more to carry around. I can't have anything to lug around except what will fit in my bag."

Even while I said it, I hated the thought of ever having to pick that bag up again, and I prayed that part of my life was over. Just one more time, hopefully. Daddy had been scurrying all around Newport News, looking for us a rental. Our time was about up, because the preacher and his First Lady were expected back in three days' time. Daddy was engrossed in the classifieds while Bell was practicing vocabulary flashcards with Bean because she was set on helping him with all the words he somehow missed along the way.

Maize wasn't home yet. He had been asked to a friend's house after school, and he didn't ride the bus home with me. Something about his absence wasn't wearing on me well. The other pea in my pod was missing, and something about my heart seemed missing, too. Maize wasn't like a kid to me. He was a part of me. He had always been my best of friends, my one true. I'd been sick with worry because he didn't have any cellphone to carry around, and Daddy said Maize didn't need one. He was a boy.

"What time is it again, Daddy?" I asked impatiently.

"Stop worrying about Maize, Mother Hen." Daddy swatted the newspaper at me. "He's due home soon."

"You said home." I frowned at him, feeling the word swirling around on my tongue. It sounded right delicious, like a warm cherry pie. "Daddy, we've got to find us a real place this time, no dilly-dallying around."

"I know it. I've got two possibilities tomorrow morning. One on Maple and one on Twenty-ninth Street."

Ray shifted uncomfortably. Maybe it was because he'd been sitting on the oriental rug since nine without moving a muscle. Or maybe he didn't like those locations.

His voice was decisive. "Maybe you should try Maple, but it's a little farther out."

"Well, I won't try Maple, then. I like the walking distance to Soul Food. It makes my life less complicated."

Daddy really meant that would save us money on all the transportation fares. Living at the Holiday over the weekend took all those greenbacks right out of his billfold, I imagined.

"I could see if Momma would let us both go looking in the morning. I know the area very well, and I could assist you if you would like," Ray offered.

"No, thank you." Daddy put his hands across his chest, resolute. *Oh no.* Here was the I-don't-need-help-from-nobody speech. "I know what we'll need. I can do this, Ray."

His tone was condescending, and I knew Ray didn't mean Daddy was incompetent. By no means. Ray wasn't that way at all.

"That's fine, sir." Ray clapped loudly and stood up. I wanted to grab him and pull him right back down, but I knew it was getting late. It was a school night, and the youngins should've already been in bed, but something about Maize not being here had us all probably a little restless.

"Can I speak to Bell in private? I'd like to talk to her about Sweet Potato's birthday."

Bell squealed and threw the cards at Bean. "You know me. Let's get this party started!"

She grabbed Ray's hand and dragged him through the swinging door to the little kitchen. Pastor and First Lady Anderson's house was a perfect size for our family. But it was beyond anything that we'd ever have. Daddy was going to be looking for us a place, but we wouldn't have the fixings to go with it. It would take us years to get to this. Curtains and rugs and sofas and beds … that would take time. But the place was a start.

Daddy motioned for me to come nearer so that Bean couldn't hear. He didn't need to worry. Bean was already dozing with the cards sprawled over his chest.

"He know about your birthday?"

I answered, "Mm … hm …"

"And he still wants to do something big? I don't get people, you know." He shrugged. "But how can we stop the wind from blowing? Once it starts, it can almost take your breath away."

I didn't know if he was trying to tell me he was already beginning to suffocate here. I prayed not. That meant he was feeling the itch to run. Red flag raised.

"Maize isn't here yet." I paced the floor. "We don't even know this friend of his. You didn't ask him any questions about it, Daddy? Why do you have be so lax about Maize?"

"Why would I get up into his business?" Daddy asked accusingly. "I trust Maize. He ain't never had this opportunity to have a friend. Are you jealous?"

My eyes grew large as state-fair-winning taters. "Jealous? No! I'm worried, Daddy. He's out there by himself."

"No, you're wrong. He said he was hanging out with a friend."

"But who?" I tried to give him an evil eye, but he cracked me a smile.

"You stop acting like the momma. You hear me, child? You start being you." Daddy placed the paper down. "It's right near eleven. These kids have school. You have school in the morning, so you are off to bed yourself. I'm getting rid of that boy of yours."

"Don't start playing Daddy now," I whispered. I wanted to add *In somebody else's house*, but I refrained.

He was going to try to send me to bed? Without Maize home? And apparently not bothered that it was near eleven? I wasn't down with double standards.

"I've gotta wait up for Maize." I crossed my arms defiantly.

"Well, play stubborn. I can be stubborner." He hit my butt with the newspaper.

"You know that ain't no word."

"I know you ain't trying to give me no grammar lessons, Sweet Potato Jones." Daddy picked Bean up with one arm. Bean was already out. "Go get that boy gone before I embarrass him."

I took off toward the kitchen. "Bell," I announced. "It's bedtime now. Ray, I'm sorry, but …"

"I know. I know. We have so much planning and so little time. Just a couple of weeks away, you know."

"I know." I rolled my eyes. "You remind me every day."

"You gonna love it, Sweet Potato."

Bell pranced proudly around the kitchen with a hum that would make a *prima donna* envious.

"I'm sure of it," I said.

Ray kissed me softly on the cheek. "I'll see you right after school, okay?"

This time we were taking the kids to a movie. That was Ray's idea.

We'd never been to an actual cinema house before, and I was sure the experience would blow their minds and distract them from what we wouldn't have in three more days.

"What's happening after school?" Bell asked with eyebrows raised.

"You'll see." I couldn't help but spin her around myself. "Ray's full of surprises, that one is."

Daddy was back. "Sure, sounds like it. Now get, before you're grounded."

Bell laughed. "You can't ground Ray, Daddy."

"He wasn't the one I was threatening."

Grounded. *Ha! Pathetic.* Daddy had never disciplined us before, and he used the word *grounded* in a sentence? What parenting book had he been reading up on lately? Not to mention we still had a missing party that I might grind right into the dirt when he did get home.

Ray said, "I'll see you tomorrow, Mr. Eli."

The rooms turned dark. Daddy didn't believe in keeping lights on without necessity. *Oh, Lordy.* How would it be when we had a place of our own? How were we to survive it, truly, when I knew there would be many responsibilities all at once? Daddy never had to think too much about being extra when we lived in a shed, but a place would take lots of effort and energy to keep burning, which meant light bills and water payments, and things of that sort. It might get too hot in the kitchen.

"Where are you, Maize?" I asked right past the ceiling, up to heaven.

I should've been so pleased that Maize had an invite to go play ball with a friend after school. When I'd asked him more about the details—like the name of this person—he'd quickly changed the subject. I walked to the kitchen about five hundred times, looking at the blaring, blue light of the digital clock that told me something wasn't right. Daddy was snoring softly on the couch, his feet fully covered in them borrowed blankets. Not a care in the world.

"Daddy, he's not here." I couldn't believe I was saying this.

He said, "Go to sleep, Sweet Potato."

Bean was knocked out next to him in a fort he had made from blankets. Bell was asleep in the next room over. Why was I the only one caring about this?

"Daddy!" I pulled the covers off him. "It's two thirty."

"Okay," Daddy said as he wiped his face. "And?"

"He's not home, and it's after two o'clock in the morning," I whispered urgently in his ear.

"He's gone." Daddy shot up. Fumbling in the unfamiliar surroundings. Too much furniture meant new leg bruises. "I can't believe that fool done run away. Now that we 'bout to settle this."

"Don't say that, Daddy." Even though I knew it was true.

He had never pulled a stunt like this, and right now my brain felt like it was the ringmaster trying to control a panicking crowd when the lions broke out of the cages.

"What else could it be?"

"It could be he got in trouble, or he got lost. You know he doesn't know this address. Do you know this address? I don't even know this fool address. If the cops had to try to take him somewhere, he couldn't say Pastor's house, and they'd know the deal. Maize probably doesn't even know Preacher Anderson's name. You know his mind hasn't been on spiritual things for a long time."

"I know where he could tell them, though. He could say Soul Food."

I wiped a tear from my cheek, imagining him riding in a cop car, scared out of his mind. He would have a panic attack without me around to talk him down, without Bell to sing. *Oh, Lordy!* Bell would lose it if he wasn't here when she got up.

"I gotta go, Daddy." We were already all dressed, like always. "I have to look there."

But I knew he wasn't there. That was too easy a fix, and nothing about loving this family was easy.

"No, I'm going." He pointed to Bean. "You got to stay here with the kids. Don't wake them up. They don't need to know about this. It'll be solved by first light."

But I knew he couldn't guarantee it. Runaways were smart if they were street, and Maize was street personified. Maize would camouflage into the darkest shadows like a super ninja. He might even have trucked it back down to North Carolina, by now. No, he'd never go back there. Too much pain in that lucky bird state.

My mind went to all kinds of places as I waited for news from Daddy. In the space of ten minutes, I felt myself losing all sense of reason.

Ray answered on the first ring. "Are you okay? I'm coming."

"Is he there?" My voice was broken. He knew I was not okay.

"No. I'm coming to you. Stay there."

Like I could move and leave my children. What was wrong with Maize? After what happened to me at The Home, he'd seemed so livid with Daddy. He was seething mad and withdrawn, even from me. All the encouraging words I threw his way seemed to bounce right off him, but he hadn't had any attacks for two weeks, either, so I'd thought maybe he was growing stronger emotionally. I didn't know what to make of all of this.

Daddy should have talked with him, but Daddy had been so distant, too. I knew he was hiding something, and I didn't like it one bit. We'd never been a secretive lot. Secrets led to mistrust and judgments. Secrets led to three o'clock panic attacks. Everything had been fitting together, moving right along. Now it was all falling apart again.

The knock on the door 'bout scared me out of my skin. It was Ray. I buried my face in his chest as he held me against the doorframe.

"Oh, baby. I'm so sorry."

"Wait? Is he dead? Oh, God. He's dead?" I sobbed, becoming fainter by the second.

"We haven't seen him, Sweet Potato. We don't know where he is."

That meant he was gone from us for good, evaporated into thin air. Ray's protective arm was warm around me, yet I was chilled to the bone.

"I've got to get him back. This is my fault." I pulled my knees up against my chest and hid my head in shame.

"What happened?" he whispered in my ear. "Tell me what happened."

"It's my fault because I don't know what happened. I'm supposed to know everything. When he stopped telling me, that's when it became my fault."

I was now choking on guilt for not having seen what he was up to. He would've left a sign—something. I jumped from the couch and went to the room he shared with Daddy. His bag was there, placed neatly beside the other two matching, drawstring, canvas bags.

I snatched his bag up quietly and tiptoed out of the room, so afraid that Bean would wake on up and find his brother gone. When I got back to the living room, Ray was on his phone, and his face was grim.

"Momma said Mr. Eli and Daddy left for the police station."

"Did they get a call?"

My hand came to my throat. I could've strangled myself for allowing all this mess to happen. I should've somehow stopped it.

"Momma's called all the places she knows. The hospitals, the principal, the church people are out everywhere, combing the streets in teams."

Ray quit talking. He startled me when he suddenly yelled, "Where did he get that?"

I was rummaging through Maize's bag, looking for any clues. Maybe a phone number of that girl. She might have known where he was. She might be the friend. *Oh, Lordy!* Ray grabbed the wadded clothes and held up a shirt.

"Sweet Potato, where did he get this?" He balled it up in his fist and threw it against the wall.

"Why did you do that?" I grabbed the shirt and stuffed it back in the bag.

He pulled it right back out. "Do you see this? This isn't a regular, black shirt."

He pointed to the right sleeve, to a tiny, silver scythe patch that I wouldn't have noticed if he hadn't drawn my attention to it.

"Mrs. Sunshine didn't get this one for Maize when we went shopping. I ain't never seen it. Why are you so mad? Ray, I've never seen you this upset before."

His eyes weren't laced with fear, but with disgust. He took the shirt in his hands and ripped it straight down the middle, as if it was made of nothing but notebook paper.

"It's the East Coast Grims, Sweet Potato. It's a Reaper shirt," he spit out, his eyes dark and menacing.

I put my hand on his arm and shook him. "What are you saying?"

"Don't you know what I'm saying? Listen to me."

My heart stopped in my chest. I hadn't heard of no Reapers. But I'd heard of The Tanks and City Dimes and Forks back in North Carolina, and from the way Ray snarled *East Coast Grims,* I knew right away it was a gang. My head fell back against the pillow, and I turned my head as the tears fell silently. I didn't lose my baby to a gang. I didn't. I didn't. I didn't. *Oh, God.* I couldn't help but rock this pain. It wouldn't go away.

I must have spoken His name aloud, because Ray replied, "You are right. God is the only one who can save him now. They have a special set of rules for a specialized crew—methodical, deadly. Once you are in, the rest of your life must disappear. They make you cut off your whole family, connections. Clipped. Oh, Sweet Potato, I'm so sorry."

He fell on his knees, right on that fancy rug, and prayed to the Lord until the sweat was pouring off his face. All I could see was Maize with his little group of friends from The Dream that he walked with every day. The ones he told me he ate with at lunch. The ones who had his back and already felt like brothers to him. I thought they were a blessing. They ended up being a curse.

"Why didn't I see it?" I cried. "He's my boy. He's done this. You're right. I know he's done this."

"He wouldn't have this unless he's done something. They just don't give out their colors to the choir boys."

He went through the swinging door with force that might have knocked it off its hinges, and I heard him stuffing the shirt in the trashcan.

I can't handle this, Lord. You always told me you wouldn't give me nothing I couldn't handle. I can't handle this gang, God. You got to take my baby out of this mob. He can't cut us off like a light switch. We've always been so tangled up, me and him. He was my live wire, my light, my source of power. But I knew what Ray said was true. Maize had done this because he wanted to get away from all of us. Even me.

"Maybe he's not in it yet. Maybe he spilled something on his clothes, and he had to borrow a shirt." I was trying to rationalize this craziness, even though I knew I was lying to myself. "Maybe it ain't too late. Maybe he'll come to his senses and remember all I taught him. What we stand for."

Ray put his arms around me. "Baby, I know this world. The Grims don't let you walk away when you up and please, and if Maize chose them, he's disowned you. Do you understand what I am saying to you? The East Coast Grims aren't some little, lollipop gang. They take you in and mold you into sellers and hustlers and bangers against their enemies—and they have a slew of enemies. They are notorious killers, death-row types. They protect those streets with their lives. Momma is going to lose it when she finds out about this."

"You know gang life? You?"

I couldn't imagine it. He seemed the most sheltered soul in America, with a smile on his face and a word of the Lord on his lips.

His face fell, tears forming in his eyes like he was reliving a sudden memory that he'd tried desperately to repress.

"Denise has a brother."

That was all he said, but it was enough. He started dialing but was respectful enough to take the call outside. I knew the reason. He didn't want me to have to hear him tell his momma. His words keep coursing through my veins as his muffled voice carried through the open window.

Maize, come back to me. Find a way, whatever it takes. Find your way back home.

TWENTY-FOUR

Daddy was talking to Pastor Anderson in the church study while Bell, me, and Bean were waiting for him on the front pew. Bean had been crying, even though he would never admit it to anybody. Bell was flipping through the hymn book, and I knew she was trying to busy her mind. I sat pulling a string on the knee of my jeans.

"He's coming back. Right, Sweet Potato?" Bean whispered against my arm.

"I don't think so, baby." I leaned my head against his and pulled him in closer to me.

"Don't say that," Bell said, breaking the eerie silence around us. "He'll be back. We gonna pray him back. He's coming back, like Jesus's second coming. It's a guarantee."

I said, "There's one thing I know about this life. Another day ain't promised. We have no assurances about this world. Haven't you learned that in our walk?"

I wanted to hurt Daddy for telling Bell our walking was the Lord's doing. For him putting Maize in a gang way. What was he doing back there with that preacher for so long? Oh, let me guess—asking for forgiveness? Finding his calling?

Ray never talked about Denise's brother, and I couldn't ask. I didn't really want to know. *Tell me lies. Tell me he went off on a fisher boat in Maine to catch them crabs. Tell me he hitchhiked across the States to California to see the sunrise on another ocean. Don't tell me he joined a gang, robbed, killed, in any order.* And I thought Denise was an only child. Oh, right. I guess she was.

But Maize was my best friend, my true, and these last three days of my life, since he'd vanished, had been the hardest I'd ever had to face. Picking out Momma's casket wasn't anything compared to this. I'd expected her to OD anytime. I didn't see this one coming—but that might be the biggest lie I'd told myself yet. We were 'bout on our way, doggone it. Daddy had to keep moving, even though I'd stopped.

Our free ride at the preacher's house had come to an end. Him and his pretty wife with her nice suit and matching bags had come back. We left. Daddy had us at the motel at the end of West Fifth until …

Bell took timid steps up to the pulpit. Step one, her voice got confidence. Step two, she started to fly. Step three, her voice was on angel wings. She was singing from the hymn book, and I hadn't heard it before. She probably didn't know the right way it was supposed to go, but she made those lyrics her own. A call-out for Maize.

When she finished, she collapsed on her knees, her little head falling into her hands like an old woman praying for a miracle. *Oh, Lordy!* My heart couldn't take much more of this. The preacher and Daddy were out now, standing down at the door frame, watching Bell. The preacher was more grief-stricken than Daddy, who seemed cool during this chaos. It made me seethe with resentment.

I went to Bell, picked her up, and held her in my arms. Bean came and curled up like a baby by my feet. They knew Maize was gone, but we hadn't the heart to tell them he'd chosen the gang life. Daddy stood in the doorway with some papers in his hand. What had he done? He'd signed us away. That's what he'd done. He signed us away and had already made peace with it. That was why he seemed so blank-faced in our time of turmoil. He had failed, cut his losses, and was moving on ... without us.

"Sweet Potato, why don't you take the kids out the back to Patty? She's got lunch ready for all the volunteers, and maybe the little ones will want something to eat."

Why was it that any time there was some kind of death or disaster, the only thing anybody could blessed think about was filling their stomachs? I needed somebody to fill my soul, and He'd turned his back on me.

Ray came in with a stack of flyers he'd been copying from the church computer. It had a picture of Maize and contact information for the church. What person out there on the street would contact the church? But for some reason they didn't want the Soul Food name on it. We couldn't put the motel phone number down, because that was another stupid temporal. What messes did we tend to make with our lives?

Daddy stepped forward. "I'll take them back. Maybe you could sit here with Sweet Potato a minute until I get back."

Oh, the old stalling technique. He was going to tell me he was shipping Bell and Bean off to Mr. and Mrs. Foster. Well, we'd have to see about that. I couldn't even look at him as he pulled Bell and Bean away from me, shushing them as he took them on out the back door to the parsonage.

"I'm almost eighteen," I said softly to the preacher.

Never had a birthday meant so much to me in my life. I was dreading it before, but now I was counting down the days.

"Don't run, too, Sweet Potato." The preacher patted my hand.

"I'm not talking about running, sir. I'm talking about claiming." I pointed to the door. "I'm taking them from him."

"You can't do that." He bowed his head. "He gave them to Patricia and me."

"What?" I shrieked.

I flew from the pew and headed out the door. Daddy was coming in, and I collided against his six-foot-three frame.

"How dare you? How dare you do this to me?"

"I freed you. You're free." Daddy took me by my arms and sat me back down beside the preacher.

"Free!" I cried. "I ain't never been free, and I won't be. I am chained to them. My life is connected to them. My very being is in them. You can't go giving something away that never belonged to you in the first place. They have always been mine."

"I am their father. I gave over my rights to Preacher and First Lady, because I have to go to the street. And where I'm going, they can't follow, and for what I've been told I might not even make it back myself. I had to think this through the right way, and for the first time in my life I think I did it."

"We have been to the street. We are the street." I beat against his chest, and he let me.

"I'm going to find Maize. If I have to go to the depths of hell and pull him out burning, I will do it." Daddy wiped his brow, already sweating at the thought of it.

"Well, then, you are giving the kids to me," I told him.

"No. You're not their mother. You're their sister." He leaned in close. "God is leading me to give them to the Andersons. They have a place for them, a home. They have a love for them. God has directed my heart to give them a true home with curtains and rugs, and that's what I'm doing. It's for the best, and I know it to be true. Where I'm going, I might not make it back, so I gotta know I finally did something right and gave them a proper place."

"I am their home. I'm what Bell knows. Bean will go backward, Daddy. We can't have him losing the ground he's found here. His feet will give way, like Maize's did."

Pastor Anderson spoke softly. "Patricia and I never had children, Sweet Potato. We tried for many years, but the Lord held out on us. Maybe it was for this time, this place, so that we could be here for your family who are in need. We will provide a Christian home for Bean and Bell. We'll care for them like they were our own—you included."

The preacher talked the talk. I knew they were good people, or Mrs. Sunshine wouldn't have stuck around there. But they weren't my people.

Ray was stepping in again, and I cried out. I ran to him and put my arms around his waist, not caring where we were. I needed him. "Daddy gave them to the preacher. He gave them away like an old pair of shoes. He's buried me. Maize killed me, and now I'm buried."

Ray looked over my head. "Is this true?"

Daddy's voice was heavy. "Yes, Ray. It's true. It's legalized and all set up."

He had to know he'd done wrong. Whatever his intention, he was still giving them away.

Pastor Anderson spoke up. "He's going to be leaving now to go find Maize. He knows what he's walking into."

"Sweet Potato, I might not make it back. I might not walk out of this one. Do you understand what I am saying? The Grims have a reputation, even though I've been told they are a small, localized group not affiliated with some of the bigger gangs. They have a unit here. It's smaller, so I may have that opening of a chance to snatch him back." Daddy cleared his throat. "But I know once you swear your allegiance, it's to the death. They can kill me for Maize's life, for all I care. They can take a substitute."

"Oh, Daddy," I sobbed against Ray, "I can't take this. Maybe we can call Maize out, somehow. We're the running kind. They've never met the likes of us."

But that hadn't worked so far. Not a soul had turned up any information about him. He hadn't shown up for school on Friday, and we'd spent the next three days combing the streets full force with about forty other godly people. The police had been circling the street with the flyers, but they had no information to share, either. Informants weren't talking. Daddy must have his back against the wall.

"Bell and Bean can't go on the street again. I've decided." Daddy spoke firmly.

But I was soon to be eighteen, and I could be their legal guardian then. I would quit school and work full time. I could do it. Somehow.

"Sir, you know that Sweet Potato and I are prepared to raise Bean and Bell."

Ray rubbed my arms, and I collapsed against him. He put his arms around me and led me to the pew, but that was the last place I wanted to park. I didn't want to sit near the backstabbing traitors.

"What you want and what is best for them are two different things," Daddy answered. "She has to finish school. She will be the first Jones with a diploma, and that is mighty big. She has to finish out this year. That is best for her."

"Don't talk about what is best for me. Like you knew how to raise us. Don't you sit here and try to tell me you think I'm incapable of taking care of them youngins," I spit out at him.

Pastor came in with the counseling tone. "I don't think that's what your Daddy is implying at all. You're still in school, Sweet Potato. You have to graduate. Ray has already signed up for the Army and will be leaving soon. Mrs. Sunshine said that she would take them, but we already have the room at our home. Patty doesn't work. She does all the pastoral care as my wife to assist me in the ministry. And even though that takes a lot of her time, she would have the proper time to devote to the children. Mrs. Sunshine has the Soul Food to keep up all day and night. We are the perfect place. God has provided."

"Tell God to bring Maize back, if He's providing," I cried.

Ray let out a sigh. He knew we were facing an impossible situation. "God is working through this as we speak." He hated to meet my gaze.

Ye of little faith, the girl of a soon-to-be preacher man.

"Daddy, let's go on back to the motel. I'll keep the kids while you go off searching."

"No. We checked out. And I've got something else to tell you, too."

I was defeated. My match was over. I was learning some tennis language, since it was strange requirement for all of us project and homeless kids to learn how to play tennis at The Dream. I was at Love-40 on a match point. No chance of a comeback.

I knew what I had to do. I knew how to run, too. After I found Maize, I would take the kids and never look back. Daddy would never be able to find the four of us. This was a big world, and I could get lost in it.

Daddy was more vulnerable than I'd ever seen him. "I want you to listen to me, now. I want you to hear all that I have to say. I'm going to try to get it out the best I can."

His hand was outstretched to mine—those strong hands I'd always admired. But I didn't reach for him. I clung to the only lifeline that meant anything to me now, my Ray. And I knew that when I ran, I would have to leave him in the dust, too. For my family, I would have to sacrifice it all. Ray would wait for me to get the kids settled and safe. I knew he loved me that much. I might not ever understand the reasons why he did, but I knew he would understand if I ran. God would make way for us. I had to get Maize and the kids back first.

TWENTY-FIVE

"It's not your fault that Maize did this." Daddy shook his head. His eyes were strong, despite the way his voice was shaking.

"Yes, it is," I said, as I sunk deeper down into the ocean depths.

Nothing he could say would ever convince me otherwise. I was Maize's best friend, and I'd let him down. Running off on some date with Ray, working to be close to Ray. He'd distanced himself and lost his way. I hadn't been there to hold him close, to ease his panicking heart. So, he'd found a haven on the street. *Lord, those Reapers better be good to him.*

What was I even saying?

Daddy exhaled. "It was mine. It's as simple as that. I own it."

He opened one of the folders he had with him. I was sure the first one held the copies of his giveaway receipt. This was something different entirely. I watched as he flipped through the pages. "Daddy! What are you doing?"

He sighed. "This place was never meant for us."

"What? We ain't staying? That's what I tried to say to you and

Maize before. Do you remember when I begged you to leave, and you told me to go to sleep? If you would've moved when I said, Maize wouldn't be in this death sentence. I said to you that we might as well go on now and save them the heartache later. The longer we stayed, the harder it was for Maize to breathe. I can barely gather up the oxygen it takes now, and for the life of me, Daddy, I don't know how I'm going to make it after this."

My voice broke, and the tears were on the ready. "I don't think I can live if he doesn't come back. Not after this."

"I ain't letting that happen no more. There's something I never told you, Sweet Potato. That I ain't never told anybody."

He passed me a folded-up document, and I flipped over the blue paper to find a deed to some farmhouse. Marigold Jones's name was typed on the first line.

I frowned. It was strange to see Momma's name on a paper. "What is this for, Daddy?"

He pushed it closer to me. "Just look at it, will you?"

I did as he asked, scanning it, trying not to focus on her name, because it was hurtful to see it printed there. But then I saw something else. In case of her death, her inheritance would pass to her oldest child.

"I don't understand this, Daddy. Ray?"

I handed Ray the paper. He read over it all and folded it right back up, shaking his head. I could feel his heartbeat and his body tensing. What was this all about? We didn't have time for this now.

"I couldn't face it, Sweet Potato. So, I put it away, and I ran. I grabbed you youngins and swore I'd never been able to touch my feet on that land. That was ten years ago, and now all it has done is grown and grown. And I've done this to you for what? For my own prejudices."

He put his hands on my shoulders. "No more. It stops now. I stop now. I'm done."

"Daddy, what are you talking about?"

Was he trying to say that we had always had a home to go to?

That he'd taken us all around the desert when the promise land was right down I-95? I couldn't take that. Just like I bet Moses couldn't take the truth when God denied him that land at the end of his journey. Daddy couldn't have made us believe we didn't have a roof over our head. For what? Was he plum out of his mind? I'd believed I was in some dream. Now I knew it for sure. But it was turning more nightmarish by the second, and I wished somebody would wake me up right quick before I lost it.

"I was. And maybe I still am. Them Parkers hated me. They disowned Marigold when she ran off with me, because they said I would ruin her and wouldn't provide right by her. For that, I never forgave them closed-minded people. I didn't want nothing they had. I didn't want their charity."

He wrung his hands in front of him like he was cleaning out a dirty dish rag.

"Charity? That's not charity, Daddy. When her parents left her their possessions, that was her right. And then it was our right. Regardless of what color we are or whether we ever met them people before in our life. So, what you are trying to tell me? That in the heart of all of this, we've had a home? For how long? How long you been carrying this paper around?" I could hardly get the words out. It was inconceivable.

"After your Momma died and I had to go down to the social services office, the news was waiting for me there. They'd been looking for us. Apparently, lawyers of them people had already contacted Marigold before. That was how she was able to score so much cash, which became the death of her. It's not like I gave her money to buy drugs with, Sweet Potato." He shuddered, and a look of disgust crawled across his face.

"Those people were our family. That was Momma's people, and I don't care how you looked at them in the past. They were who they were. They meant something to her. It hurt her to walk away. She told me so."

I couldn't help but say everything that was on my mind now. How could Daddy have done this to his own flesh and blood?

His voice was defeated. "We could've been making it the whole time. Done the whole time on the farm instead of tramping the road. Now, I have to tell you, because this here farmhouse and all that land will go to you on your eighteenth birthday. It was all left to the first grandchild. It's out of my hands now. Here."

He handed me the papers and turned from me, his shoulders slumping.

"What? You think this is a bad thing? You think this is wrong? I can see it on you. Daddy, wake up. We've lived in every filthy, rat-infested, deserted, desolate place possible because … because of your pride?"

But this wasn't about pride. This came down to family, our family. And Daddy had let me down. Yet again. Pedestal knocked down. Toppled.

"Pride is a hard thing. I couldn't go to that farmhouse down that long, dirt road and see them workers out there in them fields. Most of them migrants being taken advantage of. I bet them Sunday-dressed fools sat up in that two-story house, looking out their windows, imagining themselves still in them slave days. I couldn't go there."

"Who's been caring for the place all this time, Daddy? It would have been our responsibility to take care of our momma's home." I shot him a glare. He'd lied to us all these years, convinced Bell that we had a purpose for the Lord. I couldn't go there.

"There's a caretaker there. Mr. Steele Watson. He contacts me through the services we use from time to time, giving updates on the property. It seems that it's done well under his care. Just like Marigold had wished it."

"Wait—and you're saying that she wouldn't have wanted to go back there? To raise us kids in the place where she grew up, instead of them slums in Charlotte? She loved to sell those vegetables with her daddy at the roadside stand. She loved the land, and the smell of cut grass, of fresh plowed field dirt. She told me."

"That's not the life I envisioned for myself." He refused to turn around to me. He spoke so quietly that I thought I'd missed it.

"Excuse me!" I wailed to his back. "You stopped her? You wouldn't let her go home?"

Oh, God. Please let this not be true. That meant Daddy could've sent Momma over the edge. Her crying all the time. She'd probably found out her family had died off, and she had a chance to take us back, but Daddy had stopped her, holding us all back.

"We were more than farmers. We could've had our own restaurant, the two of us. She could've been a Mrs. Patterson, if only she would have tried." His voice trailed off, mixing in with my broken sobs.

"Daddy, please tell me that this life you've dragged us through for the past ten years has served some greater purpose than your pride and inability to forgive."

There'd been so many times where I'd felt overcome, rejected by society, but I had held on to one true constant: Daddy loved us. Now ... I wasn't too sure. I knew nothing about Daddy. That meant everything I had built up was all a lie.

He came and sat down beside me, his knee touching mine. I flinched like I'd been scorched by a hot iron.

"It's not as simple as you make it out to be, Sweet Potato. I'd had a hard life on a farm with my own family. You don't know that about me and my folks."

He wiped away tears with the back of his sleeve. "I never told you nothing about me. You don't know your daddy's raising, and I couldn't risk you there with the workers to be taken advantage of in a bad way."

"But, Daddy. You've taken advantage of us. You've stolen a life of peace we could've had. It couldn't be that bad on a farm. Hard work, I'm sure. But don't you think walking these roads has been harder for us than breathing? And now Maize is branded to the street. Do you think it's going to be easy to bring him out? You throw those precious children away like a bag of trash, like they mean nothing to you."

His voice rose. "You think it's been easy for me to watch you all? Bell and Bean are babies. Maize and you are tough, but those two are just babies."

"No, Maize isn't tough, Daddy. That's where you're wrong. He's scared. I was the one driving them on with the hope and the happily-ever-after stories—Neverland and Peter Pan. You were Hook the whole time, stealing our hopes and collecting them in your treasure box while I was trying to give them faith in our darkness. You've pulled one little string and started the fray. I'm unraveling now, and I know if this is getting me like this, the rest of it will dissolve."

I didn't even want to find out how Bell and Bean would take this. I should've shielded them from nothing and told them the harsh, cold realities of the world, without flashlight fantasies. Told them how their momma preferred the crack pipe over lullabies in the rocking chair. I did that for them. I held them when they were tiny babies. I never told them, but maybe I should have—how their momma died in a fit, a convulsion of suffering after all of her organs shut down, how she'd let out tiny gasps of breath like puffs of smoke from a train stack. Should I tell them now that their daddy was a liar and a con? *Oh, God. Not Daddy.* Maize first, then my two babies, and now Daddy. My whole family was forsaken. Cursed.

"When I ran, I didn't think it would be for long. I thought I needed one place to get away from her demons, but wherever I moved, her evil spirits followed me. I lost me with every mile we took, and the more I lost myself, the more you had to step up. How you ever going to forgive me, Sweet Potato?"

"Stop talking about me. What did you tell the kids out there?"

Was he going to tell them the truth, the whole story from beginning to end? And if and when he did, what would be the fallout from it? I was sure I was going to be the one to pick up the pieces, which meant I had to find a way to deal with this myself.

"Preacher Anderson helped me trace it all today and make some much-needed calls. That's what we've been doing, and now I know how we must proceed. I'm done now." He rubbed his hands across his forehead.

"You are done with us, Daddy?" I braced myself up against the high-backed pew.

"Done with this life. Marigold would kill me if she knew I was this stubborn and this stupid. She would be so ashamed that I'd let you live like this because I didn't want to face she was gone. She's gone, Sweet Potato." He was trying to convince me. "She never hated me for not wanting that life. She knew my scars and wouldn't have dreamed of forcing that kinda life on me. So, you think I pushed her over the edge. That wasn't me, Sweet Potato. She made her choices. Her own way. I loved that woman, and I love you youngins with all I have left."

It was my turn to shake his shoulders. "You can't say you love us now. It's too late to love us. You had years to show us you loved us, and what did you do? You hid us from what was rightfully ours? A normal life! Oh, God. The pain we've felt. I saw it sucking the very life out of Maize, and I know you weren't blind to it, either. You tell me now you ain't felt this on us? That you didn't see how Maize was about two feet tall?"

He interrupted me. "How are you ever going to forgive me for this, Sweet Potato?"

"Don't talk to me about forgiveness. You're a liar. You stay away from the kids and me. I don't want you to look at us, talk to us, call us yours ever again."

I wanted him to have a future of guilt for all that he'd done to me, to us. How dare he do this and think he was in the right all this time? To think because he was our father, he could lead us out into the desert, when we could have been slurping on sweet honey?

He was right. It wasn't my fault all along. I was the innocent victim this whole time. It was all him.

TWENTY-SIX

"I can't do this alone." I put my hands against my cheeks, trying to hide the evidence of my tears. What was the use? I'd been crying for days.

"You'll never be alone." Ray took my hand and led me to the back bedroom.

"What am I going to say to them?" I choked. My feet stumbled again, and he steadied me.

He answered, "I don't know, but it will somehow work itself out for good. Say that when you don't know what else to say."

If I could pull some of the strength from him and wear it like armor. If I didn't have Jesus and Ray Patterson ...

When he opened the door, I let my gaze fall on their faces. Bell was in the twin-size bed that she had claimed when we first came here to stay for our week-long retreat. She had her drawstring bag sitting beside her. Her little, white earpieces were stuck in her ears, and the music was up so loud I knew she was listening to Mahalia Jackson. Bean was staring at me, biting his lip. He was on the other twin bed—the same one I had slept in the week before, when I thought we were blessed to have such friends. Conspirators that would steal my children right from under me. That was probably the plan all along. Come to find out you never knew people, really.

I picked up Bell's iPod to lower the volume and sat down beside her, reaching across to pull Bean to me. Ray sat down in one of the swivel desk chairs and put his hands on his knees, bracing for the storm approaching.

My life had always been like a tornado. Unpredictable. Scary. Violent. Touch-and-go. *Oh, sweet children. Precious, innocent children.* I closed my eyes and saw visions of them in the trucker seats, scarfing down pie with Maize, singing in the choir, break dancing. No memories from before Newport News, because we had never really lived before this. *God, show me their future.* I squeezed their hands before I started. I could see love. Protection. Care. Provision. I could envision that for them, because that was all I'd ever prayed for. I didn't ever think that I wouldn't be the one to be their lead.

My voice caught as I began, and I tried to start over. My breath came out in a ragged rush. Bell pulled off her earbuds and leaned in closer to me. "Don't cry, Sweet Potato."

And that made me cry even more. I was here to comfort her, and she was comforting me instead. "I can't lose you."

"But we are going to be right here at Pastor and Patty's house," Bean said, like he had already accepted his fate. "You gonna be right down at Soul Food."

I hadn't even thought about me, nor did I care. "I want you with me, always. I'm going to get you."

"Daddy told us everything," Bell said softly. "We can't go to the farm. Maize is out there. We got to wait for him, so if this is our waiting spot, so be it."

"Did Daddy call this a waiting spot? Like you're in some bus terminal? That's not what he did. I'm not gonna lie to you no more. He signed you over to the preacher. I'm going to have to fight them to get you back. I'm almost eighteen."

"You can't fight the preacher," Bean said. "That ain't right, Sweet Potato, and you know it."

"Daddy wasn't right for signing you away. He wasn't right for hiding that farm from us, neither."

Bell squeezed my hand, and in her ten-year-old wisdom she spoke words of a wise woman. "But don't you see, Sweet Potato? We had to walk that walk to bring us closer to the Lord. If we hadn't made our journey, we wouldn't be who we are today. We wouldn't be here."

"Exactly," I cried. "Maize is missing. Daddy is a lie. Both of you are lost to me now, too."

"We aren't lost to you," she continued. "My life on the road has been a blessing, not a curse."

How could she say that? How naïve and brainwashed was she?

I couldn't tell from her sing-song voice whether she was being honest or not. She said, "It's been some ride, but Daddy says it stops now. Maize said he was tired, remember. It's time we stop. We got us what we prayed for, sister. We got us home. Right here."

Bean knocked his knuckles on the wall. "You hear that solid sound? That's a place for me."

I'd lost them. "But we aren't home if we aren't together. Bell, I need to look after the two of you. I'm gonna fight for you."

"No," Bell said firmly. "We both decided today. We want to be here with the church people. No offense to you, Sweet Potato, but you've got Ray. You've got to live your life, too. We still gonna see you all the time. We right here."

"What are you talking about? Did Daddy tell you to say all this stuff? You really want to stay here?" I screamed out. "You don't want me?"

"What are you talking about, Sweet Potato? Stop being a drama queen," Bean snorted. "We love you like wine loves cheese, like goats make cheese, well … like cheese. You know I love me some cheese." He was trying to be funny, but I couldn't laugh.

I said, "I love you both so much. Bell, you are like a daughter to me. Not like a sister. I think of you both like my own kids."

They had to know that, even though I had never told them so.

"And that's why it's time you let us go. We want to be here with Pastor and Patty, and we both decided, so it's done." She smiled at me. They weren't crying. What was this? Some post-traumatic stress disorder come to town?

I wiped my tears. "You sound like Daddy."

"Don't be hating on Daddy. He's doing this so that he can find Maize." Bean took up for him.

I didn't believe anything Daddy had said. I would never trust him again. But I knew I had to push my feelings aside about Daddy around them. They already had enough to deal with. My resentment should be the least of their worries.

"So, you are saying that you want me to leave you here, and you'll be fine." I sighed. *Don't cry again. Let me wait, Lord. Calm my spirit, Lord.*

"You're walking down the street to Mrs. Sunshine's house when you leave here. It's not like we're five hundred miles away." Bell laughed. "You know you're about to be married to Ray anyway. You gonna go off to some military place, and we would've had to stay behind with Daddy if all this stuff wouldn't have happened to Maize."

"But that would've been different. And me and Ray were already talking about fighting to get all of you to come with us when that happened."

"But what if we don't want to be up and moving all the time? What if we want Newport News to be it? Or maybe even that farm with chickens and cows and sheep. Couldn't you see Bean riding on a horse with a cowboy hat on, herding sheep in a pen?"

I sighed heavily, remembering me wanting to name him Cactus Jack.

Ray said, "I guess we need to focus on finding Maize. That's the priority right now."

I nodded, trying to signal I was about to stand up, which meant I needed him to stand up. He came up right beside me and put his arms around me. I knew he could sense my weakness.

Bell handed me a slip of paper. "You plug this number into your cellphone, and you call us before you go to bed," she whispered, putting her earbuds back in.

Diversion. She was holding it back, too. Our nightly ritual of singing and playing was over. We were never going to be the same again. She didn't know my phone was lost from the close call at number seven. I would have to find another way to call her.

"Goodbye," I whispered. "I love you."

Bell leaned against the wooden headboard of the bed and ran her legs against the wall, and I turned sharp from her and practically dragged Ray out of the house. I hit the grass and wailed.

"Baby. Oh, baby," he said, as his arms came around my waist.

I pulled at the grass, imagining I was clawing Daddy's eyes out. Some of the volunteers were still under the tent in the backyard. They stopped their jabbering when they saw me, but I didn't care. Dirt felt good against my fingertips. I wanted to destroy the earth beneath me. I wanted to rip it apart. I fell flat to the ground, feeling my cheek against the prickling of the grass, whispering into the very earth that God had formed.

"They took them all from me, Jesus. You give them back to me," I cried.

My body was shaking so that I was losing my breath. Strong arms circled underneath me, pulling me, turning me, and shielding me from all the eyes of the world.

"I'm taking you home," he whispered against my cheek.

With all the strength I had left, I pushed against him, before he could pick me up and try to save the damsel in distress. I had a prince out there who was lost, hurt, possibly dead. And this time, I wasn't going to wait around for Daddy to save the day. He wasn't my hero anymore.

I took off running before Ray could even realize what I had decided. "I'm gonna find him, Ray. Let me go."

He ran after me for a couple of blocks, keeping right on my heels. Even though I didn't know these streets and alleyways, I listened to the street and let the sounds take me. I ducked into a boarded house after the fourth block and peeked out of the broken window to see my sweet Ray still running past.

A rough voice startled me. "You want a bag?"

It was a thin dealer with a face hidden in a hoodie. How easy it would have been for me to take one. I could have made it all go away, as Momma did. But my life was never easy, so I chose the hard way.

I said, "No. I'm looking for my brother, Maize Jones. You know any East Coast Grims?"

His eyes widened. "You better stay away from the Reapers. You not far from their neighborhood, but stay away, I tell you. They the 666 around here."

"Which way?" I asked, as I pulled him out onto the broken planks of the porch.

"About three blocks east. But you don't need to go that way."

"Thanks, mister," I whispered with gratitude. I squeezed his hand. "You know God loves you," I said as I bounded down the steps.

"Yeah, I know it. He loves me this much." He spread out his arms wide, pulling his sleeves up to show His veins and track marks tattooed all over his arms. "That he died for me like this."

"That's right," I called out. "Jesus died for you. And he loves you. Come by The Assembly Revival one Sunday. I want to see you there. You can sit with me and my family when I get them back."

As my feet hit the pavement, all I could think of was the name of my brother. The ways of my brother. *Spirit, take me there.*

TWENTY-SEVEN

It would be approaching dark soon. This might not have been the best idea—not after all that Ray had warned me about. He told me they didn't care about me being Maize's sister no more. That they didn't want anybody on their turf that could steal away their fresh recruits. "Seek and ye shall find," said Jesus. I was set on finding Maize, with or without God's help. I was praying that He had decided to come along for the ride. The streets were tagged, and every concrete place—walls, columns, and sidewalks—showed a silver scythe sprayed boldly. What happened to hopscotch boards and four squares?

A few blocks farther on, I saw a couple of men wearing plain, black shirts, like the one Ray had found in Maize's bag. I bet I'd see that same patch on the right sleeve, on closer inspection. "Oh, thank God! Thank you, Jesus!" I raised my hands up to the sky.

They stood in silence, watching me, their eyes shifting and turning.

"Hey, hey."

They turned straight to me, one leaning over a chain-link fence. Dogs snored lazily on the front porch of the yellow house, close by.

"You callin' us?"

"Come here, baby," the next one taunted. He was holding a bottle, and I could see the butt of a 9mm pistol hanging out of his low-riding pants. "What is a girl like you doing in the snake's nest?"

Don't be afraid. They won't hurt me. I'm not a threat to them, right?

"I'm looking for my brother, Maize Jones."

"We don't know nobody by that name."

The one was still leaning over the fence when I approached, and I could smell his breath. They both had been at those bottles for a while.

"Of course, you don't." I laughed out loud at my stupidity. "He wouldn't have used his real name. Thank God."

"We never do." Another man approached me from behind. I hadn't seen him coming.

He looked me up and down through dreadlocked hair. His eyes were the color of dark clouds, and I hated the look of them. Gray, unnatural eyes, overcast with death as sudden as a lightning strike. Everything about him was sin. He had to be the leader. His confidence was overbearing, and I could feel the power exuding from him.

"I'm Pale Rider, and my momma sure didn't name me that. Who are you?"

"Sweet Potato," I said quickly, holding my place as he eyed me, feet planted firmly on the pavement. I took their laughter, not allowing the sting to affect me. "I'm looking for my brother. He's only fourteen years old."

"Old enough to carry. Old enough to pop." He pulled his trigger finger.

I shuddered. "He needs to come home. He ran away."

"Well, maybe he doesn't want to come home. Or maybe he's found his home." The man stepped in closer to me. "Why don't you go on back to where you came from? You don't belong here, and you clearly don't know the rules. I'll let you get by with this today, but don't you be coming around here no more. We don't give second chances."

He rubbed his finger against my cheek, and I flinched, snapping my head away. "But you are a little, dirty-faced, sweet-eyed thing. That could count for something."

"Look," I said, my voice rising out of fear. I couldn't hide it, no matter how much I tried. "I've got to have my brother. They took my other little brother and sister for this and signed them off. I got to get him back so that I can save my family. Can you please help me?"

"I ain't never had a pretty thing like you ever say please to me." His evil laugh chilled me all over. "I kinda liked that."

He grabbed my arm. "Say please one more time, and I might see what I can do."

"Please," I whispered; eyes closed.

I could smell the depravity on him—that fresh blood smell. I knew his hands were stained with it, never to be cleansed no matter how much he scrubbed. Only Jesus could clean something like that, no bar soap would do.

I heard a car approaching before I could see it, and I prayed it wasn't Ray seeing me here on the street. I knew he would lose it, and that would mean they would kill him. *Please, Ray, don't come.* It was the first time and the last that I hoped that Ray wouldn't find me.

"Hey, Rider. What you picked up?"

I heard the young voice of the driver, but it wasn't my boy. But he was somebody's boy, a little thing with a thin face and bright eyes. My heart went out to his momma, if he had one, or his grandmother or his older sister. From his baby face, I knew he was no older than twelve, but he was driving the car.

A yell came from the backseat, bringing me crashing back to reality full force. I'd found him. Maize was pushing up the driver's seat and climbing out of the black Impala.

He had a blackened eye and a cut across his left cheek that could have come from brass knuckles or even a knife. He'd only been gone three days, but there was something different about him. He seemed to stand tall.

"Sis, what are you doing here?" He came and tackled me, separating me from the others. "Go home, now," he ordered through clenched teeth.

"Daddy signed Bell and Bean away, Maize."

I watched his face fall for a second, and it was almost like I hadn't even told him anything. Stone. Blank. Dead. He stared through me. *See me, Maize! Hear me!*

"Maize?" questioned one of the men. "Maize? Your name is Maize, and her name really is Sweet Potato?" The men rolled on the pavement.

One of them hollered through tears, "What were you? Some sort of Veggie Tale Gang? She was up in here saying God's name and all. 'Save me, save my family, Jesus.'"

They were hooting and mocking God, hollering out, "Praise Jesus," their hands raised. I realized what Maize was doing. He was pushing me to the farthest corner of the street, out of earshot. I allowed him to.

"It ain't safe for you here. Don't you know that?" he whispered.

"And it is for you? I'll take care of you. Momma left us a farm. Daddy kept it from us, but it will be mine on my birthday. We can go there. Please. Please—we have to get the kids back. Please come on. Please."

Tears fell, and it was harder to see his face.

He turned over his arm, palm lifted, and fear closed around my body like a boa constrictor, slowly taking life from me, crushing my lungs. The sign of the scythe was tattooed across his entire inner arm, the words *Slash to Kill* scrawled underneath. I could see the clear tape still stuck to parts of his arm, telling me the ink was fresh.

"Oh, Maize," I cried. "Why did you do this?"

"I didn't have no choice. I don't belong to you no more. My name ain't Jones. You are not my sister, so you better get before you get got." He spoke through clenched teeth still. "Just get out now. Swear to me you won't come back down here. If you love me, you won't come back down here. That me is dead. Call me dead. But don't come down here, because you'll be dead, too."

"I love you. That's why I'm here. I won't leave without you." I put my arms around his waist.

I could sense the change in his body. His panic had been replaced by an inner strength, a confidence only a gun could give. I felt it before I saw it, as it brushed against my fingers when I tried to wrap myself around him. It was tucked in the back of his pants. *Oh, Lordy!* Not a gun.

"Maize, please turn from this. We'll run. Together," I whispered in his ear, "I'll take care of you. Me and Ray. I promise we'll leave tonight and never look back."

"I can't leave. You know that. You know what would happen if ..." His voice trailed off when he heard his new name called.

"Shack."

His eyes turned from me. Did they call him Shack? *Lordy!* "Shack, bring us that big sister of yours."

"Nah, man. She's gone. She ain't nothing."

But his eyes told me I was everything as he pushed me into the street.

"Run," he mouthed to me.

I didn't have to be told twice, because I saw the young driver slide into the car, eyes warning me he could catch me if I took off. *Let him try.* I bolted and never looked back. I couldn't face seeing Maize for the last time. His blank, cold expression, his stance. Those bruises and cuts from some kind of fight already. His tattoo sealing his fate.

They yelled as the engine roared. "Get her!"

I ran through a few yards, knocking over a patio table and tearing some clothes off a line. I hit fences and circled back, knowing if I let my feet lead me, I'd find my way back to Soul Food. It had to be that way; I could see the overpass leading to the interstate. And, as if a miracle had appeared, I saw Big Red rolling slowly past. Ray's arm was hanging out of the window, his head turning this way and that.

I screamed, "Ray!"

He knew I was in trouble and slammed on the brakes, climbing over to swing open the door.

"Get in."

As soon as I scrambled in, he barked, "Climb in the back seat and stay low. Do you hear me? Don't you look up."

I did as he instructed, putting my head down, but I could feel the rocking of the big SUV turning around in a driveway. I heard the accelerator picking up. We moved faster and faster, away from a scene that would replay in my mind for the rest of my life.

When the car started to slow, he called out, "Climb back up. We're all right now." And I knew that meant we were safe from any East Coast Grims, safe from my own brother.

I was too devastated to cry. My well had run dry. "I found him."

He reached across and grabbed my hand. "Promise me you won't go down there again. Promise me. I swear I was about to lose my mind."

He pulled over on the side of the road and put the car in park. "Come here." He reached across and grabbed me, kissing me full on the mouth. "I can't have you going down there ever again, do you hear me?"

"Maize is gone," I said quietly.

"Wait—you said you found him."

"He's not Maize anymore."

I put my head on Ray's shoulder and watched as the cars passed by. The world was moving on, even as mine had stopped.

"I'm so sorry, Sweet Potato. Everything seemed to blow up. Bombs are hitting from every direction." His arms held me tightly.

I cried, "How can things all get better and then worse at the same time? How can God do this to me? I've been His faithful servant. I've believed, even when I shouldn't. I believed more here than in any other place."

"Believe without ceasing, Sweet Potato. God is still here with you. Maize made his own choice, and now ..."

He didn't finish what I knew he was about to say. *He'll have to live with those choices or die by them, one or the other.* But I would be the one living with them, too. Bell and Bean thought Daddy would be able to go down there and pull Maize out from their clutches, and our life would go back to our un-normal existence. Daddy was going to get himself killed if he didn't watch it. Those Grims would have hurt me if they had caught me. I remembered the blank look in Maize's eyes when I told him about the kids being signed off. He'd acted like he didn't even care. I'd lost my little brother for good. Before, he would've fought anyone—a dragon, a giant—for Bell and Bean. The venom was spreading in his veins, and I feared we'd never find an antidote to fight it.

"I told him if he came back, we would hide him. We would go to the farm. They'd never be able to find him."

I sat back in my seat, and Ray set the car moving on down the road to Soul Food.

"And what did he say?" I didn't hear any hope in his voice.

"He said he had no choice. He had this sickle tattooed on his whole arm. You know what they called him?" I sighed. "They called him Shack. That broke my heart."

"Why? Shaq was one of his favorites. Didn't he have a card he carried with him?" He tried to smile at me, but it didn't feel right for any of us to be smiling.

"We came from a shack, Ray. He'll be reminded of it every time somebody plays tag or calls his name."

I sighed, drawing my feet into me. I wanted Ray to keep driving—to hit the interstate and never look back.

"What if they saw him playing basketball and called him Shaq after Shaquille O'Neal? That was probably what they meant. I remembered Maize saying he wanted to be a basketball player for the NBA."

"Oh." I exhaled in relief.

"We have to keep moving on from our pasts, Sweet Potato. Whatever life throws at us, God will find a way to turn this into a message."

He pulled up in his garage. It was Sunday afternoon, and the Soul Food was closed. Mrs. Sunshine was sitting out on the back patio with a tall glass of lemonade, talking to Mr. Joe while he grilled some steaks. Life was going on. My heart was still beating.

"Well?" Mrs. Sunshine stood up, walking quickly to me. "Baby, come here."

She knew without me having to say a word. I guessed she was right when she said she could read me like a book. My drama had come to an end. It was over, no cliffhangers. She took me in her arms and cradled me as a momma would.

"You hush now, you hear?"

But I didn't even know if I was crying, at this point. Ray's hand was on my hair. Mr. Joe was coming over to put his arms around me, too.

"I ain't had one of these huddles since my high-school football days. Feels kinda girly."

I laughed again. How could I make that sound? They squeezed me harder. "I've got to tell Daddy what I saw."

That meant I would have to face him. Never mind. Well, maybe Ray could. I honestly never wanted to talk to that man for as long as I lived. I could write it down for him—tell him not to waste his time going down there to bring Maize back. Maize didn't exist anymore.

"He's out. Left right after stopping by here around two. He said he would check in on you and the kids by calling," Mr. Joe said. He stepped back, straightened his apron, and went off back to cooking.

Ray grabbed my hands and pulled me into an embrace of his own. "You're staying with us, if you haven't figured that out yet."

"I don't want to be a burden." I looked over his shoulder at Mrs. Sunshine. "Did you fight for my kids?"

"Your Daddy did all that behind our backs, Sweet Potato. But I believe it's God's way for those precious children. We know full well they'll be taken care of." She blinked hard. "What are you going to do?"

"They told me not to fight for them, but that's like telling me not to breathe air."

I fell on the grass again, not wanting to sit in them patio chairs. I wanted to be connected to something godly, not man-made. Not steel.

Ray reminded me. "You need to call them. It's getting late."

I dialed the number quickly with his phone, and my heartbeat quickened with each ring. When Mrs. Patty answered the call, she told me I could come over to see the kids any time, day or night. She tried to assure me they'd wanted me to stay with them, as well, but Daddy had said I would rather stay with Mrs. Sunshine and Ray. He didn't have any right to make any of those decisions. I would've chosen those kids, but it was too late now. My life had been decided for me—yet again with no control on my part. Soon, that was going to change.

The kids told me all about their supper with the Andersons. Bean was hollering in the background that Pastor laughed at his joke about the blind man. I would've laughed if I could've been a witness.

"That sounds nice," I said, feeling the lump rise in my throat. When they asked me what I had been up to, I lied and told them, "Nothing at all. Just boring old stuff."

Telling them I'd seen their tatted brother in the middle of becoming a street soldier wouldn't be a good-night story worth sharing. "Well, goodnight then, my two little turtle doves, sweet loves from heaven above," I said to them both on speakerphone.

The plates were set out on the patio table, and I stared down at the food. Did they expect me to eat this? They all took hands around the table, and Ray blessed the food. So that was how it was done in a normal house. The conversation was all about Maize and what the church had been doing to look for him.

"Call them off. Call it off, Mrs. Sunshine. Tell Pastor it's a lost cause." I pushed at the food on my plate. "Somebody is going to get hurt if they go down there."

"Clarence has been down talking to your daddy some." Mrs. Sunshine patted my hand.

I had to know the whole story about Denise's brother. "Tell me about what happened, please. I have to hear it all," I begged them.

Ray said, "She needs to know. Devon being in The Five is something we don't ever discuss. You know how you told me Maize was dead. He was lost. Devon has been lost to that life for three years."

"The Five? What is that?" It didn't sound like no gang—more like the Jackson Five or a boy band.

"Devon was a bright boy with a future of gold," Mrs. Sunshine said. "He would've been on a scholarship to play ball. He even helped Ray when he was first on the JV team. He was my sweet nephew that always had joy in his step."

Mr. Joe said, "They call him the Joker, and the last time I saw him, he got a tattoo of a joker card on his whole back. The fool."

"He joined The Five when he was sixteen. Not much older than Maize. Those gang members would seek out the kids they thought were weak and would pull them through the fence like magicians."

"Like Maize," I whispered. "He'd told me he was going to run away, but I didn't believe nothing he said. He told me he was going to get lost. And that was what he did."

"You know the path that he's on is self-destructing." Ray paused, trying to judge my reaction.

"I know gang life. I'm a street-junkie's daughter, a shelter queen. Don't you think I knew what I was walking into today? That man told me I didn't know the rules, but I know that Maize signed over his blood and guts and will give it all to them for the sake of that name. That life. He's dead to this world, and the Devil has him aholt." I shivered, my breathing ragged and voice hoarse.

"The Five have a special initiation. Five killings in five days, and you're in," Ray said. "My cousin, a cold-blooded killer. He played war with me in this backyard. I looked up to him. Five in five days."

"Oh," I cried. "The beating that Maize took. His eye, his cheek. He'd been in some fight. What if he's killed somebody already? He's just a baby."

"We don't know how the East Coast Grims work in their initiations, but we know they have been gaining strength, even though they're a local gang. There are always warrants out for them—newsflashes. Their tags are coming closer and closer as their territory mounts."

Mrs. Sunshine reached out to me. "And they are enemies to The Five."

At my previous school, we had a gang that wasn't any joke. They brought their name to the school, and not a single campus officer or teacher even tried to stop them. How was Maize handling all the pressure and the Devil's work around him? I knew my chances of ever having him back were none to none.

"He's gonna die," I said quietly. "Or go to jail. I know the result. So did he. That's what kills me about this. I know why he joined the gang."

"He told you? Devon jumped head-first into a world unknown to him. By the time we tried an intervention, he had already murdered and was a top seller on the street. He seemed to be loving the taste of that thug life. He was too far gone."

Mrs. Sunshine said, "That's why Clarence is out there with your daddy, looking for Maize. They might get him before he's initiated, and to somebody that might make a difference."

Reality was sinking in. "He knew he could get lost in a gang, and that once he was in, I wouldn't be able to interfere. That's what he wanted. He wanted to be free of us, but he was too scared to make it on his own. It makes sense to me now." I pitied their hopeful hearts. They should have known from their own experience with Devon that Maize was never coming back to me.

Mr. Joe stood up. "Well, if we aren't going to eat this meal, we best wrap it up for later. Let's get you settled."

He grabbed my hand and pulled me up.

Mrs. Sunshine said, "I know you've had a tough one, Sweet Potato. Let me run you a bath."

She said that so normal—like that was what mommas did for their children. If the bath had bubbles, I might lose my mind up in here.

Ray smiled at me. "Anything that is here is yours now. You know that, right?"

I tried to fight off the dull throbbing starting at the base of my neck. How my feet moved down the hallway into that tub, I didn't even know. Maybe I was in shock. None of this was happening to me. *Dear God, let me wake up and let me be ... where? The motel with them kids all huddled up with me on one bed? Give me the shed, Lord, at that old abandoned house. Give me those woods where we played Peter Pan with broken limbs and sticks for swords, fighting off Captain Hook. Let me be Wendy and take Maize's hand and fly away with our own little Tinkerbell over the pines and through the swamps of North Carolina again.*

Give me those days when I could make up a story, weave them into a spell and a smile. I'd make them forget their existence for a little while. Give me a chance to show the kids I could make us a new way, a reality that gave them all they needed. All we needed was love and being together. I always knew that. That was what the road taught me. I had to get us back together, but was that what God had in store for us, after this?

Maybe what Bean and Bell could get was what they had deserved all along—a replacement family, but a family all the same. The Pastor said he would take care of them, and his words moved in my spirit even though I denied them. I knew they both wanted that. I always thought I was their life support, but Daddy had pulled my plug. Miraculously, I was breathing on my own. How come?

Daddy. I pounded the water with my fist, watching how the ripple went out around me. That was like Daddy sending shock waves all throughout our lives, without taking any responsibility for it. How could he have denied us that farm? How could he have strung us along, tearing us down emotionally when he should have been building us up? And I had loved him. I had trusted his leadership, never failing to encourage and support him. He was more lost to me now than Maize was. I would have to face the fact that the life I once knew was now over. I had to learn to cope and maneuver through this new set of obstacles. How I was to do that, I wasn't quite sure. I remembered what Ray had told Daddy and me before—that we needed to pray ourselves through it. I guessed I could always start there.

TWENTY-EIGHT

I dragged myself out of the bath and into a set of clothes Mrs. Sunshine put up for me. It was a VCU t-shirt with a pair of plaid pajama pants. The closest things to pajamas I'd ever owned.

When Mrs. Sunshine heard the bathroom door open, she came out to me right away.

"Can you come in here with me and sit a spell?"

She led me to the couch, which was already made up for Ray. She had piled him up some sheets, and he had a couple of pillows waiting for him. It had been decided I'd take Ray's room for the duration of my stay.

She smiled sweetly at me. "Let me see those eyes. Come here, baby. I know you feel like a caged bird singing sad tunes, but you've been free all this time. You just have to realize it."

"Free?" I loved the way her arms felt around me, safe. I hoped Bell felt that when Mrs. Patty reached out to her. I hoped they were sleeping soundly. "I've never been free."

"What you have lived, Sweet Potato—that life that you brought along with you—it has made you who you are. You are beautiful in spirit, a testimony to God's handiwork."

"You speak like you know what kind of life I lead. You have this." I waved my hand around the room, and my eyes fell on her Jesus picture.

My boat was surely rocking, but I didn't feel like having no party on top. I was diving headfirst into the ocean and letting myself float away with the shipwrecked parts of my family. "You have pictures on a wall. You have matching curtains and an armchair. You've planted yourself in one place your whole life, and you see what you want to see. You see me free, but I've been a prisoner to this world, and I don't think I'll ever be let out on parole. I'm serving a life sentence, Mrs. Sunshine."

"What's in your heart? It's not this piece of furniture, or even those pictures. It's what is inside of you. Your heart, Sweet Potato. That's what makes you who you are. It's the value of a person, their ability to give to the world, not what the world can give them. You give freely, openly. You love with all your might, not halfway. God's never left you alone, even in an abandoned house. He's been your walls, your chair, your bed, your breath ... even when you might have felt you couldn't breathe, you took the next one."

"Before coming here, I didn't have my faith right, and I'll be honest about it with you. I ain't told nobody that, but it's true." I was ashamed to even to say out loud that I'd went through a dry spell. I wondered if that was why I was being punished now.

"There are times in all of our lives when we find ourselves maybe not at our truest spiritual connection with God. We allow other things to take precedence over what is the most important. I've had those times, and to tell you that I've walked every step of the way in perfect harmony would be a lie. But I've always come back to Him. We are imperfect people serving a perfect God who loves us just the way we come to him. When my feet hit away from His path, I've had a gentle push of the Spirit to bring me back to the narrow road. That's the way we get through this, and we are not alone."

I knew exactly what she meant. "But I think the only thing I had going for me was the kids. They kept me steering us along. They kept me believing when I didn't even think I deserved to say the word 'Jesus.' And now ..."

"They are in God's hands, like you are. Do you want a life on the road for those kids? I'm not talking about Maize and what he has chosen. I'm talking about your little ones. Would you want them at a motel or the parsonage?"

I said, "I guess I'm selfish. I want them wherever I am. I want them with Ray and me. And I guess what I'm saying is it ain't about them, really, is it? It's about me." I put my hand over my mouth. "Wow."

"Go on, baby. What you getting at here?"

"A dose of that soul food, I guess." I laughed, pushing tears away. "If I had them to look after, it made what I was moving in less dirty. I had a purpose, and I kept my eye on it. I watched over them like a hawk, like you wouldn't believe, Mrs. Sunshine. And now, if I don't have them right here and I know Maize is lost, my heart is flashing a vacancy sign."

"I hate Maize has run off to that gang. I hate how that will tear you apart the rest of your life. If I thought it would do any good, I'd take my shotgun and go hunting him myself. But I know better. I hate them kids aren't down there in that bedroom, all cuddled up for you, but this is the life you have right now. You have to take it. You have to hold on them reins as tight as you can and ride it out with faith in your heart and peace in those eyes. Ride that wind, Sweet Potato."

"But it's hard." I put my hand across my chest. Yep, it was still in there beating. "It's so hard."

"Love is hard every day of your life, whether you have a wall with pictures or a backpack or a full luggage set. Baby, don't lose yourself in all this. You talk about all those lost to you. Losing yourself would be a crime." She kissed me on the cheek and stood on up. "You act like you don't know who you are without those kids, but you are so much more than a protector of your family."

I couldn't speak anymore. She wanted me to say who I thought I was when I'd always questioned that. Daddy kept reminding me that I wasn't their momma. He told me to be me. But who was I?

Ray padded down the hall, looking handsome and tired.

"Are you okay?" I asked, sadness still overwhelming me heavy. He didn't deserve my weight. I'd sink him to the bottom of the ocean if he didn't watch out.

"You're asking me that?" He sat down on the couch beside me, and I slid closer. "These past three days have had to be so awful for you."

"Can you pray with me?"

"Yes, baby."

He got down on his knees and leaned against the oak coffee table. I followed him, my head lowered, and my eyes closed. I didn't think I'd be able to speak a word to the Lord. He would have to take my attempt, Ray's words, and my heart. That was all I had to give.

Ray prayed for peace, for comfort, for care, for Maize's deliverance. Through the prayer, I saw no images, only a white peace behind my eyelids. I fought against the thoughts wanting to cave in on me and take over the light of prayer that was hovering above me. I didn't know how I would be able to sleep, because sleep would mean closing my eyes away from prayer and from Ray's soothing voice.

"I don't want to go to bed." I yawned, and Ray laughed. "I love that," I said.

"What?" He smiled.

"You. Your laugh. Your smile. The way you make me feel like I can face anything." I squeezed his hand.

"I heard you and Momma talking earlier." I swatted at him, and he kissed my cheek. "I wasn't eavesdropping. It's a small house."

"And was it entertaining for you?"

"Every day I want you to know who you are. You're a woman filled with the Spirit of the Lord. You're the love of my life, my soul mate that completes me. You're a sister to three kids who will always love you and look up to you, no matter where they sleep tonight. You are a daughter to a man who has depended on you to be more than should have ever been placed on you. I just want you to know that you can be all those things and so much more."

"If you want to keep giving me these confidence talks every single night, I think I'll allow you to do so." I kissed his cheek.

"If you ever feel like you're losing ground, you've got all of us. The Lord first, the little ones, my family, the church. You'll never have to stand alone, trust me."

"I'll try to believe you on that."

"You don't trust me, and you're about to marry me? I'm wounded, woman," he joked back.

"The one person I trusted with all of my heart and soul turned out to be a man I don't even recognize. That has shaken me up a little—well, a lot. My core is rocking." That was an understatement.

Mrs. Sunshine came down the hallway in a bright yellow robe, with big blue slippers on her feet.

"Rock yourself on to sleep, Sweet Potato. You've got school in the morning. Ray is going to drive you and pick up the kids, and you'll be off work until you can get yourself to feel better."

"I don't want off. I need to earn my keep." I stood up, feeling an emptiness at the mention of school without Maize. I hated the thought.

"Earn your keep. Ain't you soundin' a trip. Go on to bed, Sweet Potato." Mrs. Sunshine kicked out her foot at me, and her slipper flew right off. We all laughed as I headed off to bed.

Surprisingly enough, I slept without dreaming and woke up feeling I could face whatever lay ahead. Maybe some pretty major prayers had been spoken over me. Whatever it was, I needed it to keep going if I was to make it in this new world.

Ray made me breakfast as I sat at the little corner table in their kitchen.

"Why the special treatment this morning? You know we could've stepped on through to the Soul Food kitchen."

I squinted at the walls like I could see straight through them with x-ray vision. I could make out the shadows of life behind that sheetrock. Without stepping foot into it, I could still feel the vibrations of that miracle-working place pumping through my heart. What did that farm mean to me now? Would I be able to leave a place I'd grown to love so much?

"I've gotta make that walk down to the bus stop. I better get going." I began to clean up the dishes, and Ray stopped me.

"I didn't want you riding the bus anymore. I'd rather drive you. It will give us more time to see each other, and you'll get to spend more time with the kids this way." He pointed to his watch. "We better hurry, though."

Seeing Bell and Bean all dressed in their Dream clothes and clear-eyed—well, it made my heart feel good.

I pulled on Bell's hair bow. "You guys are looking mighty sharp."

She had never looked prettier, with her little plaits and matching barrettes. Bean was polished up squeaky clean. I wanted to tell them how much I missed them, but I didn't want to start sad on a Monday morning. I didn't want to ask them if they'd seen Daddy, either. Maybe it was best if we all had a little break from him until we could sort this mess out.

I frowned. "Lookie who's here."

When we pulled up at the drop-off circle, Daddy was in the corner lot, talking to the principal. His disheveled frame slumped with weariness. He still had on his same clothes from the day before, and he looked like he hadn't slept a bit. Served him right.

Ray squeezed my hand. "You have to forgive him, baby. It's the only way to move forward."

"What if I don't want to? What if it's not fair if I do?" I whispered so the kids couldn't hear me.

They were already climbing out of the back seat and running full force to their daddy. He couldn't save them, because he couldn't even save himself. Maybe that was why he ultimately gave them away. He knew he didn't have it in him anymore to be Superman. Maybe

Daddy was ready for retirement.

"If you don't forgive, your heart grows a little bit colder by the minute. We'd miss out on so much if you let it freeze, baby. We've got many miles to go."

"Stay on, brother ... roll on, sister ... just for a little while ... we've got miles to go," I sang to him before kissing him on the cheek and sliding out the door.

"I'll be here at three," Ray called out. "I love you."

"I love you, too."

Everyone was looking in our direction, and I could tell the teachers already had wind of what had happened to my baby brother. We were big news, the lot of us.

Daddy motioned me over, and I felt my bookbag droop off my shoulder and down my back. My pride began to fall like old granny pantyhose. "Sweet Potato, let's go on into the office," the principal requested.

"Well, Daddy, find him?" I questioned.

"No!" I could see the stubbornness in his eyes. He wasn't going to give up. Maybe he would after I told him what I saw.

"Mr. Jones, have a seat here." Principal Newberry directed Daddy and me to sit down. "I hate to hear this about Maize. He seemed like he was off to a positive start here. I spoke with some of his teachers over the weekend, and they didn't see any signs."

"He's turned," I spoke quietly. "He's theirs."

"Not if I have a say in it." Daddy balled his hands up into fists.

"Sweet Potato, you saw him?" the principal asked me.

Well, I didn't want to have to tell it to Daddy directly. He could hear it second hand.

"Yes, sir. He's wearing the signs of the East Coast Grims. They chased me away, and he told me never to go back down there again. And I promise you, I never will. Maize is lost. He's decided, and there is nothing we can do about it now."

It all came out so fast. I figured if I said it like that, it wouldn't have time to settle down into the deep parts of me—like I could run these words off like a line in a play. That was how I was going to get through this. I was an actor in some elaborate production about street life. Drugs, homelessness, poverty, gangs ... I was the epitome of the street. Look up "street" in the dictionary, and it would be on the same page as "Sweet Potato." Ironically, Webster already put us on the same page. How considerate.

"What did he say, Sweet Potato?" Daddy was so shamed he couldn't even look me in the eye. "Was he okay?"

"I told him that you gave the kids away, and that still didn't make him come back with me." I challenged him to look at me.

"If that didn't bring him back, nothing will." Daddy stood up. "Well, Mr. Newberry, I want you to look after the rest of my children." He held out his hand to me. "You take care of yourself."

"What are you planning to do, sir?" The principal shook his hand when I would not reach out to him. I would show him no support. He would have to live with what he had done to us.

Daddy said, "I'm going on ahead to get some things ready."

"You gonna learn how to milk a cow?" I chided. "Too late for that, Daddy."

The principal was already calling in the guidance counselor. I was sure they thought I needed to be talking to somebody right about now. But they didn't know me. All I needed to do was talk to the Lord. I would have a direct call with Him later.

"It's never too late to walk the right road," Daddy said.

"But this time you're going to be walking it alone," I said.

I pushed past him and ran down to my first class. I made it right before the bell rang. How was I to face the looks? As the eyes of some of the students met mine, I realized that I might not be the only one who had lost a brother to the Grims. Or maybe some were taken over by The Five. I could see looks of understanding and fear. One student left the room once Ms. Joann began the discussion on French and Indian War. I wondered if they couldn't bear to be in the same room as me, because I reminded them of their own little street soldier or someone close to them they'd lost.

My day at The Dream was out of focus. It was like I was looking through a camera lens that needed repair. Colors were distorted. Ray was all I wanted to see. Those kids came and held my hand, one on each side, as we waited for Big Red to drive around after the last bell rang. He was here right on time.

"How was your day?"

He asked the kids, not me. I guessed he knew better than to ask how my day had been. I sat back, intently watching their little faces as they recapped every single detail, memorizing every nuance, every rise and fall of their chests.

Ray slowly pulled up to the church. Pastor was out fixing the sign. It read, "Want to know the game plan? Come inside for details."

"Well, hallelujah. Let's all clap." I turned away.

"It's choir night," Bell reported. "Can you come, Sweet Potato?"

"No, baby. I have to work. I'll see you afterward, though. Why don't you stop in for some ..." I almost said pie, but I caught myself. Everything was going to remind me of Maize.

"We'll ask Mrs. Patty," Bell said quietly. "I'm sure she won't mind."

Ray opened his door and helped the kids out. He walked over and started talking to the pastor, who raised his hand to give me a wave. I had to turn my head.

When I turned back, Bell and Bean had already disappeared behind those big, wooden double-doors. A haven for them in a church home. I had to find some peace in that, knowing the spirit of my Bell. I bet her inside brass bells were ringing with the eternal joy that seemed to spring from her inner well. I bet she was at some deep kind of peace now. How could I ever take that away from her? No matter how I tried to figure things out, she belonged in a place like this, to people like this. I knew it, even though it was the hardest thing I'd ever have to accept in my life.

Be free, Bell. Be free.

TWENTY-NINE

"They seemed okay," Ray said. "You did good raising them."

Maybe the road had made them both a little tougher than I'd imagined. Or maybe they were so filled with the love of the Lord that they could see good in even the worst of times.

I spoke my mind, "Well, I'm not okay. I don't think I can go back to school. It's not right there anymore. I don't have a purpose there."

"What was your purpose there before, Sweet Potato?" He was already pulling into the driveway.

"Making sure Maize knew I was fighting for something worth having. I'd always told him that education would get us out of our tramp life. We could upgrade with that piece of paper. Maize will never be back in a school, and I know that for sure. That seems enough for me to finish the race early."

I threw my books into my room and quickly changed into my work clothes.

Ray followed me through the kitchen door and out into the dining room. I stopped, trying to let the place take me in again. To feel that sense of belonging, that comforting vibe. The rhythm was still the same, but my dancing had long dried up. I made rounds as he followed me, and no matter how I tried to shoo him away, he would not leave me alone.

"What?" I yelled, and the whole place got quiet. "You want me to tell you I'm gonna stay in school? You want me to tell you I have a future?"

I threw down the pad at his feet. "I ain't got nothing to live for now except..."

The words *you* never left my mouth. Glass shattered, customers screamed, and surreal flashes of color flew before me, knocking me senseless. Ray fell backward, hitting a bar stool, reaching out to me as he scrambled across the floor on his belly. I felt my body being jerked unnaturally hard as hands gripped my sides and my hair. My head was wrenched back. Tears stung my eyes from the force of the tugging.

I knew something was happening, but I couldn't conceive what it was. I knew I wasn't inside the restaurant any longer, and I watched as my feet dangled over the busted doorframe, my leg catching on the glass. Blood began oozing down my calf. I should have screamed in pain, but I felt nothing.

He called out my name, and it rang in my ears in slow motion—a drawled-out name that lasted twenty syllables. Then *rat-a-tat-at-a-tat*. Shots fired? No. They were toward Soul Food. I couldn't see anymore, because cloth was now covering my face. I welcomed the darkness.

I was pushed into a vehicle, and my body bumped into something hard and warm. They took hold of me, and I couldn't find my voice to call out to them. *Kill me,* I wanted to tell them. *Just get it over with. Don't drag this out.*

Nobody in the car answered my silent pleas, but they were reenacting every single move that they'd made. I heard the young voice of the driver. I would bet my life that I was in an Impala—and I wouldn't even mind losing.

As soon as the vehicle stopped, I was pushed out forcefully, my knees cracking to the curb, and I could feel my feet moving sideways in the grate of a drain hole. Let me sink down under to the sewer system. My hands were scratched and bleeding. Burning sensations ran on my arms, and my leg was starting to throb. They dragged me by my hair like I was some kind of animal, my body flipping and turning. I didn't try to fight or resist them. I knew there was no point.

"How many did you take?" A sneer came from the shadows.

"This one makes the fifth one," a voice said. "I claim two. I got the most hits."

Vomit rose in my throat, spilling out of the side of my mouth, staining the gag.

"I got this one for Tiny."

He ripped away the gag, allowing me to gasp air and push my sickness out.

"My, my, my," the voice said, as my vision began to clear. He tied my hands behind me. My shoulders strained, the muscles feeling they could snap any second.

I was in what looked like a metal box. The Devil was whispering to me I would die today in this shed. I told that voice to get behind me. If I died, the Lord would take my soul.

"Ain't that the girl that come the other day looking for Shaq?" the driver questioned.

"Oh, that's Shaq sista. You claimed the wrong girl. You were supposed to get that Denise girl. Joker's sista. Joker's the one that done in Tiny. She's the target, and now you've marked this one. You know what that means. Once a mark, we got to finish it."

"This isn't Denise," another one said, coming closer. "Yeah, that's Shaq's sister. Look at them eyes. But he can't take back his rights to the girl. You know the game. He called her. It doesn't matter if it was Shaq's mother. He called her in tribute, and now she'll have to answer to Charon."

"But ..."

Before the boy could finish his sentence, he was shoved violently out the swinging door.

The door slammed, and I heard a master lock click on the other side. My face hit the wooden-plank floor, and I closed my eyes to oblivion, drowning in the river Styx. The ferryman was coming to claim my soul.

Four dead, I heard them boast. *Oh, Lordy.* I would be the fifth. Five. What had I said last to Ray? I screamed at him—something I'd never done before. I lost it with him and told him that I had nothing to live for. *Oh, Lordy.* I prayed he knew what I was about to say to him. I was going to tell him I had nothing to live for except him. But I didn't get to finish my words.

What had I told the kids last? I didn't tell them I loved them when they were getting out of the car. I mocked the Lord. *Oh, God.* Even though Daddy didn't ask for my forgiveness, I knew I'd have granted it to him eventually. But I was going to act it out for a while, stubborn as a mule, letting him sweat it. For what? When I knew that I would end up forgiving him in the end, why couldn't I have just thrown my arms around him, like Bell? Why couldn't I have told him I knew why he gave them away—because he knew what they needed more than even me? He could let them go because he loved them that much.

My mind went to that sinner on the cross. I was more of a sinner than him. I had faith right in the palm of my hand, and I let it slip through my fingers like a fine sand. Jesus promised that man He would see him in paradise. But I needed another chance at this life, so I could say all I ever needed to and more.

I prayed, "God, forgive me. Give me another day to make it right."

Words spilled from me—from a well within me that spoke of all of my doubt, and fears, and unworthiness. I prayed for those people back at Soul Food. Ray. My second family. *Oh, Lordy, let them all be safe. Let none of them be dead, let them not be claimed. Let that little boy have no blood on his hands. Let them ...*

The lock clicked, and Maize came busting in, the door slamming against the metal frame. "I told you! You don't ever hear me!"

He kicked me as I lay there in tears. I felt the brunt of his shoe against my side, but I didn't even flinch.

"Maize," I cried out.

He fell to his knees in front of me and pushed the hair out of my face. My hands were bound and bleeding, and he pulled out a knife, clicked it open with ease, and cut through the rope.

"I've got to get you out of here. Why did they mark you?"

"They thought I was Denise. Ray's cousin is in The Five." When I said that name, he spit at my feet as if he'd had a long-running feud with them all his life. "They called out something about Tiny."

Maize said, "Tiny was shot last night. We got to retaliate. It's what we do." He pulled me to my feet. "But not with my sister. I told you not to come here."

"Can't you stop them?" I whispered, watching him looking out through the door. I was sure there were more Reapers about.

"I haven't completed my initiation yet. I have no voice." He wiped sweat from his face—or was that tears? "You are marked and done for. I can't believe I got you into this mess."

"No, I can't believe you got yo'self into this mess. I would've still been working in Soul Food today. It could have happened even if you weren't in this gang. You being here is going to get us both out of this. Maybe that's why God let you do this—to save us both."

"I can't be saved." Maize silenced me with his hand across my lips. "I'm done, Sweet Potato. When I get you out of here, you run as far as you can. They'll put a bounty on your head. You hear me? You got to take them kids and run."

"What's this?" I heard a call from the yard. "Shaq? What are you doing?"

"She's my sister, man." Maize squared his shoulders.

"Oh, that's right. But what you think you are doing? Charon

already called this dog to slaughter. What are you doing opening the door for?" He put his hand in his pocket, and I knew what was there, waiting for an invitation.

"I had to see if it was her." He darted his eyes at me. "I had to tell her I loved her before I said goodbye."

"A family reunion." Pale Rider was back. "Did you get out all you wanted to say?"

"No," I choked out as fast as I could before Pale Rider permanently shut me up. "I love you, Maize. You're my best friend. You find a way to get those kids back for me. You tell them ..." My voice broke, and he flinched. "You tell them I'll always love them, and I'll be watching them from heaven with Momma." *Even though Momma might sure be in hell.*

"How you so sure you going to heaven?" A Reaper came from behind me, wrapping my hands back up.

This time I cried out in pain. "Because I believe in Jesus Christ, my Savior and Lord."

Let them do to me as they willed. They wouldn't take faith from me now. That was all I had left.

"You hear that, Shaq? Your sista's got Jesus. I guess you got the Devil." They flashed signs at me, and I turned my head from them.

One said, "You go on and finish this quick, Charon. She gets to go meet her maker."

I could feel the energy in the air, hear the rapid beating of hearts racing. Everything seemed so distinct to me—so close to my face. I could feel Maize's fear and hopelessness rising.

"Please," I heard him beg. "Don't."

Charon stepped forward. He looked like he had years of torture scarring him. He slammed Maize in the nose, and Maize's head snapped back. I flinched for his pain. I was sure his nose was broken.

"She's mine. We gonna do this like it was done to Tiny—execution style." They grabbed me by my hair again and dragged me out to the middle of the dirt yard.

I heard cries of rage from the other Reapers, and my mind closed to their voices.

Pale Rider stepped in front of me. "Wait!"

His hands came up, and I prayed for a pardon. Would this Caesar let me go free?

"Let Shaq show us his loyalty. Let him be the one to pull the trigger. Give him your gun."

"But ... I ..."

He was interrupted sharply. "Take the gun, or you go down with her."

Oh, Lordy! How did it come to this? I watched Maize's hand—the hand that could grip a basketball like no other I'd ever seen, that hand I'd held through so many panic attacks. The hand that grabbed the gun that was going to take my life.

I didn't know how I was able to speak, but I was. "Maize, I love you. Just do it fast. Get the kids and run."

He put the gun over his head and fired three shots. The other members raised their weapons and let off another volley of shots. I heard some of them paying tribute to Tiny, their fallen warrior. The gun was slowly lowered, and I watched as Maize's black pant legs brushed up against my shoulder. I tried to lean into him, to feel the comfort of my baby brother one last time, but I swayed and missed, falling to the ground.

Somebody kicked my head, and I felt the brunt of a shoe crushing my skull. My body was moving in slow motion again, pulled and dragged and set upright. He was behind me now. The boy I'd loved from the first second I'd seen his crystal-blue eyes. I had never been alone in this world, because I'd always had him to protect—always had his back. And now he was against mine. I could hear his ragged breath, feel his fear creeping up my spine, even as the muzzle of the gun was shoved hard against the back of my head. I stared straight ahead, waiting for death to come. Waiting for the end. Somehow, in the midst of this, I had found my peace.

God, let Maize be forgiven for this. Let Maize make it out. Please, Jesus, put your arms around ...

Pop.

The shot rang in my ears. A steel-toed boot shoved me violently, crushing me, pushing me down. My face hit the grass, and I braced myself for the rush of pain that coursed through my body. I heard sirens and the sounds of a gate being busted—scraping metal and clanging chains.

"Raid!"

I heard shouts from every direction.

"Don't move."

Dogs barked.

Were they friendly, or should I be scared?

My thoughts crashed together like clanging cymbals. I could feel the pressure of a bookbag. Was I at school? No—it was too heavy for a bookbag. My books weren't that heavy. What was it? I tried to force myself to rise, but I was tied to the ground with invisible cables.

A body was lying over me.

Dead weight.

Oh, my God!

Was it Maize?

I tried to lift my head, but I couldn't. Those big shoes truly did leave a mighty fine impression on me. My vision was blurred. I caught a glimpse of black pants moving past me. Faded jeans. Black work boots. Tight, black pants with blue stripes down the sides. Why would I catalog clothes at a time like this?

"Miss, are you okay?" A firm hand was on my shoulder. "Miss, can you hear me?"

The weight lifted off my body. I floated like a bird in the storm. My eyes closed, and I succumbed to the darkness, praying that when it was all over and done with, I would see light at the end.

THIRTY

Suffocating. My body jerked and heaved upward like I was breaking free of the river Styx that filled my lungs with black water, dragging me under. I let out a noise, but it didn't sound human.

"Sweet Potato." His hands cradled my face, and I could feel his fingers running down my cheek. "Oh, baby."

I tried to focus on his face. Nothing felt like it was working right. The haze felt like permanent tears clouding my vision.

"Ray." I tried to speak, but it only came out in a broken whisper.

"Momma," he called out, without taking his hands from my face. "Momma!"

"I'm here, I'm here." Mrs. Sunshine came busting into the room. I heard her enter, but I couldn't turn my eyes from Ray. My head wouldn't turn if I tried. I felt duct-taped to the pillow. I needed for him to know just how much …

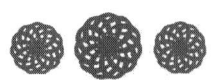

Did days pass, or was it a moment?

The scene was the same. Still suffocating. Still hurting—but at least this time my eyes could clearly register the face of the man I adored. Could I speak?

"I love you, Ray Patterson. I love you. I was saying I ain't got nothing to live for except you. You are my life, Ray. I love you."

My voice still hadn't gained its momentum, and I squeaked like a little field mouse.

He cried, "I know, baby, and you are mine. I love you, too, baby."

He kissed my mouth eagerly, the wetness of his tears against my cheek.

"Joe, she just woke up. Come on." The phone slammed down on the table beside me.

The room was filled with nurses and a doctor with flashlights and probes and big, old black arm cuffs. Questions were being thrown at me.

"You suffered head trauma, Sweet Potato. Do you remember what happened?"

When the doctor asked me that one, it only took one look at Ray for me to know the truth of what had happened behind my back.

"He's gone."

I knew it was true, and I knew what he had sacrificed for me. *Oh, Maize, why did it come to that? Your life over mine. You could have taken mine just fine if it meant you would have lived.*

The doctor patted my hand. "You have been in a coma for over a week. You are one lucky woman."

Mrs. Sunshine said, "Hush up. There was no luck about it. She is blessed and blessed indeed."

The mouth of the doctor kept on moving, but I missed everything else he said. I heard something about not rushing things or talking about anything that would upset me. My head was still feeling woozy. The room was spinning like a record. My body fell back against the bed, and I felt my head roll to the side like I hadn't yet learned how to control my muscles.

I watched as a man in a white coat put something from a needle into this long tube attached to me, and I was gone again, searching out Maize in my dreams. The boots were crushing my skull. Weight. He was holding out his hands to me. The gun dropping at my side. The smell of the sulfur. All I wanted to tell him was how sorry I was I couldn't save him, and how brave he was for giving his life for me. I wasn't worthy of that.

He wasn't wearing black at all. His arms were outstretched to me. He joked, "How you like this get up?"

I smiled at him. "White looks good on you."

"We prayed me out and upwards." Maize's grin was more than I could take.

I wanted to feel him, touch him.

But the closer I tried to come to him, the farther and farther away he went, until he was out of my reach completely—and I knew he was gone. Gone, but not lost.

When I woke up this time, I made sure I did it slower. I focused on my surroundings and let the room come to me. My eyes fell on Mrs. Sunshine. She had her Bible spread out on her lap and her hand over her chest as she leaned over to Mr. Joe, both using each other for props as they slept. Ray was closer to me, and I turned my head the other way to find him. He looked like death warmed over, and I wanted so desperately to comfort him. Daddy was standing behind him, watching me with those giant, dark eyes. I tried to smile at him, and I knew my face twitched, but I wasn't quite sure if the corners of my mouth came up in the right way.

"Hey, Daddy," I whispered. My voice was foreign to my ears, but I knew he could make it out.

"Hey, Sweet Potato Jones. Welcome back." He choked back tears.

"I'm sorry, Daddy."

I tried my best to keep my face in the smiling position, no matter how it hurt me to do it. My face was bruised, and my jawbone was already starting to ache. If he asked me what I was sorry for, I wouldn't be able to answer him. I was sorry for all the wrongs in our lives. For all the paths he should have led us on but didn't. I was sorry for not standing up to his nonsense long ago, stepping along with him when I did have a voice. For enabling him more than helping. I was sorry for all of that, and for so much more, but I would never be able to say it aloud. Some things just had to be understood.

"I'm sorry, too," he said.

And I knew it was for all those things and more. The burden he had carried on his back for all those years must have been a heavy load. I hoped now it could be lifted and we could somehow find a place where we could start over—and I wasn't talking about leaving Newport News. I meant a place in the heart where forgiveness could heal, and love could find a way.

Ray rubbed my arm and leaned in close to me. "Are you feeling okay? Do you need anything?"

"The kids? Are they all right?" I whispered to him. My throat felt like I had swallowed burning knives in a carnival show.

"They're with Pastor. We've been calling them. They're too young to come here, because of the hospital rules and all the flu protocols, but they're worried sick."

He rubbed his face with his hands and said, "We've all been sick with worry. If I would have lost you ..."

"Well, it's over now." I put my hand to my throat, trying to massage it so I could talk better. I sipped the water Ray gave me, but it did me no good.

"I'll call them now for you. Do you want to hear them? Why did I ask? Of course, you do."

When their voices came on the line, my eyes overflowed with tears. They sounded fine. Ray was talking to me, telling them the tube they'd used down my throat made it hard for me to speak right now, but I could hear everything they were saying, and I was smiling. So that must have meant my face muscles were still working, no matter how strange my bones felt.

Bean said, "Why did the cookie go to the hospital?"

Ray asked, "Why?"

"Because she was feeling crummy." He laughed on the other end, and I couldn't help but try to laugh along with him.

"Hey, do you know if you fart for six straight years, you could power up an atomic bomb?"

Ray laughed. "Well, is that what you been learning in school this week?"

Even though he wasn't funny, and I would never tell him how silly his jokes were, he was my boy, and he was doing what he knew best. He was giving me his gift right there.

It took me another week before the doctors said I could go home, but that week was spent with me resting in and out and not remembering much of anything. That was what I needed most, I believed. It hurt too much when I saw the way everybody was looking at me. Better living life with my eyes closed.

When the release papers were signed, I had to sign my own forms. Daddy wasn't anywhere in sight, and I was sure it was because he was still getting things in order. I guessed that meant he had to see to Maize's arrangements and burial. I hated he had to face that alone. I'd done all the work for Momma's funeral and would have probably had to do it all for Maize, if I wasn't stuck in this hospital.

Ray said he'd been a hospital camper this whole time and was trying to tell me all about what I'd missed, but he knew I wasn't listening to anything he was saying. It's not that I didn't want not to concentrate; it was too hard to settle my mind on one thing. Sleeping felt much better.

Ray said, "Yep, that's right, Sweet Potato. You missed your birthday. You're already eighteen."

The nurse helped me into the wheelchair, even though I didn't need one. She said it was the rule, and I wouldn't be making it out of here unless I followed it, so I didn't fight her on it.

"I'm glad I missed it." I knew he would never understand that about me. Some days weren't meant to be celebrating.

"Don't think you're getting out of it that easy. I've got something special planned for you," he whispered in my ear as he helped lift me up into Big Red. I could tell whatever it was, it was eating away at him, and the excitement seemed to grow on him by the second.

I didn't feel like talking on the way home, and I was glad I didn't have to. There were so many questions I had for him. The first was to find out what had happened to Maize's body. Had they had a proper burial for him, and did they know just how much of a sacrifice my boy had made to save my life? He'd bought me time by firing those shots. He alerted the police with all that shooting. He took his own life to spare mine. I would be the one that would have to tell Maize's story.

I had other questions, too. Who were the bodies claimed at Soul Food that day? Was it customers I knew? Had they caught the crew responsible for it? I knew the driver was a trigger man. I could pick him out. And what did this mean for my family and me? Would I be taken again? Was it over? Would any of us ever be safe with a mark on my head? I knew too much.

Hiding out might still be our only choice in life. What was that on Ray's apron? *Rescue me from my enemies, O Lord, for I hide myself in you.*

Through the windshield, I stared out at the crisp, October sky and watched as the world changed colors without me. Time was passing, still on its celestial plan. Life was moving along at its pace. Who was I to think I could control it, anyway? I lived to say *I love you*. I lived to say *I'm sorry*. I would see Maize on the other side. God was still an awesome God. I gave Him all the glory.

Ray pulled up to the entrance to the church and stopped the car. He was already getting out of the car to help me out.

"What are we doing here? I know it's Sunday afternoon and all, but I'm just not up to seeing anybody. I need to go home."

"You are home," he answered me. "I've got a surprise for you, remember?"

I put my hand on his face and drew him into me for a kiss. "Ray Patterson, I love you."

He replied, "I love you, too," as he picked me up and cradled me against his chest. "You're going to be my wife soon, don't be forgetting that. Was waiting for that legal age. We gonna make it official."

"You know I can walk," I whispered into his warm neck.

"Baby, I believe you could fly, if you wanted to. But let me do this right now, Wonder Woman."

I felt a little piece of my soul returning to me. *God, help me through this. I need you, Lord. I just can't do it alone.*

"Maize's doing all the flying for this family right now," I told him.

I believed what I'd dreamed was true. I would never tell a soul about it, for fear they would take me to the loony bin. I felt his presence, the essence of him in my spirit, even as I was being carried up them church stairs. If he was in the dark place, I didn't believe God could allow him close to me. So that meant he had to be waiting for me by the pearly gates. Maybe he had found Momma. Maybe they had both accepted the Lord before their last breaths. Who was I the one to judge or question? God knew it, and I guessed I would have to be patient and find it out someday.

I gasped. "Oh."

The church was filled solid with people. Candles lined all the aisles, the front of the pulpit, every windowsill. Arrangements of morning glories were all over this place of worship, and I knew all about that flower. I'd looked it up after Daddy had told me about my name. A morning glory symbolized somebody loving in vain. I knew that all too well. I loved despite myself, without deserving it, whether it did me any good. I loved because I had to, even when it was returned harshly. I had no other choice but to love and pray. Even if it was in vain, I would love anyway.

I knew our walk had led us here to this place, and God was with me every step of the long road. Love was washing over me. Prayer was hovering over me again, and the Spirit of the Lord was there. I had to be open to it and let it in.

Mrs. Sunshine announced, "We've been keeping the candles burning day and night. Burning for Maize and burning for your recovery."

It was so quiet in the sanctuary. Everybody was standing up as Ray walked me down the aisle. He set me softly down on my feet, and I walked unsteadily to the front of the church.

Ray was right to bring me here. It wasn't because I was a miracle walking. It was that Jesus was my miracle-maker. Being here made perfect sense to me in this imperfect world. At the end of the aisle, Ray didn't turn me back to face the people or give some great speech about how thankful he was I was out of that hospital. He let me stand there, waiting, wondering.

Bell came out from the choir door, dressed in a lavender dress with a white coat and little gloves, pretty as a princess, her hair done up in twisted knots. She let out a squeal of pure joy, and I closed my eyes, trying my best to hold in all of my emotions.

Bean was now with her, dressed in a white suit, purple tie, and sideways hat, looking all stunning, like a Blues-singing boy. He took his little sister's hand, and they stood up at the pulpit together. The piano played, and Bell's little voice came out like a warm, summer melody drifting lazy on the wind. Not the kind that would take my breath away—more like a soft, gentle breeze blowing against my face. I stared into her eyes lovingly, proud, and in that second, I knew what her freedom felt like against my broken heart. Against all odds, we were fighters, the whole lot of us. Fighting for a purpose that was not our own. With God on our side, no one could be against us. We were going to be okay. There could be no other way.

Their voices rose together in unison—such a beautiful duet.

Battered log drifting in the river wild, crashing aimlessly from riverbank side to side. That's how I feel sometimes, like a motherless child,

holding on to the hope where the river ends, when freedom calls
only God knows when
here's a turn around the bend, Lord just pull me out.

The door opened again, and I cried out in wonder. "Maize?" I screamed out his name as he stepped out all in white like from my dream.

Bell and Bean kept singing, their words speaking my heart.

I find my feet and start to feel my place.
I recognize the Lord has made this race not for the faint of heart,
so I trudge on.
I find the spirit call, grant me wisdom and a loving heart,
courage for a brand-new start.
The Lord is faithful, and He hears my beating heart.
Lord just pull me out.

Daddy was standing behind him, and he gently pushed Maize toward me. Maize burst into a run, toppling down the steps. He took me up in his arms, knocking me back into Ray. His tears wet my face. My hands came up to run through his hair, across his neck. His pulse was there. He was bruised, scarred, but he was alive. *Thank you, Lord. Amen.*

My beginnings might not have been the best there ever was. My middle was still uncertain, that was for sure. But I did believe, with all I had in me, that God had given me and my family a second chance. My boat may still have been rocking on the waves, and the storms were sure to follow us, but Jesus had my back, and I was finally ready for the party.

"Bring on life. I'm ready now," I whispered to the Lord.

Maize cried against my neck, sobbing how sorry he was for everything. Bell and Bean held on to my waist, and Daddy and Ray stood looking on. I started singing the song Bell would often sing to us as encouragement. This time, Jesus was without a doubt coming along for the ride.

"Stay on, brother ... roll on, sister ... just for a little while ... we got miles to go."

Acknowledgments

There are so many I could name that deserve rooftop praise, but in doing so would actually create the longest manuscript printed in history! First, I must thank the Lord for opening doors and connecting me with Georgia McBride. I must spend this time thanking Georgia for believing in *Sweet Potato* and giving me a chance. There are no words that can express my gratitude for your belief in me. For the rest of my author career, which I pray is a long and successful one, I hope to have you as my publisher! To Amanda McCrina, my editor, all I can say is *wow*. The labor of love you poured over *Sweet Potato Jones* is amazing. You took my manuscript and polished it to a jewel I'm even more proud of today than I could have thought possible. My family and friends are beyond phenomenal, and I am truly blessed to have you in my life. The support you give me in all that I set out to do helps fuel my passions. You get me through the tough days and inspire me. I love you all, and I thank God for you. To those of you that read *Sweet Potato Jones*, I hope you'll always remember to treat everyone with kindness, help a stranger, and give words of encouragement. You never know what someone else is going through. Be a light.

Jen Lowry

Jen Lowry is North Carolina born and raised, still holding on to that country slang that is unique to the small town of Maxton she loves so much in Robeson County. She an avid enthusiast of all things horror, UFC, and binge watches old episodes of Quantum Leap. She finds herself comfier in a pair of pajamas and would make all public appearances in them if she could get away with it. When she isn't literacy coaching, life coaching, or homeschooling her two fabulous boys, she can be found napping or singing loudly, probably napping. Jen has her doctorate degree in Christian Ministry and is a member of Raleigh First Assembly. Check out Jen's official author sites all over the net from podcasts, YouTube, Instagram, and more by searching up Jen Lowry Writes or follow her on @jenlowrywrites. Contact Jen for special author appearances and teaching opportunities or stay up to date with her journey at:
www.jenlowrywrites.com.

CONNECT WITH US

Find more books like this at http://www.myswoonromance.com

Facebook: https://www.Facebook.com/swoonromance
Instagram: http://www.instagram.com/swoonromance
Twitter: https://twitter.com/SwoonRomance
Tumblr: http://swoonromance.tumblr.com/
Georgia McBride Media Group: www.georgiamcbride.com